"Suddenly ... **had the c** ... **ence."**

There was the faintest hint of sympathy in Mingus's tone as he answered, "I know."

Joanna blew out a soft sigh. She took up her fork and began to eat. She suddenly paused, the utensil stopped in midair. "You said we're going to figure out your brother's next steps. What are you going to do? And what am I supposed to be doing?"

Mingus narrowed his gaze, amusement sweeping across his face. "You are going to sit tight and stay out of trouble. And you're not going to worry about what I do."

Her gaze skated across his face, trying to read the emotion staring back at her. She finally shook her head, rising from the table as she grabbed his plate and hers. "Well, I can tell you now, that's not going to happen, so try again, Mingus Black. I need answers and I don't plan to leave your side until I get them."

* * *

**Don't miss future installments in the
To Serve and Seduce miniseries, coming soon...**

* * *

**If you're on Twitter, tell us what you
think of Harlequin Romantic Suspense!
#harlequinromsuspense**

Dear Reader,

No lies! This story *worked* me! *Hard!* It was challenging from start to finish, the characters continually turning left when I was trying with everything in me to herd them right! But I absolutely *love* the final product. Once again, it was about family and the strength of their love and their commitment to doing right, when it would be so much easier to do wrong!

I loved fleshing out Mingus Black. He's a bad boy to his core and yet he's a big softy when it comes to the delightful Joanna Barnes. The two are sheer perfection in all their flawed beauty. Together, they are fire! I hope you enjoy them as much as I enjoyed writing their story.

I really love this book! I hope you will, too!

Thank you so much for your support. I am humbled by all the love you keep showing me, my characters and our stories. I know that none of this would be possible without you.

Until the next time, please take care and may God's blessings be with you always.

With much love,

Deborah Fletcher Mello

www.DeborahMello.blogspot.com

TEMPTED BY THE BADGE

—

Deborah Fletcher Mello

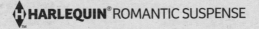

HARLEQUIN® ROMANTIC SUSPENSE

Recycling programs
for this product may
not exist in your area.

ISBN-13: 978-1-335-66192-0

Tempted by the Badge

Copyright © 2019 by Deborah Fletcher Mello

All rights reserved. Except for use in any review, the reproduction or utilization of this work in whole or in part in any form by any electronic, mechanical or other means, now known or hereafter invented, including xerography, photocopying and recording, or in any information storage or retrieval system, is forbidden without the written permission of the publisher, Harlequin Enterprises Limited, 22 Adelaide St. West, 40th Floor, Toronto, Ontario M5H 4E3, Canada.

This is a work of fiction. Names, characters, places and incidents are either the product of the author's imagination or are used fictitiously, and any resemblance to actual persons, living or dead, business establishments, events or locales is entirely coincidental.

This edition published by arrangement with Harlequin Books S.A.

For questions and comments about the quality of this book, please contact us at CustomerService@Harlequin.com.

® and TM are trademarks of Harlequin Enterprises Limited or its corporate affiliates. Trademarks indicated with ® are registered in the United States Patent and Trademark Office, the Canadian Intellectual Property Office and in other countries.

Printed in U.S.A.

www.Harlequin.com

Writing since forever, **Deborah Fletcher Mello** can't imagine herself doing anything else. Her first novel, *Take Me to Heart*, earned her a 2004 Romance Slam Jam nomination for Best New Author. In 2008, Deborah won the RT Reviewers' Choice award for Best Series Romance for her ninth novel, *Tame a Wild Stallion*. Deborah received a BRAB 2015 Reading Warrior Award for Best Series for her Stallion family series. Deborah was also named the 2016 Romance Slam Jam Author of the Year. She has also received accolades from several publications, including *Publishers Weekly*, *Library Journal* and *RT Book Reviews*. With each new book, Deborah continues to create unique story lines and memorable characters. Born and raised in Connecticut, Deborah now considers home to be wherever the moment moves her.

Books by Deborah Fletcher Mello

Harlequin Romantic Suspense

To Serve and Seduce

Seduced by the Badge
Tempted by the Badge

Harlequin Kimani Romance

Truly Yours
Hearts Afire
Twelve Days of Pleasure
My Stallion Heart
Stallion Magic
Tuscan Heat
A Stallion's Touch
A Pleasing Temptation
Sweet Stallion
To Tempt a Stallion
A Stallion Dream

Visit the Author Page at Harlequin.com for more titles.

To Kay Edmondson

You are a joy and a blessing to know!

Know that you are much loved and valued!

Chapter 1

The noise level in the small classroom rose substantially as the door flung open and students began to parade inside. Joanna Barnes looked up from the papers she'd been grading, a bright smile pulling at her lips. Greetings rang out warmly as one student after the other found their way to a seat for the third-period history class.

"Good morning, Ms. Barnes!"

"Hey, Ms. B!"

"Ms. Barnes! What up?"

She twisted the cap back onto the red pen she was holding and slid it and the test papers from her previous class into her desk drawer. Rising to her feet, she returned the gesture, greeting each student warmly as she moved to stand by the door.

"Mr. Parsons, good morning! Miss Hayes, how are you? Take a seat, please, Mr. Tolliver!"

The energy in the room was palpable, everyone anxious about the test they would soon be taking. This was one of the honors classes, the students all exceptionally bright and especially motivated. Over half had already been notified of their early acceptance into college, with most of them headed to Ivy League institutions. They were considered the elite of their graduating class. They challenged Joanna to insure the curriculum was one that would not only boost their individual class rankings but also kept them interested; boredom was easily the kiss of death for any teacher.

The test they were taking was on the early Industrial Revolution in England and Wales, with the emphasis on the plight of women during that time period. Joanna had no doubts most, if not all, would pass with flying colors. There were one, maybe two exceptions determined to buck the system, no matter where they were in life.

The last student through the door was one of her more challenging pupils. Standing a foot taller than most of the class, Damon Morrow was one of their star athletes, playing varsity football and basketball in the fall and baseball in the spring. Keeping him off academic probation had become a full-time job all on its own and, despite his obvious intellectual genius, his was an issue of effort, or rather lack of. He was smart and talented, but he was lazy as hell. Damon Morrow was content to fly through life on his dashing good looks and the trust fund he would inevitably inherit when he turned twenty-one.

"Mr. Morrow, good morning," Joanna said warmly. "You studied, I hope."

The young man shrugged broad shoulders. "Do we have to take this test today, Ms. Barnes?"

"Yes, we do," she said matter-of-factly. "Everything under your desks, please. And get your pencils ready."

Damon sat, still scrolling through messages on his cell phone instead.

"Phones away," Joanna said, tapping her nails lightly against the desktop. "If I see any phones during the exam, I will confiscate them. Your parents will have to come get them from me at the end of the semester, and I mean it."

Damon shot her a quick look. "Hey, Miss Barnes, did you hear?"

She blew a soft sigh. "Did I hear what, Mr. Morrow?"

"Everyone's talking about it!" another student interjected.

Joanna looked around the room, her eyes scanning their faces as she mentally took attendance. "Has anyone seen Mr. Locklear?" She gestured toward the only empty seat, going off topic for a brief moment.

There were shrugs and looks of disinterest, no one seeming to care that one of their own was missing.

She shook her head ever so slightly. "So, what is everyone talking about?" she asked, her eyes shifting back to the student staring at her.

"One of the teachers is getting fired," Damon stated. "Someone's been giving it to a student on the side," he said with a snide laugh and an inappropriate hand gesture. He slapped palms with the boy beside him. "I bet it was Coach Peterson. Which one of you girls has been giving it up to him in the locker room?" he quipped.

Laughter rang around the room and the noise level rose slightly. Joanna winced, unable to fathom how any adult could even consider taking advantage of a student's trust. That her kids were piqued by such an abhorrent rumor didn't sit well with her. It didn't sit well with her at all. She shook her head. "That will be enough of that, thank you."

"He's serious," a young woman named Shannon Heigl said. "One of the teachers has been having an affair with a student and the student reported it to the administration."

Another student added her two cents. "They're going to press charges and whoever it is plans to sue the teacher and the school district!" she exclaimed.

Joanna's gaze skated from one face to the other, everyone suddenly looking at her to either confirm or deny the rumors she was hearing for the first time. A string of expletives suddenly rang through the air, Damon cursing as he continued to scroll through his phone. "This is so effed up!" he said with a snide laugh.

"Mr. Morrow! Watch your mouth!" she chastised. She held out her hand for his cell phone. "I said no phones."

The young man eyed her sheepishly. "I was just shutting it off. I swear," he said as he shoved the device into the top of his book bag and the book bag under his desk. He dapped the palm of her hand and gave her a wink of his eye.

Joanna met the look he was giving her with a stern stare, her eyes narrowed. She shook her index finger in his direction. "You're walking a very fine line with me, Mr. Morrow. You do not want to test my patience."

As she turned, she saw him leaning to whisper to the boy beside him. "The student is male! The teacher's a woman!" he quipped, the two giving each other a high five as if that was something to celebrate. A titter of laughter and hushed whispers swept through the room.

"All right, that will be enough," Joanna said as she

moved to the front of classroom and began to count off test papers at the head of each row. "Let's focus on something useful, please. It doesn't matter who did what to whom, regardless of gender—if such a thing happened, it's wrong! Let's not waste any more of our energy on unsubstantiated accusations. Spreading rumors only serves to hurt people unnecessarily. You all should want to be above that." Her eyes connected with each student, finally coming to rest on Damon Morrow's face. He was still grinning from ear to ear, his chest pushed forward arrogantly as he and his desk mate whispered one last time.

"Take one and pass it back," she said to the students at the front of each row.

Minutes later their heads were down, pencils scribbling away as they diligently tackled question after question. Joanna moved back behind her desk and took her seat. She'd been teaching since forever at Riptide High School, the Chicago, Illinois, staple rich with history. She'd also been a student here back in the day, the senior class president of her graduating class and a cheerleader. Her parents had both been graduates, as well, and before them, her maternal grandfather, one of the first to integrate Riptide classrooms before it had been court mandated.

Joanna came from a long line of educators, beginning with her paternal great-great-great grandmother, who'd taught other slaves on a Georgia plantation how to read and write. Her mother had taught English at Riptide's rival high school for most of her career, only recently retiring from her assistant principal position to tend her beloved gardens. During the spring and summer, she grew the fruits and vegetables she intended to can in jars while catching up on her reading when the weather turned. Joanna's father was a math professor at the local community college, determined to trek to his day job until they laid him in his casket. Both loved what they did, and so did Joanna.

She had always known she would be a teacher, even preferring to play classroom instead of house as a child. Despite the challenges of students who were self-absorbed, more abrasive and less focused, she enjoyed everything about sharing her love of history with the students who came every September and were gone by June.

And Joanna loved history. She found it fascinating that if you examined the past closely enough you could find a precedent for most current situations. She loved helping her students discover that for themselves. It was thrilling when she could show them a correlation between their own challenging academic environment and the courts of the Italian Renaissance, giving teens philosophies on how to survive in their dog-eat-dog world. When there were questions of integrity they studied Martin Luther King, Gandhi, Thomas More and people who, through the ages, epitomized the fight for what was right. When students bemoaned their home situations, she made them research life in the Middle Ages and its lack of comfort and convenience. There were lessons to be learned from the past and Joanna enjoyed everything about exploring them.

The time passed quickly and when the bell sounded, announcing the end of class, a few of them jumped in surprise. Joanna stood. "Pencils down, please, and leave your tests in the basket on my desk on your way out. There is no homework tonight, so enjoy the break!"

Chairs slid against the concrete floor and the noise level rose as the class marched single-file past her, sliding exam papers into the wicker container on the corner of her desk. As the last student made his exit, they were still spreading gossip, cell phone messages and social media updates being shared. Joanna couldn't help but wonder if there was any truth to the allegations, but figured she'd learn more before the day ended. She had no doubt there were as many teachers gossiping as there were students trying to dig up information.

As Joanna bound the test papers with a large rubber band and a sticky note detailing the class and time, her friend and associate barged into the room.

"You're on break now, right?" English teacher Angel Graves gushed, tossing a look over her shoulder.

Joanna nodded. "I'm chaperoning fourth period study hall and grading these test papers. What's up?"

"Haven't you heard? The administration is in an uproar and there's been two police detectives in the principal's office since this morning. Someone's in some serious trouble. Mrs. Magee says it's about to hit the fans!"

Joanna shook her head from side to side. "Mrs. Magee gossips too much! I don't know why you pay that woman any attention," she said, referring to the office secretary.

"I pay attention to her because she's that inside line to everything that goes on in this school. You should give her more credit. Besides, aren't she and your mother old friends?"

"Which is how I know she gossips too much!"

"Yes, but she always has the best gossip!"

Joanna laughed as they made their way out of the classroom and down the hall toward the other end of the school building. Their conversation was easy and casual as they maneuvered their way through the throng of students hurrying to their next period class before the late bell sounded. "So, who did what this time?" she asked.

"It's serious. They're claiming teacher misconduct and inappropriate contact with a student."

"Are they saying who?"

Angel shrugged. "Only that the student is a senior."

"I just can't believe it. I know some of the men around here are slimy, but I can't imagine any one of them doing such a thing. That would just be horrific!"

Angel shrugged her shoulders. "You're preaching to the choir! I wholeheartedly agree but you just can't trust people like you used to."

Joanna shook her head. "I swear, if it's not one thing around here, it's another. Last week it was all about the district wanting to close our doors and sell off the building, and the week before that our accreditation was supposedly in jeopardy. It's anything that will get the school board up in arms. That last school board meeting lasted an hour longer than necessary. I can just imagine what a scandal like this will have them ranting about."

"Yes, you can. They'll revisit the dress code, insist on psychological background checks to detect predatory tendencies, maybe even contemplate a no-touch, no-tell policy. You know the drill."

"No touch, no tell! Now you're being funny," Joanna said with a soft chuckle.

Angel laughed with her. "You have to have a sense of humor if you plan to make tenure."

"I already have tenure."

"Retirement, then. Either way, if you don't laugh at foolishness like this, you'll go crazy."

Their banter was suddenly interrupted by someone

calling Joanna's name loudly from the other end of the hallway.

"Ms. Barnes! Ms. Barnes!"

The two women exchanged a quick look before turning in the direction of the high-pitched squeals piercing through the thick chatter of students crowding the hallway. Marion Talley tossed up a slight hand as she stomped her size-eleven heels in their direction. Before reaching their side, she admonished one student for cursing, a second for groping his girlfriend inappropriately and sent a third to the office for the length of her skirt. She herself wore a black knit dress that hugged one curve too many, remaining baby weight from her two middle-school-aged daughters still clinging to her midsection and hips.

Joanna forced a smile to her face, her mouth bending upward as she feigned interest in the woman who chaired the school's English department. Marion Talley spent every opportunity she could find to make Joanna's life miserable. The two of them had history that took them both back to their own high school days, resentment harbored over teenage antics that should have been long forgotten.

"Mrs. Talley, what can I do for you?" Joanna asked, mindful of all the ears shuffling past them.

"I was hoping to catch you before you left your classroom. You must have rushed out before the students. You do know leaving early without permission is grounds for disciplinary action. If someone were to tell, of course."

Joanna bristled slightly, the little hairs against the back of her neck rising.

"Cut the crap, Marion," Angel snarled under her

breath. "You know she left her classroom the same time you left yours. You're always trying to start something."

Marion narrowed her gaze on the other woman, her face skewing with irritation. She bit back a comment, turning her attention onto Joanna instead.

"Mrs. Donato would like to see you in her office. I'm headed down to cover your study hall."

"Did she say what it's about?" Joanna asked.

Marion smirked. "No. But then there's so much going on around here today. I'm sure it's nothing, though."

Joanna gave her another smile. "I'm sure, too."

"Humph!" Marion grunted as she turned on her high heels and stomped back in the direction she'd come from.

When Marion was out of earshot, Joanna muttered under her breath, "I really wish she'd fall into a large hole and disappear."

Angel laughed. "I know two sophomores who would gladly make that happen for you. Just give me the word."

Minutes later Joanna sat in a wooden chair across from Valentina Donato, the school principal, and a police detective from the Chicago police department. A uniformed officer stood at the door. Joanna was shaking and on the verge of tears.

"Your union rep will meet you down at the police station, but you might want to consider hiring your own attorney," Valentina was saying.

Joanna shook her head. "I didn't do anything."

"I'm sure this is just a misunderstanding," Valentina said, "but we have a legal obligation to have the charges levied against you investigated. The allegations are very serious, Joanna! David Locklear claims you had a sexual relationship with him and that you held that relationship over his head and threatened his grades. We can't just ignore that."

Joanna turned to the man standing at the edge of the desk. "Am I under arrest? Because I certainly didn't do what you're saying I did!"

The detective cleared his throat. The man was short and slightly obese. He wore a gray suit that was ill-fitting. He was sweating profusely, his eyes darting around the room. He was clearly uncomfortable and he refused to look directly at her. His gaze finally rested somewhere on the wall behind her head. "For the moment, we just need to ask you some questions, Ms. Barnes, and under the circumstances we need to do that down at the station."

Joanna could feel herself nod but everything seemed like an out of body experience. Her arms and legs were heavy and she was shaking. Her nerves felt completely fried. The wave of shock that had washed over her was consuming and, for a moment, Joanna wasn't sure she could keep her emotions in check. She took a deep breath and then a second, filling her lungs with air as she struggled not to cry, or worse, rage aloud.

The detective rose from his seat and gestured for Joanna to do the same.

"I have my car..." Joanna started. "I can meet you—"

The detective shook his head. "I need you to ride to the station with me, Ms. Barnes."

Her eyes widened. "I don't... I can't... I need to..." she stammered, suddenly unable to complete a coherent sentence.

"It's not an option," the detective added. "Right now, this is just a formal questioning and I'm willing to spare you the embarrassment of handcuffs as long as you co-operate."

Joanna stood. She took another deep breath. "I need to make a call," she said, her voice a loud whisper. She reached into her handbag for her cell phone. "Please? I need to call my attorney to meet us there."

The detective nodded. "That is your right."

Mingus Black rolled his eyes skyward, not at all amused by his sister Simone. The sixth child and the youngest girl in his family, Simone Black was being a proverbial pain in the ass as she pranced around his office, giving orders to his staff like she paid the bills. Despite him being older, his attorney sister was notorious for bossing him around, wielding control when it was least wanted. She got that from their sister Vaughan. He was grateful when her cell phone rang, announcing an incoming call, because he was just seconds from throwing her out the door on the heels of her Manolo Blahniks.

"I need to take this," she said with a light laugh. "But when I'm finished, we need to talk about you incorporating this business. You can't keep running it all willy-nilly like you're doing." Mingus rolled his eyes a second time as she depressed the talk button on her phone. He went back to signing the checks his secretary had dropped on his desk earlier that morning.

Simone's lighthearted expression suddenly deflated like air being sucked from a balloon. Her brow furrowed, shock and concern flooding her face. She was listening intently and from where he sat he could sense the anxiety of the person on the other end of the phone line.

Mingus met his sister's stare as he shifted forward,

lifting himself upright. "What's wrong?" he asked, his voice a loud whisper.

Simone held up her index finger, still listening attentively to the party on the other end. Rising, Mingus rounded the desk and moved to stand beside her. He brushed a large hand against her back and shoulder when he realized she was shaking, something having moved her to distress.

"Everything's going to be fine," Simone said, clearly fighting to contain the worry in her voice. "I will meet you at the police station. Don't say anything to anyone. Don't answer any questions until I get there. I'm on my way." There was a moment of pause, the other person speaking, and then Simone said, "It's going to be okay. I promise," before she disconnected the call. "Mingus, I need you to come to the police station with me."

Mingus eyed her with a raised brow. "What's going on?"

"Do you remember my friend Joanna Barnes? She and I went to Western Illinois for undergrad. Joanna is one of my sorority sisters. She went to the Center for Teaching at the University of Chicago for her graduate studies."

Mingus shrugged, having no real interest in putting a face to the name. "Sorry, it doesn't ring any bells," he said as he moved back behind his desk and sat.

Simone frowned. "Well, she's been picked up for questioning. They're alleging she had a sexual relationship with one of her students."

Mingus shot his sister a look. "She's a teacher?"

"High school, and she didn't do it," Simone said matter-of-factly.

"How do you know that?"

Simone scowled. "I know her. Joanna is not that kind of woman."

"Are you sure you know..." he started.

Simone waved her index finger at him a second time. "I know." She reached into her purse and pulled a dollar bill from inside, dropping it onto his desk. "I need to hire you to help prove she's innocent."

Mingus laughed as he picked up the currency, smoothing it between his fingers. "You really don't expect me to work for free, do you?"

"Of course not. That is just an unofficial retainer. We'll work out the details later."

He laughed again. "I'm not an attorney, Simone. I'm a private investigator. There's no privilege that needs to be established."

"I know that," she answered, irritation rising in her tone. "I just need you to come to the station with me. Please."

Mingus blew out a heavy sigh. He had a lengthy list of things he needed to complete and taking on another case was not something he had planned to do. He watched as Simone headed for the door.

Simone tossed him one last look over her shoulder. "So, are you coming?"

Mingus tossed up his hands in frustration, knowing that if he were honest with himself, he really didn't have any other options. His sister knew there wasn't anything he would not do for her. Even when she irritated him. She had already banked on him saying yes. He'd follow her to the station and he would work whatever case she needed him to work. She had him wrapped tightly around her little finger and, despite his best efforts, he had yet to unravel the string to set himself free.

"I'll meet you there," he said, reaching into the desk drawer for his keys. "I need to drive my own car."

Despite his reservations, Mingus was at least willing to show up. He didn't know Simone's friend, but her relationship with the woman was already a cause for concern. He always kept his distance when dealing with people he knew personally in a professional capacity and knew that friends weren't always truthful if there was something they didn't want you to know. He didn't want to be the bearer of bad news if Simone's friend wasn't everything she believed her to be.

Chapter 2

Mingus shifted into fourth gear, his Nissan 370Z Coupe picking up speed. He'd kept straight instead of turning right when his sister did, Simone believing the shortcut through downtown would shave some ten minutes off her travel time. He knew they'd arrive at their destination within minutes of each other, Mingus parked in the lot when she pulled in. It would irritate her to no end and that gave him the slightest bit of satisfaction.

The Chicago Lawn district police station was on West 63rd Street, around the corner from the West Communities YMCA. The surrounding neighborhood was a modicum of small businesses and modest single-family homes. During his brief stint on the Chicago police force he'd been stationed there and then at the West Harrison Street station.

Mingus had followed his father and older brother into

law enforcement after graduating from Loyola University Chicago with a bachelor's degree in criminal justice. His parents had expected he would join the ranks of detective, eventually climbing the law-enforcement ladder to lieutenant before heading his own precinct as commander. But the rank and file of being an officer hadn't been for him. Mingus didn't play by the rules that others did. Even when he was on the straight and narrow, he wasn't above deviating down his own path to get a job done. His work ethic was impeccable, just not necessarily above board. He approached most things, including his relationships, with a wary eye. He defied expectations, rebelled instead of acquiescing, and often took shortcuts others had issue with. He often thought he was simply wired differently from everyone else. The uniform and badge had often tied his hands and Mingus didn't take kindly to his hands being tied. Giving it up had been the best decision he'd ever made, even if it had disappointed his parents.

Mingus came from a family of high achievers. His father, Jerome Black, was the Superintendent of the entire Chicago Police Department. His mother, Judith Harmon Black, was a federal court judge, and both were well respected in Chicago's judicial system. They were all in the spotlight, doing their civic duty to make Chicago a safer place. Mingus was just as dedicated to the municipality. But he worked alone, sometimes in the dredges of the community, beneath the cover of darkness, getting his hands dirty. He sometimes did what others weren't willing to do and he did it exceptionally well.

When Simone pulled her car into the empty parking space beside his, Mingus was standing against the hood of his vehicle with his arms and legs crossed. As she stepped out the driver's-side door, he stole a glance at his watch, a sly smirk pulling at his mouth. His sister was not amused and she said so.

"You're going to get another speeding ticket and they're going to pull your license."

"My license is already revoked," he said matter-of-factly.

Simone blinked, her lashes batting feverishly. "Are you crazy? And you're driving?"

Mingus laughed. "No, I was joking. You need to stop being so serious."

"You play too damn much!" Simone snapped, suddenly unleashing her frustrations on him. For a good two minutes she recapped everything that had ever been proclaimed about him. He wasn't focused or driven, and he was too unpredictable. He took too many risks, played too many games and was surely headed to hell if he didn't change his life around. For two good minutes Mingus let her rant.

"So, are you done?" Mingus finally asked, his tone even.

"Sorry," Simone muttered softly. "I didn't mean…"

"Yes, you did. But it's all good." He wrapped his arms around her shoulders and gave her a warm hug. "Are you okay?"

"No." She stepped out of her brother's grasp and took a breath. "No," she said again, her head shaking. "I was just on the phone with Danni," she said, referring to their brother Armstrong's bride-to-be. "They're going to formally charge Joanna with sexually assaulting a student."

Mingus nodded. "But you knew that was a possibility."

"I was praying that it was a horrible mistake. But this also means I can't represent her. I've called Ellington to see if he can take her case. He's on his way."

"Have you talked to your office?" Mingus asked.

She nodded. "I had to make sure I recused myself. I can support her as a friend, but it's a conflict of interest with the prosecutor's office for me to do anything more."

Mingus nodded as she continued.

"I really need you to work your magic, big brother. I don't know what's going on, but I do know Joanna is not capable of what she's being accused of."

"No promises, Simone. I know she's your friend and you say she's innocent, but that might not be true. We don't even know what they have on her yet."

Simone took another deep breath. "Let's go find out!"

Joanna couldn't stop shaking as she wrapped her arms tightly around her torso. She'd been sitting alone in an interrogation room for almost an hour, no one speaking to her until her attorney arrived. She'd called her bestie, Simone Black, because she hadn't known who else to call. She'd only needed an attorney once before, when she'd purchased her townhome. She doubted highly that the man her parents had recommended, who'd represented her at closing, would be able to help her through this situation.

Despite knowing she hadn't done anything wrong, Joanna sensed things were not going to go well for her. For the life of her she couldn't begin to understand how she'd come to be in this position. Never in her wildest dreams could she have fathomed anyone believing she would take advantage of one of her students. But they did. She'd seen it on the principal's face, and the detectives were treating her like a pariah. No one was answering her questions and she had dozens she wanted to ask. The room's door suddenly swung open. She didn't recognize the man who stepped through the entrance and she felt herself tense.

"Ms. Barnes, my name is Richard Pearce," he said as he extended his hand to shake hers. "I'm an attorney with the teachers' union. I've been assigned to your case."

Joanna gave him a slight nod of her head. Richard Pierce was of average height and slightly overweight. His suit was expensive, a polished black silk partnered with a white dress shirt and red paisley necktie. "Thank you for coming," she said, her voice a loud whisper. "That was fast."

"Actually, it's your lucky day. I was in the area on another matter when I got the call. Typically, it takes a day or two for us to get to you."

"I don't feel lucky," Joanna muttered.

"That's understandable. Obviously, I'm going to need to get up to speed with the case, but I'm told they have a significant amount of evidence against you. Eventually we may try to plea it out and hope that—"

"I didn't do it."

The man looked up from a manila folder he'd pulled from a brown leather attaché and had rested on the table. He seemed surprised to be interrupted. "I'm sorry?"

"I didn't do it. I did not have a sexual relationship with any student."

"Obviously, I'll need to do some investigating, but the evidence—"

"I didn't do it," Joanna repeated even more adamantly as her tone rose significantly.

Mr. Pearce stared at her for a quick minute. He leaned back in his seat. "Ms. Barnes, I'm here to represent your best interests. Clearly, we want to do everything we can to minimize the damage to your reputation. I understand that you're probably still in shock right now, but eventually we will need to discuss your options and pleading this case out may be your best recourse. I'm not sure—"

Joanna interrupted him a third time. "Am I required to use you, Mr. Pearce? Is it a condition of my union membership?"

The man bristled, his eyes widening. "No, of course not. You have the option of hiring a private attorney if you'd be more comfortable doing so. But the union is here to protect your interests."

"You're not protecting my interests if you're already talking about me taking a plea deal. I didn't do anything wrong and I certainly didn't do what's being said. I have no intentions of pleading this case out. I don't want to go to trial, but I will if it means clearing my name."

Before Mr. Pearce could respond there was a knock on the door, the entrance swinging open a second time. The two men moving into the room surprised both Joanna and the union representative. Joanna recognized the man who stepped forward, greeting her warmly.

"Joanna, I don't know if you remember me, but I'm Ellington Black. Simone's brother."

Joanna nodded. "I do remember you. We met once at an Alpha Kappa Alpha event. I appreciate you coming."

Ellington smiled. "Simone said you needed an attorney. She thought I might be able to help."

"She's not coming?"

"She can't represent you. She works for the state prosecutor's office and it would be a conflict of interest. But she's waiting to take you home." He extended his hand to the other man. "Ellington Black, and you are…?"

"Pearce. Richard Pearce. I'm with the teachers' union. I've been assigned to Ms. Barnes's case."

"Wonderful. We can use as many people on the team as we can get." Ellington reached into the breast pocket of his suit jacket and pulled out a business card. "Here's my number. I'm sure we'll need all the help available as we rev up the investigation. I look forward to working with you."

Pearce traded business cards, seeming flustered by the turn of events. "I was just telling Ms. Barnes that we might want to consider a plea deal if one is offered."

"That's not an option," Ellington said. He extended his hand in a firm handshake. "I don't mean to be rude, but I'd like to speak with Ms. Barnes privately. So, if you'll excuse us, I'll be in touch when we need you."

The moment was immensely awkward as Pearce rose reluctantly. He'd been summarily dismissed and as the three of them stood staring at him, he said his goodbyes and sulked. When the door was closed shut behind him, Ellington took the seat across from Joanna. It was only then that she turned her attention to Mingus, who stood against the wall, his arms crossed over his chest. He'd eased in quietly, settling into the background as he stood in observation.

There was no missing the family resemblance. Both men stood well over six feet with lukewarm complexions that were a rich tawny with just the barest hint of mahogany undertones. They had the same chiseled features—sculpted cheekbones and strong jawlines. Both had solid builds and broad chests and shoulders. Ellington wore a navy-blue suit, the silk fabric expensive, pristinely tailored and polished. The other man was dressed more casually in black denim jeans, a collarless black shirt and black varsity jacket. His hair was cropped close and he sported a hint of mustache and a goatee. He met her stare, his expression hiding any trace of emotion. But there was something simmering in his eyes. Something hiding behind the blinking of his lashes. Something that captured Joanna's attention and held it tightly.

"I didn't do it," she said softly. "No one believes me, but I did not sleep with my student." She was still staring at the second man, her comment more for him than her attorney. She introduced herself. "I'm Joanna. Joanna Barnes. Are you an attorney, too?"

Ellington looked from her to the other man and back. "I'm sorry. I assumed you two had met before. Joanna, this is my brother, Mingus Black. Mingus is a licensed private investigator. He's going to help work this case. We're going to trust him to help us figure out what's going on and why you've been targeted."

The slightest smile pulled at Joanna's lips. Her bottom lip quivered and tears pressed hot behind her eyelids. She gave him a slight wave of her hand. "Hi."

Mingus nodded in response, his expression unchanging. But something burned hot in the pool of light dancing in his eyes. Had he been anyone else, his silence would have been unsettling, but Joanna found his presence eerily comforting and she had never before been

attracted to the strong, silent type. It gave her a moment
of pause as they seemed to be measuring each other up.

Ellington continued, Joanna focusing her attention
back on him. He reached across the table for her hand and
held it. "Here's what's going to happen," he said softly.
"When I open that door, the police are going to come in
and you'll be formally charged and arrested. They will
handcuff you and then they're going to take you downstairs to the jail to fingerprint and mug-shot you. After
you're processed, we're going to go before the judge and
I'm going to ask for bail. I don't think we'll have a problem getting it. Once we're able to bond you out, Simone
is going to take you home."

Joanna closed her eyes. "I can't believe this is happening," she muttered. "Don't I get to make a statement or something? I thought they wanted to ask me
some questions?"

"What they were hoping was that they could push
you into making an admission of guilt. They believe
they have more than enough evidence to prosecute you.
Them asking you questions was only a polite formality,
the end goal being to discredit you."

"But what evidence do they have? How can they have
anything? I didn't do this!"

"We'll know more at your arraignment. I do know
they believe they have a credible statement from your
accuser."

She took a deep inhale of air, blowing it out slowly.
"Will I have to spend any time in jail? I mean, how soon
will I be able to get bail?"

Ellington shook his head. "I'm going to do everything I can to make that happen very quickly. It's still
early. The judges are back from lunch, so once the po-

lice do what they need to do, there is no reason we can't head right to the courthouse for a bail hearing. If all goes well, you'll sleep in your bed tonight."

He cleared his throat before he continued. "Unfortunately the press is all over this. They're going to try to get you to make a statement. You have no comment. You are not to discuss this case with anyone. Not your parents, not your best friend, Simone, not your husband or your boyfriend. No one! From this moment forward the state will try to find anything they can to use against you. We don't want you to give them anything they can use. First thing tomorrow morning, you, Mingus and I will sit down and go through what we know and figure out how to proceed. Do you understand?"

As she nodded her head in concurrence, Joanna's tears finally slipped past her lashes, beginning to rain in a steady stream down her face. "I swear," she said, her gaze shifting back to stare at Mingus. "I didn't do this." She wiped at her cheeks with the back of her hand. She then wrapped her arms around herself, hugging tightly.

A uniformed officer gestured for Joanna to stand and put her hands behind her back. She was a stunningly beautiful woman: long and lean with a petite frame and mile-high legs. She had delicate facial features, killer cheekbones, dark eyes and a warm umber complexion. Her skin was slick as glass with just a hint of pink undertones. Mingus imagined that if she ever blessed him with a smile it would be wide and full, showcasing the picture-perfect teeth currently biting her bottom lip anxiously.

Mingus watched the detective read Joanna her Miranda rights, his voice echoing around the room like an annoying fly buzzing in the space. Zip ties were secured around her wrists and then a female officer clutched her by the elbow and guided her out of the room.

Mingus was still standing like stone as he watched them take her away. Something he didn't recognize pitched through his abdomen, a wealth of emotion swirling like a cyclone through his midsection. Before anyone had come into the room, Joanna had asked his brother for a tissue, tired of swiping at her tears with her fingers and not wanting anyone else to see her cry. For a brief moment, just before she was escorted out, his eyes locked with hers and held. Her expression was stoic, her lashes batting up and down to stall the wave of saline from falling a second time. The look on her face yanked at his heartstrings. Hard.

As Ellington exited the room, Mingus moved in behind his brother, listening intently to the conversations being held. The detective was saying that the student and his parents were scheduled to come in again the following morning. Two uniformed officers were cracking bad jokes on the low, amused by the salacious details of the crime Joanna was being charged with. Mingus gave both men a look that cut their conversation short, leaving them red-faced and slightly anxious that they might be called out for the indiscretion.

Moving back to the lobby area where Simone sat anxiously waiting for an update, Mingus was surprised to find himself conflicted. Something about the case wasn't sitting well with him. Despite the assumptions of guilt and what little he knew of the evidence, Mingus had believed Joanna when she'd said was innocent.

Simone pressed him for information. "How is she holding up?"

"She's not unraveling, if that's what you want to know."

"Joanna's a very strong woman. And she'll fight this with everything in her. She'll be fine."

"How close are you two? She knew Ellington, but we had never met."

"She's one of my best friends. She was around more that year you spent in South Africa after you left the force. We talk often, and we hang out every chance we can, but our career choices keep us running in different circles. I think you, and maybe Armstrong, are the only siblings she hasn't met."

"Ellington mentioned her husband? Or it might have been a boyfriend?" Mingus looked nonchalant as he questioned his sister about her friend, but truth be told he was curious to know more about her. To know if Joanna had a significant other. If some man had her heart and her heart wasn't available.

Simone finally answered. "She's not married and, the last time we spoke, she wasn't dating anyone special. I don't think that's changed."

"Does she have an ex who might be looking to hurt her?"

"No!" Simone said, shaking her head vehemently. "No one I can think of. She's always been very particular about who she dates, and most have been upstanding men."

"Most? What about the ones who weren't?"

Simone gave her brother a look. "Are you asking professionally or personally? Because I don't know how that has anything to do with this case."

"The more I know about her, the better I'll be able to figure out who's trying to hurt her. Is this kid acting out because she gave him a bad grade or has someone put him up to this? If someone is trying to frame her, then this is vindictiveness at the highest level. If there is absolutely no truth to the allegations, someone has gone to a lot of trouble to destroy her. A scorned lover would be at the top of my suspect list because this is as dirty as it gets."

Simone blew a soft sigh. "I'm sure she'll tell you whatever you want to know. She's one of the most honest souls I know."

Mingus pondered his sister's statement. It spoke volumes that she thought so highly of her friend. That Simone attested so vehemently to Joanna's character. For his sister to see Joanna as family meant he would welcome her as if they were kin. Family meant everything to him and for that reason alone, he would do whatever he could to help the beautiful woman.

Three hours later Joanna stood before the honorable Judge Margaret Walker and listened as the prosecutor proclaimed she'd had sex with a seventeen-year-old male student numerous times. Allegedly, sex acts had been performed in his car during school hours, in her home and off school property. The state was charging her with two felony counts of rape in the third degree and two counts of endangering the welfare of a minor. After a statement against bail from the prosecutor and Ellington pleading for leniency, the judge granted bail. Her bond was set at one hundred thousand dollars. She was also ordered onto electronic monitoring and, with the slam of the judge's gavel, Joanna knew her nightmare was just beginning.

It took another hour for Ellington to meet with the

bondsman. Joanna put her home up as collateral. Arrangements were made for her to be fitted with an electronic ankle bracelet. She struggled not to cry again as an officer explained the restrictions. When they were finally done, Ellington guided her to the front of the building where Simone and Mingus stood waiting to take her home.

Chapter 3

Women crying didn't faze Mingus one way or the other. Truth be known, he'd probably made more than his fair share sob. But Joanna crying had him feeling some kind of way and he was having a hard time reconciling that feeling with rational thought.

The technician installing her ankle monitor had left an hour earlier, ensuring the new device was transmitting a radio frequency signal with the location to the receiver and from the receiver to the service center. If Joanna breached the permitted range, the police would be notified of her whereabouts.

Despite her best efforts to not let her emotions show, they were written all over her face, the wealth of it puddled in the water that clouded her dark eyes. She was angry and frustrated. She was also hurt, unable to fathom how anyone could ever believe she could do something so foul. She cried when she thought no one was looking and Mingus couldn't stop staring.

He stood against the pantry door in her kitchen, his hands shoved deep into his pockets. He watched as Simone and Joanna made an earnest effort to prep the evening meal, both pretending like nothing had happened. His sister was tossing ingredients for a large garden salad into a glass bowl. Joanna stood at the stove stirring a simmering brew of meat sauce in a cast-iron pot. Pasta boiled in a second pot on the other burner. Joanna was going through the motions, pretending to be okay when she really wasn't. She was broken and just barely holding it together. He found himself wondering how long it would take her to snap, betting that she was probably not far from her breaking point.

Joanna's parents sat at the kitchen table, visibly shaken by the news. Their frustration painted the walls a dank shade of blue as they peppered their daughter with questions she wasn't able to answer.

"I just don't understand," Lillian Barnes was saying, her silver-gray hair waving with each shake of her head. "How can this boy say those things about you?"

"Boys lie," Vincent Barnes snapped. "Young boys lie all the time. You've taught enough of them to know that."

"Some tell little white lies about losing their homework. This is something totally different. Did you do something to lead this boy on, Joanna?"

"Of course not," Joanna snapped. "Why would you ask me that?" She'd spun around to stare at her mother, her hand fastened around a wooden spoon. "You know I'd never do anything like that!"

Joanna's father stood from the table, moving to stand between his daughter and her mother. "Calm down.

Both of you. Joanna, your mother didn't mean anything. She's just concerned about you. We both are." His gaze moved from his daughter to his wife. "You know better than most that kids these days are a whole other breed. It's not like when we started teaching. These kids will manipulate the truth faster than you can blink."

"It still doesn't make any sense to me," her mother persisted. "Clearly there had to be something she either said or did to give him the impression…"

Joanna's tears had risen for an encore, her sobs stalling her mother's words. She was visibly shaking, her last respite of calm exploding with a vengeance. She suddenly excused herself, slamming the spoon onto the counter before sweeping out of the kitchen toward the master bedroom at the rear of the house.

The matriarch stood abruptly, calling after her. "Joanna!"

Mingus suddenly stepped forward, an outstretched palm stalling them all in their tracks. "Give her a minute," he said softly, his gaze sweeping from one to the other. His eyes rested on his sister last, something he couldn't say aloud causing him to lift his brows.

He shifted his attention toward Mr. and Mrs. Barnes. "Joanna really can't discuss the case with any of you," he said. "She'll be better once she gets a good night's sleep."

Mr. Barnes shook his head. "I think we're going to go. We'll call to check on our daughter later."

"Are you sure?" Simone questioned. "I know Joanna appreciates having you both here to support her. This is just a difficult time for everyone." She threw her brother a look.

"We're sure," the matriarch said, attitude ringing in her voice.

Mr. Barnes rolled his eyes skyward. "Lil, this is not the time for you and Joanna to be at each other's throats. She needs—"

His wife cut him off. "Our daughter needs some time. Clearly our asking questions is a problem for her right now. Simone, call us, please, if anything comes up we need to know about." She gave her husband another look, then shifted her gaze toward Mingus. She looked the man up and down and his own stare narrowed as he gave her a look back. "And, please, tell our daughter we love her," she added.

The moment was tense, and awkward. Mingus sensed Joanna's parents were feeling completely out of sync and unable to be of any help to their only child. Since court, Joanna had been distant at best and neither could understand. Neither he nor Simone had any answers for them either.

"Yes, ma'am," Simone said as she watched the family make their way to the front door. "I'll call but I'm sure Joanna will ring you both later, too."

Mr. Barnes gave her a nod of his head as he and his wife stomped out the door, the structure closing harshly behind them.

Mingus hesitated as Simone stood in the doorway, watching as the couple headed toward their car. When she finally closed and locked the door, he turned and disappeared down the hallway.

Joanna's home was filled with books. Shelves overflowed with tomes in every room.

As Mingus reached the open bedroom door, he noticed the music for the first time, the sound piped through the entire house. Joanna had turned up the volume in the space.

Joanna lay in the in fetal position across her bed, a plush pillow pulled beneath her head. Her eyes were wide open, her cheeks still damp with moisture. She lifted her head just enough to give him a look, seeming unfazed by his presence. She rolled to the other side of the bed and fell back into thought.

Mingus knocked against the door frame before he stepped over the threshold. He walked easily into the room and took a seat on the settee that rested at the foot of the bed. He sat listening to the music, some country crooner singing that his woman was better than heaven could ever be. His eyes skated around the room, noting more shelves lined with books. There was a mahogany dressing table decorated with assorted bottles of perfumes and nail polish. Her closet was overflowing with clothes on black-velvet hangers and shoes lined neatly in clear plastic containers. A framed photograph of a young Joanna posed primly between the parents he'd left standing in the kitchen with his sister decorated one wall. The shabby chic decor was an eclectic mix of soft florals and hand-painted furniture. It was a pretty room and Mingus sensed that much thought had gone into every aspect of it, and the rest of her home, to ensure it reflected her personality. Joanna suddenly spoke, pulling him from his thoughts.

"I've been trying to figure out why this is happening. Why did he pick me? I really need to talk to David Locklear," she said, saying her accuser's name aloud for the first time.

Mingus shook his head. "That's not going to happen. Get the idea out of your head. They issued a restraining order against you. You can't go anywhere near that kid and, if you do, they'll revoke your bail so fast it'll make your head spin. That is not a risk you want to take. Trust me."

Joanna sat upright. Mingus was flipping through the pages of a signed, first-edition, leather-bound copy of Pablo Neruda's *Twenty Love Poems and a Song of Despair*. She was taken aback by the deep vibrato of his voice, the rich timbre like an aged cognac. It was the first time she'd heard him speak since their initial meeting.

He lifted his eyes to stare at her, the two locking gazes. He seemed taller, even though he was sitting, his six feet plus a few inches pulled upright. There was no denying the man was good looking with his chiseled features, delectable caramel complexion, haunting eyes and magnetic smile. But she didn't care much about his good looks right then.

He dropped his gaze back to the book. She was slightly taken aback by his casual disposition, Mingus seeming unfazed by her situation. There'd been something final in his comment, almost as if he was executing an order and daring her to challenge him.

"So what am I supposed to do? How do I get the answers I need?"

"You trust me to do my job," he answered matter-of-factly as he turned the page he'd been reading. "Despite what some people think, I'm really good at what I do."

"Weren't you with the police department once?" she asked, trying to remember what little Simone had told her about this brother.

Mingus nodded, meeting her stare for the second time. "I was."

"What happened?"

"That, I wasn't any good at." The slightest smile pulled at his full lips. "I discovered I work better when I work for myself. I have issues with authority." His eyes dropped back to the book, seeming genuinely interested in the poem he was focused on.

Before Joanna could respond, Simone poked her head into the room, eyeing her friend and then her brother. "Everything okay in here?"

Mingus shrugged his broad shoulders. He glanced at Joanna. "You good?"

Joanna nodded. "I'm fine. I just needed a moment to myself. My old people were just a bit too much for me to handle."

"They're just worried about you," Simone said, trying to be comforting.

"My mother is doing what everyone is doing—trying to figure out what I did that caused all of this. She hasn't once considered that maybe I didn't do anything to provoke being attacked. Why is that?"

"Because you're a woman," Mingus answered. He rested the book back into the custom clamshell box where he'd found it. He continued. "Even if the situation were reversed and the teacher were male, there are those who'd be asking what the girl did to provoke his attention. More times than not boys and men are getting high fives for having scored while girls and women get labeled as community sluts."

"Well, that's not fair," Simone said.

"Maybe not, but that's how our society is."

"It's total bull," Joanna snapped, the profanity surprising the other two.

Mingus chuckled, then he and his sister exchanged a look.

Simone moved into the room and crawled in beside her friend on the bed. "We're going to figure it out, Joanna. *Mingus* will figure it out," she said, leveling one last look on her brother as she added emphasis to his name.

Mingus moved onto his feet. "Are you staying here with Joanna tonight?" he asked, looking at his sister.

"I had planned on it," Simone said, nodding.

"That's not necessary..." Joanna started. "Really, I can—"

Interrupting, Mingus narrowed his gaze. "Someone needs to keep an eye on you. You're already plotting how to get out of that ankle bracelet and over to that boy's house to interrogate him. We can't let you go out like that."

He focused his eyes on her hands, her fingers twisting and turning the monitor around her ankle. When he looked back up, she could feel herself blushing profusely.

"I wasn't...well, not really. I just..."

Mingus suddenly laughed, the sound of his voice bringing the first rays of comfort shed felt since rising that morning. The warmth of it vibrated through the space and bounced from one wall to the other. Joanna and Simone soon found themselves laughing with him, the mood in the room lifting ever so slightly.

Mingus winked at her. "If my sister wasn't here, I'd show you how to get that off without getting caught. But since she is, it'll have to wait until we're by ourselves."

Joanna smiled, the first warm bend to her lips since they'd met. "Promise?"

"I got you!" With one last wink, Mingus gave them

both a wave. "Joanna, I'll pick you up in the morning. Simone, I will catch you later. You two try to get some rest tonight."

"Good night," Joanna said. "And thank you."

"Later, big brother!"

The two women paused, listening for the front door to open and then close after the man. When they heard him rev the engine of his car as he pulled out of her driveway and down the street, both released easy sighs.

"I like him," Joanna said, shifting her gaze to look at her friend. "Your brother. He has a good spirit."

"He's pretty special. But I worry about him and I'm not sure why because, of all my brothers, I think he's the most capable of taking care of himself."

"That's an interesting statement."

Simone shrugged. "Mingus never goes with the flow, never follows the rules, never stresses over anything and he always comes out on top. Every time! There's nothing he hasn't attempted that he hasn't excelled at. Even when he was a police officer. He was one of the best. But he doesn't like authority. He hates being told what to do and I doubt there is anything he's ever taken seriously."

"Why do you think that is? Your whole family is so by-the-book about everything. Why do you think he deviates from the status quo?"

"Wish I had an answer. Mingus just is the way he is. His way works for him. We stopped trying to figure him out when he was twelve years old!"

Joanna smiled, seeming to reflect on the comment as she thought about the tall, dark and handsome stranger who was suddenly so important in her life. Even without saying it Mingus seemed to understand her desperation, wanting to help her fix what was broken. In just the few hours of knowing him she sensed he was a man who said more with his silence than most men articulated with words on a daily basis. Despite his mysterious, bad boy demeanor, there was something about her bestie's brother that was sitting comfortably in her soul. Something that made her feel like everything would be fine as long as she had Mingus Black on her side.

She shifted her body off the bed. "I hope you didn't put all the food away. I think I'm hungry."

"Actually, I didn't put any of it away. And we made enough for an army. You'll be eating spaghetti for the next month."

"Good," Joanna said, her smile widening. "I like spaghetti!"

Simone grinned. "So does my brother. You should have told him to stay."

Joanna grinned back. "I should have. Maybe next time I will."

Mingus sipped three fingers of Conviction bourbon. It was a rich blend of corn and malted barley with a hint of sweetness that reminded him of vanilla fudge and chocolate-covered cherries. He sipped slowly, his mind lost in thoughts of the history teacher.

Papers were strewed across his living room coffee table. Copies of Joanna's arrest warrant and complaint, her employment file with the city and miscellaneous information his brother had deemed important. He'd read the report taken by police, the initial charges leveled against the educator and accounts from the victim reading like a romance novel gone very wrong. How she'd begun to pay extra attention to her student, offering to tutor him after hours. Then tutoring transitioning to something more when the young man expressed his attraction to her. Innocent flirtation and playful banter becoming more personal and then physical. David Locklear believed himself in love, consumed by desire, until he wasn't. He'd felt defenseless, alleging his favorite teacher had threatened to compromise him graduating if he tried to leave the relationship. A failing grade on a thesis paper had been the final straw leading to the boy telling his mother, who herded him down to the police station to give a statement.

When he was done reading everything for the umpteenth time, Mingus settled in his leather recliner, lifting his legs up and out in from of him. He closed his eyes, remembering the hurt that had furrowed Joanna's brow, questions steeped in the hot tears that had rained down her warm brown cheeks. She'd been adamant about her innocence, never once wavering. She had made no effort to make excuses for the charges. She'd called David Locklear a liar and had been unapologetic about doing so. She hadn't been at all concerned about the optics, insisting that the truth would prevail and redeem her. In her mind, if the kid was willing to tell such a blatant lie, then he would have to accept the consequences of his actions.

The prosecution had already offered them a deal, believing their case against her was a slam dunk. Believing a guilty plea and short prison sentence would alleviate the embarrassment of a trial. Thinking that Joanna wouldn't want to put herself, or her alleged underage lover, through the trauma.

But something about the beautiful woman told Mingus she wouldn't hesitate to get on the witness stand to tell the world her truth. In fact, he'd be willing to wager

Joanna Barnes would have no issues trudging to hell and back to prove her innocence. She was ready to battle and something about her had him wanting to get into the fight and go to bat for her. If he'd had any doubts about her innocence, her own actions had dismissed them summarily. Mingus could only hope that the teenage boy was prepared for the war that was coming.

He refilled his glass from the bottle on the end table by his elbow and took another slow sip. He knew sleep wouldn't couldn't come any time soon. He needed to put a plan together, to figure out his next steps. But for reasons he couldn't begin to explain, he couldn't stop wondering what the exquisite history teacher might feel like in his arms.

"Classroom to the courtroom! A teacher is facing sex abuse charges involving one of her teenage students. Good morning, everyone, and thank you for joining us this morning at seven. I'm Mark Miller and this is ABC7 Chicago."

The anchor sat in the news studio, his expression smug as he shuffled a stack of papers on the desk and gazed into the camera. Joanna saw her mug shot suddenly appeared in high definition across the television screen as the newscaster continued.

"The teacher in trouble is twenty-nine-year-old Joanna Barnes, accused of having an inappropriate relationship with a seventeen-year-old male student. That teacher is the third, and the only woman, from the local high schools to be charged with a sex crime in the last eight months. The ABC7 team's Leanne Garner is reporting from Riptide High School."

There was a shot of the high school as the students

entered the building, the newscaster standing on the sidewalk. Leanne was young, wearing a vibrant blue dress that flattered her petite frame. She spoke with an air of confidence, like she'd scored the story of the year. "Mark, news of the teacher's arrest has spread pretty fast and caused jaws to drop. The parents and students we talked to were shocked by the allegations."

The camera flashed on someone's father and a student Joanna didn't know.

"She seemed so nice," said one.

"I'm in shock!" said the other.

The newscaster continued. *"As the allegations involved a minor, school officials here at Riptide High contacted the Illinois Department of Children and Family Services and Chicago police. Per a statement issued by Christopher Munn, Chicago Public Schools superintendent, the teacher in question has been removed and termination is pending.*

"We wanted to know what the district is doing to ensure students are safe. The superintendent stressed the primary concern is always the protection of students, adding the district is taking the necessary steps to ensure the security of every child."

Leanne concluded, *"This case is still very early in the legal process, but according to the Chicago police and the arrest report, Ms. Barnes has denied the charges. Efforts to reach her for a statement have been unsuccessful."*

Joanna depressed the off button on her television remote, the room spiraling into silence. Rising from the bed, she moved to stand in front of the full-length mirror, staring at her reflection. She no longer recognized the woman looking back at her. Just twenty-four hours earlier she'd been contemplating a cruise to Cuba for the summer break or perhaps traveling to Italy instead for a holiday fling with a handsome stranger. Just one day ago she didn't have a care in the world, her biggest concern being whether to repaint the master bathroom finch yellow or the dull beige her mother wanted.

Today the reflection staring back at her wasn't sure if her holiday vacation would include a stint in a maximum security prison with her name on the state's sex offenders registry, or worse, the unemployment line, her teaching license forever terminated.

The bathroom was never going to be finished and life felt everything but carefree. What she did know for certain was that, for her, the school year was done and finished, and she might never be able to step foot into another classroom. Just the thought made her want to start crying again.

Joanna hung her head, her shoulders rolling forward as she felt as if she was suddenly struggling with the weight of the world. She'd risen early, having barely slept. She had tossed and turned for hours, despite her best efforts to rest. Having always been in full control of her life, she was suddenly out of control, someone else pulling her strings and intent on ruining her.

She took a deep breath. She was angry, frustration fueling rising rage. Mingus had been right. Had she been able to get to David Locklear, she would have probably been in handcuffs for murder because she really wanted to strangle the boy.

David Locklear had been a promising student, though slightly lazy and often distracted. He'd been raised by a single mother, his father having disappeared before his birth. His mother had been a stern disciplinarian and, for all intents and purposes, he'd been raised well. But he could be troublesome, using his teenage antics to impress his peers, no matter the consequences.

The attention Joanna had given the kid hadn't been any more or any less than she'd given any of her other students. She had offered to tutor him when he was struggling. Had disciplined him when necessary. Had often reached out to his mother to keep her abreast of his progress and she'd advocated for him when others had been ready to write him off. He'd excelled, his grades better than average, and Joanna had been ecstatic for him when he'd been accepted to college. His accusations made no sense and she had no clue what had motivated his lies or what proof had been given to justify her being charged.

The smell of fresh coffee suddenly assaulted her senses and she realized she desperately needed a cup, maybe even two, if she had any hope of getting through the day. Pots and pans were rattling in her kitchen and she whispered a silent prayer of gratitude for Simone. The two women had talked for hours. Simone had made her laugh and had let her cry. There had been no judgment and the woman's calming presence had been exactly what she'd needed to keep from losing her mind. Shortly after midnight Simone had retired to the guest bedroom and Joanna had been grateful to have someone else there with her in her home.

Joanna moved toward the door, swinging it open eagerly. She headed down the short length of hall to the kitchen. Her eyes widened in surprise when she found Simone's brother Mingus standing room center, a foam container of eggs in one hand and a stick of butter in the other.

He gave her a nod of his head as her gaze met his. "Good morning."

"Hey! Good morning! I was expecting to find Simone in here making all that noise."

"She had to leave. She has a trial starting today and needed to get to her office to prepare. She said to tell you that she will call and check on you later." He turned to the stove, resting the eggs beside a glass bowl on the counter. He threw a glance over his shoulder, deliberately eyeing her from head to toe. A slight smirk crossed his face, something carnal seeping from his eyes.

The moment was intensely awkward as Joanna suddenly realized she was standing there in sheer panties and a tank top, her bathrobe forgotten in the bedroom. The attire hid very little, all her goodies on full display. She cussed as she spun on her heels and hurried back in the other direction. Behind her, she could hear Mingus chuckling softly.

Minutes later Mingus could hear her in the other room, still muttering under her breath. Her reaction had been priceless and he was amused. Despite his best efforts he couldn't stop thinking about the visual she'd blessed him with. The form-fitting garment she'd been wearing had flattered the round of her buttocks and the hint of cleavage between her pert breasts. Her skin was a rich, warm, gingerbread brown and with the length of black hair that hung past her shoulders, she'd been quite the sight to behold. But it had been her bright smile pulled from ear to ear that had him still grinning. He liked seeing her happy.

He had cracked the eggs into the glass bowl and seasoned them with salt and pepper. A second trip to her fridge produced cheese and an assortment of vegetables to complete the morning meal. He was sliding omelets onto two plates when she returned. This time she was wearing denim jeans and a white-and-blue button-up shirt. Her hair had been pulled into a ponytail that hung down her back. She was still just as stunning. He ignored the rising sensation quivering for attention in his southern quadrant, instead reaching for the coffeepot to fill two cups with brew.

"I hope you're hungry."

"I usually don't eat breakfast, but it smells really good."

"It's the most important meal of the day. I always eat breakfast in case I don't get to eat for the rest of the day."

Joanna moved to take a seat at the table as Mingus pointed to her plate. "Does that happen often? That you don't get to eat?"

"Sometimes."

Mingus suddenly reached across the table, motioning for her hands. For a brief moment the gesture caught her off guard. She eyed him questioningly, her brows raised. He waved his fingers a second time until she extended her arms toward his. He clasped her hands beneath his own and lowered his head.

"Father God, thank You for the food we are about to receive for the nourishment of our bodies. In Jesus Christ's name we pray. Amen."

Joanna was still eyeing him curiously as he let her go and leaned back in his seat. He reached for his fork and began to eat. She reached for hers, poking at the two-egg omelet filled with cheese, spinach, onion and tomato. She rested her fork against the plate and reached for her coffee cup. After splashing it with hazelnut-flavored creamer, she took a sip, her eyes closing as she savored the rich flavor.

"Coffee's really not good for you," Mingus said as he took a sip of his own brew.

Joanna smiled. "So, breakfast is good and coffee isn't?"

"That's what they say."

"So why are you drinking it?"

"I never pay much attention to what *they* say. I do what I want, when I want."

Joanna took another sip. "Works for me," she said, tossing him a look of complicity.

Mingus resisted the urge to smile, his game face sliding into place. He swallowed a forkful of eggs, the melted cheese and vegetables bursting with flavor in his mouth. For a moment they both sat savoring the meal, neither saying anything until Joanna spoke.

"So, what's on the agenda today?"

"I'm going to take you to Ellington's office, so we can figure out his next steps. After that, you'll come back here."

"I need to get my personal belongings from my classroom and I need to pick up my car."

"You can't do that. I'll get your things for you. If you go within ten feet of the school, it will violate your bond."

She suddenly thought about the news segment, her face plastered across the television screen. People thinking she was a criminal when that was farthest from the truth. "I was on the news this morning. They called me a predator. A child molester. And they posted my picture. Suddenly, I'm guilty before I've even had the chance to prove my innocence."

There was the faintest hint of sympathy in Mingus's tone as he answered. "I know."

Joanna sighed softly, took up her fork and began to eat. She suddenly paused, the utensil stopped in mid-air. "You said we're going to figure out your *brother's* next steps. What are you going to do? And what am I supposed to be doing?"

Mingus narrowed his gaze, amusement sweeping across his face. "You are going to sit tight and say out of trouble. And you're not going to worry about what I do."

Her gaze skated across his face, trying to read the emotion staring back at her. She finally shook her head, rising from the table as she grabbed his plate and hers. "Well, I can tell you now that's not going to happen, so try again, Mingus Black. I need answers and I don't plan to leave your side until I get them." She tossed him one last look as she turned, moving to drop the plates into the kitchen sink.

Mingus watched as she rinsed the dirty dishes and moved them into the dishwasher. Her pronouncement came with much attitude in her tone and her body language showed she didn't care whether he agreed or not. Her expression was stoic, her emotions tightly contained. She was learning not to show her hand and he was impressed. He appreciated her determination, even though he sensed she was going to be a royal pain in his ass.

Chapter 4

The law office of Black, Turner and Hayes was in the three hundred block of LaSalle Street, occupying the sixty-fourth floor of a glass-and-steel skyscraper. The office boasted floor-to-ceiling windows in the exterior offices, expensive interior contemporary decor, and a library and conference room reminiscent of an old English library with polished wood-paneled walls, hardwood floors and three walls of leather-bound law books lined meticulously on shelves.

Ellington Black greeted them in the front reception area then asked the young receptionist to direct all his calls to his secretary's desk. "Were you able to get any rest last night?" he asked as he guided Joanna and Mingus to the oversize conference room.

Joanna shook her head. "No, not really."

Ellington nodded in understanding. "Please, have a

seat," he said, gesturing to one of twelve high-backed, tufted brown-leather executive chairs.

Mingus ambled into the room behind her, moving to hold up the wall as he stood with his arms crossed over his chest. Joanna tossed him a look but didn't bother to comment. His brother didn't react one way or the other to Mingus not joining them at the table. But Joanna didn't miss the look that passed between the two men, a silent conversation she wasn't privy to.

"Unfortunately," Ellington started, "we've hit a snag in the case that isn't going to help us with your defense." He gently placed the folder he'd been holding on the table as he took a seat. He took a deep inhale of air before he continued. "The state is levying additional charges against you. They're adding twenty-one counts of distributing pornography to a minor."

Joanna's mouth dropped open, her eyes widening. "I'm sorry...pornography?"

Ellington nodded. "It seems they found photos of you on Mr. Locklear's cell phone. Very explicit photos."

Joanna was suddenly shaking her head vehemently. "That's not possible!" she exclaimed, her words coming in a low hiss. "I never took pictures with that boy! Never!"

Ellington took another deep breath. "They are executing a warrant on your home this afternoon." He shot his brother a look. "I'm going to ask Mingus to keep you away while they do their jobs. I'll head on over after we're done here and stay until they're finished. I'm sure the district attorney is going to petition to have your bail revoked, or increased, based on the new charges. I'll appear before the judge to answer if they do. Hopefully we'll be able to keep you out of jail."

Joanna jumped from her seat, spinning in a tight circle around the chair. "This is crazy! I would never do something like that! Never! Why is this happening?"

She shifted her gaze to Mingus, who hadn't reacted, nothing in his eyes showing how he'd received the information or what he thought of it, or her. Frustration furrowed her brow and her jaw tightened as she clenched her teeth. She suddenly shouted, "Say something, damn it!"

Mingus stared, his eyes narrowing as they locked gazes. The moment was suddenly tense and awkward. He didn't budge, giving her nothing.

Saline clouded her view, tears welling behind her thick lashes. Joanna shook her head, fighting the wealth of teardrops threatening to flow. She turned back to Ellington. "May I use your restroom, please?"

Ellington stood, extending his hand as he pointed toward the door. "I'll show you where it is," he said as he turned the knob and led her from the room.

He returned promptly, throwing a quick glance at his brother. "It's not looking good for her," he said, reaching for the thick file on the tabletop.

"She didn't do it," Mingus answered. "I believe her."

Ellington nodded, pulling a photo from inside the manila folder. He passed it to his brother, watching him intently.

From the moment they'd arrived and he and Ellington had exchanged gazes, Mingus knew something was amiss. Something that had his brother more than concerned. As he gawked at the photo, he was taken aback by the image, but he didn't show it. He never let his blank expression break.

The young man in question was wrapped naked

around a woman, clearly in the throes of some serious sexual passion. Arms and limbs were exposed but you couldn't see the woman's face well enough to say it was Joanna or not. But what you could see clearly was a tattoo on the woman's upper thigh. The same tattoo Mingus had been able to glimpse just an hour or so earlier as Joanna stood barely dressed in the center of her kitchen.

The silence in the car was stifling and it took everything Joanna had not to scream at the top of her lungs. She couldn't begin to imagine what Mingus was thinking. Even she was beginning to have doubts as the evidence piled, making her look guilty.

She had seen the photos, the graphic images stunning her into silence. None showed her face, but the tattoo was identical, the brown skin the same tone as hers. The woman in the photos was even wearing her favorite nail polish, OPI color Barefoot in Barcelona. But even as she'd professed her innocence, doubt had punched her hard, knowing no one was going to believe her.

Now they were ransacking her home and there was nothing she could do about it. The police had already confiscated her cell phone and Ellington had warned that her computer, iPad and all her other electronic devices would be taken, as well. Despite knowing she'd done nothing wrong and had nothing to hide, knowing someone was searching through her personal possessions infuriated her.

"Why you?" Mingus cut his eye in her direction, suddenly disrupting the blanket of silence. "Why have you been targeted?"

Joanna shook her head. "I honestly don't know."

"Do you have any enemies? Have you been beefing with someone lately?"

"No. No one."

"Really think about it, Joanna. Who would want to hurt you?"

There was a stillness in the air that seemed to rise and fill the car with angst and turmoil. Joanna was drawing a blank, unable to fathom how anyone could hate her so much. She was a good person, or at least she tried to be. She treated people decently, had wonderful friends and had never been ugly to anyone, even when it might have been warranted. She shook her head, no soul coming to mind. She suddenly felt deflated, blowing a heavy gust of air past her thin lips. She had no answer to his question, so she didn't bother to reply.

"How long have you been teaching at Riptide?"

"My entire career. I graduated from Riptide and after college it just felt right to come and give back. They had an opening and I took it."

"Is that normal? I mean…do a lot of teachers do that?"

"I don't know about a lot, but a few."

"How many teachers did you work with who also graduated from Riptide?"

"There were three of us. Marion Talley, who teaches English, and Donald Patterson, one of the administrators. Marion and I were classmates and graduated the same year and Mr. Patterson actually went to school with my father. He'll retire this year, I think."

"Your dad graduated from Riptide?"

"He and my mother. And my great-grandfather."

"Interesting…" Mingus seemed to drift into thought

as he considered her comment. "So, you and this Marion Talley were friends?"

"I wouldn't say that. Personally, I can't stand her! She's just mean and nasty for no good reason. And I don't doubt that she likes me even less."

Mingus shot her another look. His brows were raised, his gaze questioning.

Joanna continued. "Long story short, James Pratt asked me to prom and not her. She's resented me for it ever since."

"Enough to want to frame you for something you didn't do?"

There was a moment of pause as Joanna stared at him. "You believe me? That someone's trying to set me up?"

Mingus had come to a stop behind a line of traffic, waiting for the stoplight to change from red to green. He shifted his eyes to meet hers. "Yeah, I do! Something about this doesn't feel right. I just need to figure out why someone would go to so much trouble."

Riptide High School was one of eighty-five public high schools in a system that supported some four hundred thousand students. The rivalry between some of the Chicago schools was renowned, but he was discovering that Riptide had recently been in the news about everything but the success or failure of its sports teams.

Two previous scandals at the high school involving teachers already had parents on edge. A former cheerleading coach was fired the previous year for posing naked in a men's magazine, the images hanging in more than one young boy's locker. Just months later an administrator had been terminated for racist views published on social media. Both incidents had made the front page of the *Chicago Tribune*, a host of national news outlets and had been the focus of school board meetings for longer than most would have thought.

Just weeks prior, that same school board had listed it as one of ten schools under consideration for redistricting and a potential closing. People were talking about Riptide and it wasn't at all positive, despite its graduate success rate and the high number of college acceptances. They also had a stellar football team, frequently placing in the top 2 percent of all high school conference districts. But even that wasn't enough to keep the clouds casting dark shadows over the school's reputation at bay.

Mingus took a deep breath as he observed the rush of students moving from their last class toward home. They were loud, slightly obnoxious and he couldn't begin to imagine having to deal with the lot of them all day. The office secretary seemed to read his mind.

"They can take some getting used to. Most of them are really not that bad. It's the end of the day, though, and they're all ready to be done and out of here."

Mingus turned to meet the look the older woman was giving him. He smiled slightly. She reminded him of someone's grandmother. Her head of thick, gray hair was tinged a strange shade of pale blue. Crow's feet adorned the edges of her bright eyes and she wore her age across her face behind the barest hint of makeup. He gave her a nod.

"How long have you been here?" he asked.

"Twenty years in November. I was at the elementary school before that."

"So you've known Ms. Barnes since she started?"

"I've known her since before her church confirmation. Her mother and I go way back. Joanna and my second son are the same age and our two families have been friends since forever."

"Is she well liked here?"

"Immensely. She's one of the more popular teachers at the school."

Mingus started to ask another question when they were interrupted by the school principal. Valentina Donato looked harangued as she rushed into the room. Her face was flushed a brilliant shade of red and perspiration beaded across her brow. She threw Mingus a quick look, her eyes widening. She took a deep breath and then extended her hand.

"I'm so sorry. You must be Mr. Black. The district office called and told me to expect you. I understand Ms. Barnes's attorney made the arrangements."

He shook the woman's hand, her palm slightly clammy. "I appreciate you accommodating me."

"This is such an unfortunate situation. Between you and me, I'm glad Joanna has hired outside counsel to protect her interests. This is completely out of character for the woman I know and respect."

"So you don't believe the allegations?"

"I honestly don't know what to believe. And, of course, I'm not in a position to offer a formal opinion that goes against the statement issued by the school district." She and the other woman exchanged a quick look before she focused her attention back on Mingus.

The exchange didn't go unnoticed. Mingus nodded. "If you don't mind, I'd like to see her classroom."

"Not at all. Most of the students are gone for the day. Ms. Graves was asked to pack up Joanna's personal possessions. The two are good friends, so she may be able to provide you with information that I can't."

"And Ms. Graves is…?"

"One of our English teachers," Principal Donato responded.

"Has David Locklear returned to class?" Mingus asked.

The woman snapped, "You can't talk to any of the students without parental permission."

Mingus suddenly felt scolded and his eyebrows lifted. "I only asked if he'd returned," he snapped back, not at all intimidated by her brusque tone and the cutting look she was giving him.

She turned and hurried out the door, gesturing for him to follow. "I apologize, but we have an issue with one of the buses and I have twenty-seven students still waiting to get home. I had a student smoking pot in the boys' room and a television news crew hovering like vultures at the corner of the property. Now the school board is talking about closing us and I have parents breathing down my neck because of the news coverage about one of my best teachers. I've had my hands full and today has just been one of those days!" She cut her gaze back in his direction, seeming to need a hint of understanding. "But yes, he's back."

Mingus gave her a nod in response.

They traversed a series of hallways and one flight of stairs into a second building. Metal lockers numbered consecutively and secured with an assortment of padlocks lined the halls at each turn. Posters meant to encourage and promote the high school experience decorated the walls. An occasional student and a few teachers eyed him curiously. One or two were even bold enough to question the school's principal, who summarily dismissed them, sending them on their way.

Principal Donato came to an abrupt stop, the walkie-talkie on her hip vibrating for her attention. She paused, reaching to answer the man on the other end.

"Yes?"

"The bus has left, but we've got a reporter heading to the athletic fields."

"I'm on my way," the woman responded. "Let them know we're calling the police to have them removed."

"Yes, ma'am."

She closed her eyes and took a deep breath, her head waving from side to side. "Will it ever stop?" she muttered.

Mingus gave her a slight smile.

"I'm sorry." She pointed to the door on the left, at the end of the hallway. "That's Ms. Graves's classroom. This should only take me a minute. I'll be back as soon as I can."

"No worries," Mingus responded as she did an about-face, disappearing quickly through the doors they'd just passed.

Mingus moved to end of the hallway, pausing to knock before entering the room. "Are you Ms. Graves?"

The woman was seated at one of the desks, completely lost in thought as she stared into space. She jumped, blushing ever so slightly as she stood abruptly. "Yes, I am. Angel Graves, but you can call me Angel. And you are?"

"My name's Mingus. Mingus Black. Principal Donato told me I'd find you here."

"You're here to pick up Joanna's things?"

He nodded as he moved to the woman's side. She

was tall for a woman, standing nearly as tall as him in flats, and he was a good six feet, two inches.

"How is she doing?"

"She could use her friends right now."

"I've been trying to call but haven't been able to get an answer. I didn't want to just show up at her house unannounced."

"The police confiscated her phone."

Angel threw up her hands in frustration. "I still don't believe this is happening. No one does."

"How well do you know Joanna?"

"She's one of my best friends. We've worked here together for years."

"Do you think she's guilty?"

"I think someone's lying through his teeth. Joanna would never violate the trust she has with any student. She's an outstanding teacher. Her peers respect her and her students adore her! She's one of the most popular teachers in this place! Joanna Barnes is no sexual predator and, if need be, I will gladly testify to her character."

"Do you know the kid who's accused her?"

"I know she would not want his trifling little behind! That boy—and make no mistake, he is a *boy*," she said, emphasizing her word before continuing, "has absolutely nothing to offer her or any other woman with an ounce of good sense. In fact, I can't fathom any teacher wanting one of these nasty boys. No manners, barely past puberty and they always smell bad!" She wrinkled her nose as if a breeze of the offensive odor she talked about was suddenly wafting through her space. "I'd bet everything near and dear to me that boy is lying through his teeth."

Mingus nodded. "Do you know where I can find him?"

"Right now? I'm sure he's down in the gym or out on the baseball field with the coach, but you didn't hear that from me. Our boys' baseball team has made it to national playoffs. He's one of the star players. Everyone's coddling him right now to ensure he plays."

Mingus was just about to ask another question when a woman suddenly barged into the room. She moved straight to the desk, pulling open a drawer and peering inside as if looking for something specific. Mingus noticed there was a standing file rack with a few file folders and someone's purse inside. Realizing she wasn't alone, the woman looked from Mingus to Angel and back, her gaze sweeping his length with curiosity.

"Oh, excuse me! I didn't mean to interrupt," she said, a wide smile crossing her face.

Angel rolled her eyes skyward. "I'm sure you didn't, Marion. What can I help you with?"

Ignoring the question, the woman stepped forward, extending her hand to shake his. "I'm Marion Talley. I head the English department. Are you a parent?"

Mingus gave the woman a look back, his gaze narrowing. Recognizing her name, he hadn't known what to expect. He was slightly surprised, knowing that she and Joanna were the same age. She looked much older than he had imagined, hiding her years behind a touch too much makeup. Overbleached hair was cut in a pristine bob and the form-fitting dress she wore hugged her bulges tightly.

He shook her outstretched hand. "No, ma'am. I'm not," he said, not bothering to introduce himself. He turned his attention back to Angel. "I appreciate you talking to me. I'll take those things now."

Angel moved to the desk and a box that rested on top. "Thank you, and if you talk to my girl, would you please let her know she can call me at any time? Day or night. And I'll stop by to check up on her sometime this week."

Marion's eyes widened as if she'd had a lightbulb moment. "Oh, you're here to pick up Ms. Barnes's personal belongings. It's such a shame! She just never looked like the type."

"What type is that?" Mingus asked.

The woman fanned a hand in his direction. "You know…"

"No, I don't. So why don't you tell me?" He eyed her with a raised brow.

"The type to be accused of such a heinous act. She just never seemed like that *type*. And that poor child! I just hate to think what he has had to go through! It really is a shame. You think you know someone until you don't."

"So you think she did it?"

"Well, obviously I don't know for sure, but why would the young man lie? He's one of our brightest students, with a promising future. It breaks my heart to think how that woman may have traumatized him!"

"Marion, I just can't with you right now," Angel snapped, extending her palm toward the woman. She gave Marion her back, her head shaking slowly from side to side. She took a deep inhale of air and held it, speaking only after she'd released it slowly. "Thank you, Mr. Black."

Mingus gave her a slight smile as he lifted the box

with both hands. He moved to the door and made his exit. Behind him he could hear the two women fussing, their conversation rising a decibel as it echoed down the hallway.

Making his way back to his car, he deposited the box into the trunk, pausing to rifle through its contents. He wasn't expecting to find anything significant but was curious to see if he'd learn something new about Joanna that he didn't yet know.

Her friend Angel had rested a note on top, encouraging her to hang in there. The words were fluff and glitter, meant to make her smile. He decided he liked Angel. She was regular people and what you saw was what you got. He understood why Joanna considered her a friend.

Marion Talley, on the other hand, was a piece of work. Her hostility toward Joanna was corporeal, thick and abundant. The woman had barely been able to keep from sneering when she spoke Joanna's name. Despite a vapid attempt to seem sympathetic, she instead came off as judgmental and disapproving. There had even been an air of revulsion in her tone that hadn't gone unnoticed.

Mingus made a mental note to do a little more digging into Marion Talley. A woman like that had secrets and he was certain whatever she hoped to hide might prove to be beneficial to the case. Or not.

Chapter 5

Mingus had moved his car to the other side of the school, into the parking lot that faced the ball field. The local police were standing in conversation with a news reporter from station WTVD, admonishing him and his cameraman about being on school property. The school principal stood off to the side with another man, looking as flustered as she had looked earlier.

On the field, one of the coaches was running the baseball team through drills, one young athlete after another perfecting the art of stealing a base. A few stood off to the side eyeing the melee of adults, laughter and cell phones marking the moment.

Mingus recognized David Locklear from his high school yearbook photo. Because of his age, and the nature of the crime, his identity was being protected from the public, although Mingus imagined it wouldn't take much for a determined reporter to discover who he was. He had no doubts the reporter being escorted back to his ride had been banking on those boys being boys and one or more talking out of turn to give him a story.

David Locklear was laughing it up with a crowd of his friends. He seemed disinterested in the commotion, unfazed by the attention as a few of his pals high-fived him or threw easy punches against his narrow shoulders. He looked anything but traumatized.

Mingus suddenly felt conflicted. He didn't think Joanna was guilty and he fully intended to prove it. But if someone had taken advantage of the boy then that made him a victim. David didn't need to be judged or criminalized for something that wasn't his fault. Too many women endured not being believed or, worse, castigated for the abuse dealt to them. Mingus didn't want to perpetuate the fallacy that David Locklear had to have done something to invite any criminal behavior against him if indeed something had happened. Until he could prove otherwise, he owed the boy the benefit of the doubt, no matter how he was behaving.

He suddenly sat upright in his seat, tilting his head just enough to peer over the tops of the metal-framed Aviators he wore. He watched as a pretty, young woman stood in conversation with the teacher named Marion Talley, their conversation seeming heated and one-sided, as Mrs. Talley appeared to be scolding the girl. Seconds later the girl moved to the fenced ball field and exchanged words with David Locklear, who seemed irritated by the intrusion. The girl talked, but Mingus didn't see the boy respond. Instead he gave her his back and moved to the outfield behind the other players. His female friend shifted her leather handbag over her shoulder, turning abruptly as she hurried across the lot to a parked car. The driver had been sitting patiently, the car running, waiting until the young woman was settled inside. They pulled out of the lot into traffic.

Mingus lowered his camera and reached for his cell phone. He dialed his brother's number and waited for someone to answer.

"Detective Armstrong Black, please."

There was a pause as Mingus listened to the person speaking on the other end.

"Tell him it's his brother calling. Mingus Black."

Another pause.

"I'll hold, thank you."

Mingus shifted his attention back to Marion Talley standing in conversation with the principal, the coach and the man he didn't know. The woman was animated, her hands moving in sync with her mouth. The others seemed to be listening with half an ear, their expressions blank.

The phone line suddenly clicked in his ear, his brother greeting him.

"Hey," Mingus responded. "I need you to run a license plate for me."

Joanna swept the last of the debris into a pile and lifted it to the trash bin. Despite their promise to not wreak havoc on her home, the police had left her with a mess to clean up. Clothes had been pulled from the hangers and strewed to the floor. Drawers had been pulled from the bureaus and emptied. Her beloved books had been knocked from the shelves. Even the toiletries under her bathroom sink had been pilfered and tossed aside. The intrusion had left her angry and frustrated and she'd been glad that Mingus had dropped her off and hadn't come inside.

She blew a soft sigh. Ellington had offered to stay and help her put things back in place, but she'd refused his assistance. She had needed the time alone, just a few minutes of respite to clear her head and put the last twenty-four hours into perspective. Putting her possessions back into place had been therapy of sorts. Now she was wondering where Mingus was and if he planned to return.

She fought the urge to call the number he'd left for her and then remembered she didn't have a way to communicate with him without leaving the house to find a phone. Her confiscated cell phone was now in a plastic bag down at the police station. She suddenly heard her mother's voice in her ear, whispering that she should have had a landline installed for emergencies. In case her precious cell phone didn't work. Her parents still had the same phone and the same telephone number from 1965, when they'd gotten married and had purchased their first home. Convincing them that they no longer needed it had been futile and now, it seemed Joanna would have to concede that they may have been right about keeping it.

She moved from room to room, checking to ensure her possessions were in their proper place, irritation still fueling frustration. She moved back to the kitchen and began reheating the leftovers from the night before. As the spaghetti sauce began to slowly warm, she pulled plates from an upper cabinet and proceeded to set the table for two. Minutes later the melding of garlic and tomatoes scented the air as slices of garlic-buttered bread waited to be popped into the toaster oven.

A rumble of noise drew her attention to the bay of front windows. There had been a small crowd gathered at the edge of her driveway since earlier that morning. A team from the local media, parents, sexual violence advocates and people just being nosey, hoping to catch a glimpse of her doing something illicit to report on social media. Some carried signs calling her all sorts of vile names. Others just waited with their cell phones at the ready to capture any image that might further the narrative that she was a bad person who'd done something awful to one of Chicago's youngest and brightest.

Peering past the curtains she saw Mingus standing in conversation with the cameraman from the ABC7 Chicago news team. The two were chatting like old friends, the other man tossing his head back as he laughed at something Mingus had said. She watched as the stranger began to pack up his camera equipment. After a few more minutes of chatter, the cameraman and the reporter climbed into their news van. The crowd had thinned substantially, most returning to their cars. Only one or two persons still lingered, finally disappearing, as well, after an exchange with the private investigator.

Joanna moved to the front door and eagerly pulled it open. She watched as Mingus turned slowly. He hesitated for a split second when he caught sight of her and then with the briefest nod of his head he moved toward the door.

She greeted him eagerly. "What did you say to make them leave?"

Mingus shrugged his broad shoulders. "They didn't have any reason to stay," he answered. His eyes skated around the space. "You've been busy. I expected to find more of a mess."

"It just made sense to get it cleaned up as quickly as I could."

Mingus nodded. "Something smells good."

"Leftovers. I thought you might be hungry. I mean, I didn't know if you might want something to eat. I mean... I thought... I don't know what I mean," she finally muttered, feeling out of sorts for reasons she couldn't begin to explain. "For all I know you might need to go home to have dinner with your wife or your girlfriend."

Mingus smiled, his gaze narrowing ever so slightly. "I don't have a wife," he said. "Or a girlfriend. I'm surprised Simone didn't tell you that."

Joanna shrugged. His sister had told her, but she figured it didn't hurt to double check. She had no doubts Mingus didn't tell his siblings everything about his personal life. She didn't bother to respond.

He reached into his jacket pocket and pulled a cell phone from inside, passing it to her. "It's a burner. Until you get yours back."

The two locked gazes for the briefest moment before she responded. "Thank you." There was a moment of pause, awkward and slightly tense, as both waited for the other to lead. Joanna finally turned toward the kitchen. "Come eat," she said. "Tell me about your afternoon. Did you make it by the school?"

"I did," Mingus said. He pulled out a seat and sat. "I spoke to your friend Angel. She's worried about you."

"Angel is good people. I need to call her."

"I also met Marion Talley."

Joanna rolled her eyes. "I can just imagine that conversation."

"She's definitely not good people," Mingus quipped. "There was nothing likeable about her."

Joanna set a plate of spaghetti in front of the man then took her own seat. "Marion can definitely be a challenge. What did she say about me? Because I know she had something to say."

Mingus pulled a forkful of food to his mouth. He didn't bother to answer, only giving her a look that said more than he needed to say out loud.

Joanna rolled her eyes a second time, turning her attention to the food on her plate.

For a good few minutes neither spoke, falling into their own thoughts. Mingus hadn't known just how hungry he was until he realized he was shoveling his food into his mouth, barely chewing before swallowing. He suddenly sensed Joanna watching him out of the corner of her eye, amusement dancing in the dark orbs. He reached for a paper napkin and wiped it across his mouth and then his chin.

"The spaghetti's good," he said. "It's really good."

Her smile lifted. "Thank you."

"Do you do a lot of cooking?" Mingus questioned.

"Not as much as I'd like. I love to do it, but it's not always practical cooking for one. Occasionally, I'll have friends over and then I can really show off my culinary skills. How about you? Do you cook?"

Mingus shook his head as he helped himself to a second helping of the meal. "When it's necessary! I wouldn't say cooking is my forte. I do, however, consider myself a connoisseur of great cuisine. I enjoy good food no matter who has prepared it. And this is exceptionally good!"

Her smile widened. "I appreciate the compliment."

Mingus smiled, lifting his glass of merlot in salute. "Question for you," he said as he rested the wine goblet on the table and leaned back in his seat. "Do you know a man named Kyle Rourke?"

Joanna paused in reflection, her fork stalled in mid-air. "No. I don't think so. Should I?"

Mingus shrugged his shoulders. "He's a petty level criminal. Been busted for some minor offenses. Check fraud, shoplifting, that kind of thing."

She shook her head again. "Not the kind of crowd I usually run around with. Sorry."

Mingus reached for the digital camera he'd rested on the other end of the table. He depressed the button for the images and passed the camera to her. "Do you know that girl?"

Joanna studied the image that filled the screen. "I don't know the girl, but that's Marion Talley with her."

"What about the next picture?" Mingus asked. "Who are the two men standing with Talley and the principal?"

She pointed with a manicured index finger. "That's John Talley, Marion's husband. He's president of the Board of Education, and that's Coach John Dyer. John runs the athletic department and coaches the boys' basketball and baseball teams. He coaches one of the girls' teams, too, but I don't remember which one,"

Joanna flipped to the next image, bristling slightly. David Locklear was standing on one side of a chain-link fence and the girl from the previous image was standing on the other; neither was looking happy. She took a deep breath, holding it for a moment before releasing it in an annoyed huff.

"And you're sure you don't recognize the girl?"

Joanna returned to the first image and stared intently.

She shook her head. "No. I've never seen her before." She lifted her eyes to stare at Mingus. "Who is she?"

"I don't know yet. But she left with a man named Kyle Rourke. I had my brother run his license plate to get his name and address."

"I still don't know either of them."

"Don't you think she looks like you? You both are about the same height, with similar body types."

Joanna stared a second time. She and the young woman in the picture shared the same warm complexion but little else as far as she was concerned. The girl had more hips and whips than she did, her curves fuller and softer. Joanna was thinner, her body more athletic and toned. The stranger was also wearing what was clearly a wig, or maybe even a weave. Thick and lengthy, the extended tresses fell to her waist. Joanna's shoulder-length hair was natural, straightened periodically with a blow dryer and a flat iron.

No, Joanna thought to herself, *I don't look anything like that woman!* She was only slightly offended by his comparisons. "I don't see it," she said. She rested the camera back on the table. "I don't know either of them…"

"Did you talk to David?" she asked.

"No, I didn't."

"Do you plan to talk to him?"

Mingus gave her a look but didn't bother to answer. He turned his attention back to his plate and the last of his spaghetti. A good few minutes passed as she sat glaring at him.

Despite her frustration she trusted that he knew best. She knew that everything he did served a purpose and his not talking to David Locklear was probably for her own good. She didn't like it, but she would deal with it. It still didn't stop her from wanting to give the kid a well-deserved tongue-lashing. She took a deep breath and rose from her seat, gathering the dirty dishes.

Mingus rose with her, taking his own plate to the counter.

"Please. Sit. I can do this," she said.

"I know. But it'll go faster if you let me help." He moved to her side, reaching for a drying towel as she filled the sink with soapy water.

"It gives me something to focus on. Otherwise I might lose my mind. House arrest is no joke."

"Technically, you're not on house arrest. They just want to know where you are at all times."

"Technically, it's still a pain in the ass!" She lifted her foot and waved it from side to side.

Mingus chuckled softly as he wiped a clean towel across the washed plate she passed into his hands.

"So, can you really get it off without setting off any alarms?" she asked.

"Are you planning on making a break for it?"

"I'm just curious."

The man smiled. "You know what happened to the cat that was curious, right?"

Joanna laughed. "Touché!"

They fell into a moment of easy quiet, moving smoothly around each other as they returned her kitchen to pristine condition. As Joanna wiped down the kitchen table, Mingus leaned against the counter and watched her. Joanna pretended not to notice but his intense stare had her feeling a little out of sorts. She took a deep breath and cut an eye in his direction. "Why are you staring at me?"

Mingus shrugged his broad shoulders. "I have a lot of questions."

"So, ask. I don't have anything to hide."

"Tell me about James Pratt."

Joanna blinked, that question not at all what she'd been expecting. "James? Why are you asking me about James? That was high school!"

"I didn't know there were questions that were off limits."

"There aren't, but I haven't thought about James in years. That just came out of left field."

Mingus shrugged again. "How long did you two date? I assume you two dated before he asked you and not Marion to the prom, right?"

"We didn't date. James was the kind of boy parents didn't want their daughters dating. To be honest, back then, James scared me. He was more experienced, had plenty of female attention and you just knew he'd be trouble. The kind of trouble your mother warns you about and you still chase. He could also be aggressive. My father didn't approve of James. But we were science lab partners and I tutored him in math. We became friends and he use to tease me a lot. By the time we graduated he was more like a big brother than anything else.

"He's married now with four daughters. The last time I heard anything about him he was doing well. He owns a fast-food franchise over on Morgan Street. It's a Chick-fil-A or a Shake Shack, I think. It's one or the other. But we don't keep in touch, if that's what you want to know. We catch up if we happen to run into each other, but it's been months, maybe even a year since I last saw him."

"And he asked you to prom?"

"He wanted to take my friend Debra Magill. Debra and I were on the cheerleading team together. But Debra had already said she was going with his friend Craig. Asking me was supposed to make Debra jealous."

"Did it?"

"Debra married him the day after graduation. They've been happy together ever since. At last count they have five kids together."

"How did Marion Talley fit into the equation?"

"Marion was a fungus. She had it bad for James, but he was not interested in her. After Debra turned him down, Marion asked him to take her to prom and he told her no. That's when he asked me."

"Did you go to prom with him?"

"Damn right! It was *senior prom*! That, and no one else asked me." She laughed, the wealth of it gut-deep.

Mingus smiled, the bend of his full lips dimpling his cheeks. He shook his head.

"So, neither you nor Marion ended up with this guy, so why has she held a grudge all these years? I'd think she'd be mad at the woman he married."

Joanna sighed softly as she leaned against the counter beside him, folding her arms over her chest. "It's felt like Marion and I have been competing against each other since the third grade. I got picked one too many times to hand out the test papers, or always got an exam grade that was higher than hers. We both ran for class president and I beat her twice, our sophomore and junior years. We both applied to Ivy League colleges and I was accepted everywhere I sent an application. She wasn't so lucky. She was also a bully and she enjoyed making my life miserable whenever she could. Prom was just the last of many instances when she felt like I had bested her. I never gave it much thought until we had an argument a year a two ago and she blurted out how she had always hated me and why. It was sad, but it explained a lot of her behavior."

"What were you arguing about?"

"There was an issue about the teacher pay structure that was going before the school board and we were both asked to speak at the board meeting. She didn't think my opinion was needed and since I wasn't a department head she felt she was better positioned to represent our peers."

"Sounds to me like most of it was just petty bullshit."

"It was, which is why I try to avoid her whenever I can. After all these years, I can't make her like me and I see no reason to try."

Joanna shifted her weight from one hip to the other. Her brow suddenly furrowed with concern. "You don't think she has something to do with this, do you? I mean, I know she can be evil as hell, but this would be a whole new level of demonic for her. She couldn't possibly hate me that much, could she?"

Mingus shrugged his broad shoulders. He didn't bother to respond.

Joanna turned, reaching for an empty glass out of the cabinet. She shook her head as he reached for his own glass, filling them both from the bottle of wine that remained from dinner.

She found it slightly disconcerting to have Mingus questioning her about her past. She hadn't thought about her high school years in ages. James Pratt was a vague memory at best, as were most of the boys and men she'd dated over the years. Not that she'd dated all that much.

She could count on two hands the men she had spent

time with and have fingers left over. There had been no long line of lovers who she'd spent time with. The last man in her life had been a friend of a friend. His name had been Patrick, a social worker with the state of Illinois. The relationship had barely lasted six months. Patrick had been looking for a life partner and Joanna knew he was not the man for her. He'd been decent in bed if that counted for anything, but the fact that he wasn't a reader and considered libraries to be antiquated and books extraneous brought their affair to a quick end. She whispered a silent prayer that Mingus didn't ask her about Patrick. That wasn't a story she was ready to share.

Mingus's cell phone suddenly chimed loudly, an incoming call drawing his attention. He answered, throwing her a quick look as he stepped out of the room.

"Hey! What's up?"

Joanna listened, still standing where he'd left her.

"Where?" He seemed to be listening intently, the few words he spoke being one-word responses more than anything else. "You sure?"

The mood suddenly felt anxious, the hairs on the back of Joanna's neck twitching, goose bumps rising on her arms. His tone had changed, something in his voice raising concern. He had barely ended the call, returning to the kitchen, when she accosted him for an explanation.

"What's going on? Who was that? Is everything okay?"

"I need to run. Are you going to be okay by yourself?"

"No, I'm not," Joanna answered emphatically, a littler perturbed by his attitude. "Was that about my case?"

Mingus stared at her for a moment.

"One of my guys has identified the woman who was at the school today talking to David. Her name is Alicia Calloway. Does it ring any bells?"

Joanna shook her head. "No."

"She's an exotic dancer at a gentlemen's club here in Chicago."

"A stripper? Why was she at the school?"

"I'm going to go ask her. So I need to leave."

"I want to go with you."

"That can't happen." He looked down at the floor and the government-issued bracelet around her ankle.

"You said I wasn't under house arrest."

"Where I'm going isn't a place you want them to have a record of you being anywhere near."

"You also said you could get it off."

"When it's necessary. Right now, I just need you to stay put."

Joanna threw up her hands, frustration dropping like a wool blanket around her shoulders.

Mingus suddenly reached his hand out, drawing his index finger along her cheek. His touch was gentle and calming. The gesture gave her a moment of pause as she stared into his eyes and felt herself sinking into the emotion swimming in the dark orbs. She nodded in agreement. Mingus didn't bother to say anything else, instead turning on his heels as he headed for the exit. Joanna called after him, his name a soft vibration against her tongue.

"Yeah?"

"Will you come back?"

"I don't know how long it'll take, Joanna."

"It doesn't matter what time. Just come back. Please?"

Looking back at her from the front entrance, Mingus hesitated for a split second. Then he nodded his head and turned, disappearing into the rising darkness outside.

Chapter 6

The dank nightclub catered to a horde of pestilence perched precariously on the edges of wooden seats and uncomfortable bar stools. Despite the early hour most inside were already lost in the hollow voids of a drunken stupor. Dubbed the Boys' Room, it was a low-level strip club with a questionable clientele. It catered to Chicago's underground, its misfits and the downtrodden desperate for a moment of respite. When one needed information on a criminal element in Chicago, answers could always be found inside. You just needed to know who to ask and Mingus always knew who would talk and who wouldn't. He frequented the place when a case called for it and sometimes when he just needed to kick back and relax, no one having any expectations of him The bouncer at the door greeted Mingus by name.

Identifying the young woman named Alicia had simply been a connection of dots that had started with

the man who'd given her a ride from the local high
school. It had taken a couple of hours and a few degrees of separation to discover his associates, his bad
habits and his obsessions. Alicia Calloway topped all
the man's lists. Discovering Alicia's identity answered
questions Mingus hadn't even asked yet and felt like
the first real break in a case that seemed like it could
go nowhere fast.

Mingus slipped the man at the door a hundred-dollar
bill and eased his way inside. Moving to the back of the
club, he settled down at a table in the corner that gave him
an unobstructed view of the bar, the stage and the exit
doors. His presence didn't go unnoticed. The bartender
had given him a nod as he poured a shot of bourbon into
a glass. Minutes later that shot glass and a beer chaser
were delivered to the table by a voluptuous blonde wearing nothing but a black G-string and four-inch stiletto
heels. Her makeup was intense: heavy foundation, an
abundance of rouge, a vibrant red lipstick, dark eyeliner
and lengthy eyelashes. Her hair was teased and sprayed
into a full bouffant mane, the blond strands framing her
small face abundantly.

She kissed his cheek, her smile pulled full across her
face. "Mingus Black!"

Mingus smiled as he greeted her warmly. "Hey,
doll!"

"Long time no see. I thought you might have forgotten about me."

"Now, Lily, you know that will never happen."

The woman giggled, her eyes wide in amusement.
"Is this visit business or pleasure?"

"Strictly business, this time."

"That's never any fun." The woman named Lily pushed her Botox-enhanced lips out in a slight pout.

Mingus chuckled softly. He downed the shot of bourbon and then swallowed a swig of the bottled brew. "We can't always play like you play, mama!"

"What do you need, handsome? And how can I help?"

"There's a dancer here. I'm told she calls herself Alicia."

"Alicia Champagne. What do you want that skank for?"

His brow lifted. "Why does that sound like you don't like her?"

"She's young and dumb. Thinks the world should revolve around her. And no, I have no love for her. Tell me you're here to bust her ass for something."

He laughed again. "I just need to have a conversation with her. Is she working?"

"It's your lucky night. She goes on next, if I'm not mistaken."

"Would you make the introduction?"

Lily held out her hand, her palm upright. "How badly do you want to talk to her?"

Mingus reached into the breast pocket of his leather jacket for his wallet. He pulled out another hundred-dollar bill and slid it across her fingers.

"You must want to talk to her really bad!" Lily exclaimed as she folded the bill into a small sliver and slid it into the heel of her shoe.

"Actually, I need to ask you a few questions, too."

"Anything you need, good-looking! You know I am always available to do business with you."

Mingus gave her smile and a wink of his eye. "Alicia have a boyfriend?"

"Alicia has a pimp. Squirrely looking guy named Rourke. He's small-time and small-minded. I haven't seen him tonight, but he comes in regularly."

"Anything unusual about their routines lately?"

"Just them bragging about some windfall they're supposed to be coming into. But he's the type who always has some get-rich-quick scheme up his sleeve that bombs and puts her back out on the streets taking care of him."

"You haven't schooled her yet, mama?"

"Like I said, young and dumb! She's determined to learn her lessons the hard way."

A spotlight suddenly filled the center stage. Seconds later Alicia pushed past the velvet curtains at the back of the stage and stomped in high heels to the pole in the center. She wore a red cape and carried a stuffed wolf head on a three-foot giddy-up stick.

The music in the room rose a few decibels, a thick bass line vibrating through the space. Alicia sloped back against the floor-to-ceiling pole, one leg curled behind the pole, the giddy-up stick between her legs. For six minutes she performed a bump and grind that revolved around the dance pole and the toy wolf that took her out of her cape and down to a red-sequined G-string and tasseled pasties.

At the end of her Little Red Riding Hood performance she was gathering the dollar bills tossed at her when Lily leaned in to whisper in her ear. Mingus lifted his arm and slowly waved a twenty-dollar bill as Alicia looked up to stare in his direction. She tossed him the faintest smile as she gave her associate a quick look then climbed down off the stage and sashayed slowly toward him.

Mingus gestured with his monetary offering, waving her into the seat at his side.

"My name's Alicia," she said as she snatched the money from his hand. She was a pretty girl. Her warm complexion was identical to Joanna's, but she sported long burgundy braids and a mountain of makeup to mask the wear and tear of the life she lived. Her eyes were large and black, like wells of ink. But they were empty, devoid of any real emotion other than strands of anger and indifference that tensed every muscle in her body.

Mingus nodded. "You look familiar," he said. "Do we know each other?"

She stared at him then shook her head. "I don't think so, but for another eighty dollars we can get to know each other very well." She slid her body closer to his, her hand sliding across his thigh, her eyes focused on the wallet he'd rested on the table.

"I graduated from Riptide High School. You look like someone I went to school with."

"I'm not her," Alicia answered. "I went to school in Detroit."

"You sure?"

"You doing an interview or what? My time isn't cheap and I'm really not looking to make new friends," she snapped. "You're either paying for my attention or you aren't."

Mingus nodded a second time. His gaze dropped to the tattoo on her thigh. "I like your ink," he said, pointing to the tattoo on her upper thigh. "That's different."

"Yeah, whatever," she said as she stood. "My play

cousin Omar did it. He's got a shop down in the West Loop if you need something."

"Play cousin?"

"We grew up in the neighborhood together. His grandma used to babysit me and my little brother. Omar's my boy. He's good people and super talented."

"Omar does good work."

"It's okay. If you like that kind of thing," she said, shrugging her narrow shoulders. Her tassels spun from side to side. "He's going to redo it in a few weeks for me. I want to cover it with a pod of baby dolphins."

"But it's new, isn't it?" Mingus sat forward to get a closer look. The tattoo was fresh and had barely healed. The coloration was vibrant but still peeling slightly around the edges.

"It was my boyfriend's idea, but I want to cover it up with dolphins."

Mingus pulled another twenty-dollar bill out of his wallet and slid it toward her. "You have a nice night, Alicia. Thank you for the chat."

"You don't want a private dance?"

"Maybe next time. I have someplace I need to be."

"Whatever," she quipped as she snatched the currency from the tabletop and turned on her high heels.

"Yeah, whatever."

Mingus watched as she walked away, sashaying her way to the bar and then behind the curtained stage. On the other side of the room, his friend Lily sat on the lap of a large, burly guy. With his fire-engine-red hair, full beard, handlebar mustache and the plaid shirt he wore, he looked like a lumberjack in training. The man was grinning from ear to ear, clearly entertained by Lily's presence and she was working it for every dime she could. With the crowd beginning to pick up, Mingus imagined she'd probably have a lengthy client list before the night was over.

He tossed Lily a nod of thanks as he rose from his seat. Reaching to the table for his beer bottle, he chugged back the last of his beverage. His attention suddenly shifted to the door and the two men moving through the entrance. Alicia had moved back into the room and she rushed to greet the man Mingus knew to be Kyle Rourke. He was heavier in the face than his last mug shot was taken, but it was him. His walk was cocky and there was a distinct air of arrogance that he exuded. Alicia pressed her body to his and his response was dismissive as he shooed her off to work, snapping at her like a chained dog. His bark was meant to intimidate her and everyone within hearing distance. The mistreatment was pervasive and Mingus felt himself bristle with indignation, wanting to reach across the room and punch the fool in his face.

But it was the man standing beside Rourke that Mingus found most interesting. He looked anxious and clearly out of place. His nerves were getting the best of him and he was trying hard not to let it show. Sweat beaded across his brow and he was shaking in the brown leather loafers he wore. He clenched his fists tightly at his sides, his stance as if he were preparing to run. The suit he wore was expensive but ill-fitting against his thin frame. He was pedigreed, eyebrows meticulously plucked, his face freshly shaven and his olive complexion looking as smooth as a newborn's ass. His companion, who was clearly not as preened, was not in his league. The two together looked like oil and water trying desperately to mix. Mingus suddenly had more questions than answers. Pretending to dial a call, he shifted his cell phone in his hand to snap a quick picture without being noticed.

As he moved to the door, passing the two men as he sauntered past the bar, he and the nervous stranger exchanged a look, each measuring the other like grown men sometimes did. Shifting his gaze away, Mingus dismissed them both and made his exit.

Joanna moved from the large bay window back to the living room sofa. She'd been pacing the floor since Mingus had left earlier. Wondering where he was and what he was doing had her a lot stir crazy. She had questions, curious to know more about the stripper he'd been so anxious to go speak with. Wondering what type of woman Mingus was attracted to. She couldn't stop herself from imaging the stripper who might have his attention and something like jealousy pitched through her midsection. She shook the sensation, desperate to focus on anything except Mingus Black.

Twice she'd gotten into her car, pulling it out of the garage and down the driveway. Twice she'd been determined to do something. To do anything that would help her feel like she was doing something because she was feeling exceptionally lost and it was not sitting well with her spirit.

Her last attempt had been stalled by a police cruiser driving past the home to do a routine wellness check in the neighborhood. Despite her efforts to maintain a confident attitude when Mingus was around, she wasn't feeling very self-assured now that he was gone. In all honesty, she was scared to death and slightly desperate to find the answers that would fix what was broken and return a semblance of normalcy to her life.

She was also tired of the pity party. Feeling sorry for herself had become exhausting and it hadn't been seventy-two hours yet. She needed to cut the life crisis short before it sent her spiraling into a pit she couldn't crawl out of. She needed to feel useful and less like a victim. She stood and moved to the window, sliding back the sheer curtains to peer outside.

There was a full moon surrounded by a spattering of stars, all illuminating the night sky. The home across the street from hers was dark, just a single light flickering from a back room. The street was quiet, no sign of Mingus or anything else moving around outside. Joanna blew a soft sigh and headed into the kitchen for a bottle of wine and a bowl of microwave popcorn.

An hour later there was a soft knock at her front door. Joanna was slightly surprised, having lost herself in thought as she navigated the pages of the most recent copy of *Saveur* magazine. Rising from her seat, she hurried to the entrance, peering through the peephole before throwing it open to welcome Mingus inside.

There was something about his presence that Joanna found exhilarating. The energy he exuded actually gave her goose bumps. He was truly one beautiful man! His hair was cropped close and his beard and mustache were meticulously edged. The black jeans and leather jacket he wore flattered his physique. But it was his eyes, the lids hooded slightly as he stared at her, that gave her pause. His gaze was intoxicating and when he bit down against his bottom lip she felt moisture puddle in the most intimate places. She felt herself gasp as she stared at his full lips, the plush pillows lifting in the barest hint of a smile.

"Hey…"

Joanna glanced over his shoulder. "Where's your car?" she asked as he eased himself past her. She took a deep breath and inhaled the aroma of his cologne. It was a decadent scent, light and fresh with a hint of citrus finished smoothly with satinwood and amber. She held her breath, allowing it to fill her lungs as he answered.

"I parked it down the road."

There was the briefest moment of quiet as she pondered his comment. "I guess it would look a little suspect if that news crew came back and found a strange car parked in my driveway."

"Maybe not suspect, but we don't want to give them anything else to talk about."

Joanna closed and locked the door, following behind him as he moved into the center of the living room. He dropped down onto the sofa, assuming the seat she had just vacated.

"Are you hungry? Can I get you something to eat?"

Mingus shook his head. "No, thank you. I'll take a drink, though."

"What would you like?"

"What do you have?"

"Juice, tea, water…"

"Nothing stronger?"

"I think there's a bottle of vodka and maybe some bourbon left from the last party I had. I'm not a big drinker, so I really don't keep anything on hand. I might have some wine left, too. I don't think Simone and I drank it all."

"Bourbon's good."

She nodded as she turned and moved into the kitchen and the pantry where she kept the booze. The bottle of bourbon was tucked in the back behind an assortment of canned goods. It had been there since Christmas and the holiday open house she'd had for her friends and coworkers from Riptide. It had been a full house, everyone in a spirited mood. Noise and laughter had been abundant and any bad behavior blamed on too much drink and a good time.

Clint Owens, the head of the history department, had dropped his pants to show off the dancing elves on his boxer shorts and Principal Donato had danced a tad too close with a young substitute teacher who'd snaked a hand beneath her blouse when he'd thought no one was looking. There had been a slight ruckus between Angel and the coach over a hand of bid whist at her kitchen table and then everyone had headed home to celebrate the holiday season with their families. It had been a good time.

Joanna prepared a quick cheese board, piling on cheddar, Camembert, Gorgonzola and Pepper Jack cheeses, a small round of Brie, prosciutto, pepperoni, crackers, seedless green grapes, olives and a small bowl of pepper jelly. She set the wooden cheese board, two crystal tumblers and the bottle of bourbon on a larger tray and carried it into the living room. She placed it onto the coffee table and took the seat beside him, pulling her legs up beneath her buttocks. Reaching for the bourbon bottle, she poured them both a shot.

"I didn't mean for you to go to any trouble," Mingus said, his eyes skating over the delicacies. "But it looks good."

"I can't drink without eating something."

"I thought you didn't drink."

"Just on special occasions."

Mingus chuckled. "And this is a special occasion?" he said as he took a sip of his beverage.

Joanna shrugged. "It's something."

The room was quiet, her favored country music playing softly in the background. Despite the pleasant lull, both were lost in thought, the two of them deliberating over the last few hours.

When Joanna could no longer take the silence, she shifted her body to face him. "So, what did you find out?"

Mingus stared. Since he'd been gone, she had showered and changed, her hair still damp and pulled back into a ponytail. She'd removed her makeup, her fresh face gleaming. She was as pretty as he remembered, her natural glow reminding him of summer sunshine and liquid gold. There was something special about Joanna Barnes, but she was also proving to be quite the distraction.

He wasn't accustomed to anyone continually questioning him on how he did things and Joanna asked a lot of questions. He suddenly felt slightly uncomfortable as they exchanged looks, falling deep into one another's stare. Her eyes danced a slow two-step with his, lashes fluttering softly. The nearness of her caused a wave of heat to ripple softly through his body, settling sweetly in his southern quadrant. He tensed, muscles tightening naturally. He shifted in his seat, crossing one leg over the other.

Few women moved Mingus Black. He had never been interested in a committed relationship with anyone. Women who shared time and space with him knew he was not their happily-ever-after. At hello he was up-front about what he wanted and most appreciated him being direct and to the point. He'd enjoyed more than his fair share of one-night stands and the few who'd gotten more than one night could be counted on a single hand with fingers left over. Now, suddenly, Joanna had him wondering what old age might be like with a woman like her. Her eyebrows lifted, her expression still questioning as she waited for him to respond. Mingus had no intention of telling her about Alicia or the tattoo. He didn't need her riled up before he had the answers to explain what was still a question mark in his own mind. Mingus answered her unspoken question with a query of his own.

"Tell me about your tattoo."

Joanna's gaze narrowed, those lashes batting rapidly. "My tattoo?"

"Yes."

"Which one?"

This time Mingus was the one eyeing her curiously. "You have more than one?"

"I have five."

Mingus shifted forward. "You have five tattoos?"

Joanna nodded. She turned her head slightly then tilted her chin down. "There's the butterfly," she said, revealing the image of a small monarch hidden behind her ear.

Mingus reached a hand out, his fingers lightly grazing the butterfly's wing. The pad of his thumb trailed across the small design and down the line of her profile. Her skin was silk and heated beneath his touch. A hint of perspiration beaded over her brow. He suddenly wondered what she would do if he were to press his lips to that spot behind her ear. As if she read his mind, he heard her breath catch, pulling him back to the moment.

He nodded, snatching his hand away as if he'd been burned. The gesture moved Joanna to smile ever so slightly.

He nodded again. "Where are the others?"

Joanna pointed toward the floor as she turned her bare foot out for him to see. The phrase *Walk by Faith* was inked in a soft font, the design simple and elegant. She leaned back and lifted her T-shirt to expose her abdomen. There was a delicate filigree that circled her belly button and a piercing: a silver cross dangling from a small ring.

Mingus found himself resisting the urge to touch her a second time. But he really wanted to touch her again. He lifted his eyes to hers and their gazes locked and held. Something between them shifted, feeling tangible and sweet like orange blossom honey. He had no doubts that if he were to be so bold she'd welcome his advances, wanting him as much as he found himself wanting her.

He crossed his arms over his chest and shoved his hands beneath his armpits. "Tell me about the tattoo on your upper thigh. The one that was in the pictures with David Locklear."

That tattoo was of a stack of intricately detailed books. The top book was open, the center pages fluttering away like winged birds. Beneath the image was the George Santayana quote "To know your future you must know your past."

"I got it done about a year ago. There's a tattoo artist down off Randolph Street, near Fulton Market named

Omar Ramos. He's not my usual person but she wasn't available and recommended him."

"Omar Ramos from Lighthouse Tattoo and Piercings?"

"Yes," she said as her eyes widened. "You know him?"

"No, but I think we're about to become acquainted." He shifted once again, clasping his hands together as he rested his elbows against his thighs. "And your fifth tattoo?"

Joanna suddenly became tight-lipped, her eyes shifting from side to side in deliberation. There was a lengthy pause as she seemed to debate her response. He gestured with his head, still waiting for her to answer.

She took a breath and then responded. "That tattoo is for selective eyes only."

"Excuse me?"

"It's not for everyone to see."

"Where is it?"

"Someplace very private."

"Someplace only a lover would see?"

Heat colored Joanna's cheeks a deep shade of embarrassed. "A lover and my gynecologist."

"So, if the kid had slept with you, he'd be able to describe that tattoo?"

"He didn't sleep with me," she snapped.

"But if he had?"

She sighed. "Then I'm sure he'd be able to describe it in vivid detail."

Mingus nodded, the gesture slow and easy. "Did Omar do that one, too?" he finally asked.

Joanna shook her head. "No. That one was done by an old friend of mine. Rebecca Carson. We went to school together. She comes from a family of tattoo artists and graduated with a degree in art. She did Simone's tattoo, too, I think."

Mingus suddenly laughed. "Simone has a tattoo?"

Realizing her faux pas, Joanna rolled her eyes skyward. "You didn't hear that from me."

Mingus stood, tapping at the screen of his smartphone. "Go change. We need to go talk to Omar."

"Now?"

"Unless you want to stay here."

Joanna jumped to her feet. "Hell no!"

Chapter 7

Late-night hours were the norm at Lighthouse Tattoo and Piercings. Mingus knew if it was a good night they would go well into the early morning hours detailing body art on their customers. Three tattoo artists were standing around waiting for clients to arrive when Mingus and Joanna moved through the gallery door. Four others were working back in their respective booths.

The young woman who greeted them was loud and boisterous, a petite body of noise and laughter. Her attire was miniscule and tight, basically string with patches of fabric to cover her tiny frame. Mingus found her exuberance off-putting, not in the mood for the good time she was trying to sell.

"Welcome to Lighthouse! How can we help you?" she chimed, her voice sounding like she'd sucked on a boatload of helium.

Mingus gave her a slight smile. "I called earlier. I have an appointment with Omar. The name's Black. Mingus Black."

The receptionist smiled widely, her bubbly personality spilling over as she batted her false eyelashes at Mingus. Her full attention was focused on him as if Joanna wasn't standing there by his side. "We're glad you could make it, Mr. Black. I'm Leslie! What are you hoping to get done today?"

"Leslie, I'm undecided. I'm sure once Omar and I have a chance to talk, he and I'll figure it out."

"Omar is great! He'll hook you up with anything you want!" She drew her hand down the length of his forearm, manicured nails tapping at the jacket he wore. "This isn't your first tattoo, is it?"

Mingus chuckled. "No. Definitely not my first tattoo."

"Mine, either," Joanna interjected. "Omar did a tattoo for me a year ago."

Mingus smiled. "My friend here has only had good things to say about him. I'm glad he could fit me in."

The girl shifted her attention to Joanna, eyeing her as if she were seeing the woman for the first time. Joanna gave her a bright smile and took two steps closer to Mingus as she leaned into his side. He found the gesture amusing and for the first time he struggled not to let it show. He took a deep breath as he and Joanna exchanged a quick look; he felt the hint of a smile quivering at the edges of his lips.

The receptionist shifted her gaze between them. "Well, isn't that special," she said facetiously, tossing the length of her brunette hair over her shoulder. Her bright smile had dimmed substantially. She suddenly narrowed her gaze on Joanna. "I know you," she said abruptly, "You're that teacher on the news, aren't you? The one doing it with her student. That's so nasty!"

Mingus took a step, the gesture protective as he put himself between Joanna and Leslie. The look he gave the girl stalled any other comment she might have been thinking of speaking.

Tension swept between them and Mingus sensed that Joanna was biting back her own retort, not wanting to cause a scene. He reached for her hand, entwining his fingers with hers. His touch was warm and possessive, and the moment gave him pause.

When he squeezed her fingers gently, a level of comfort rose sweetly between them. Joanna released the breath she'd been holding, newfound confidence sweeping over her.

They both felt the other woman bristle ever so slightly, her attitude like a confetti-filled balloon bursting through the room. She glanced down the hallway and then to her appointment book, leaving them hanging ever so briefly as she answered an incoming call. Finally she said, "Omar's ready for you. Follow me!"

Mingus tossed Joanna a look and a wink of his eye as he led the way, pulling her after him. The receptionist was still talking a mile a minute.

Omar Ramos pointed his finger in recognition. "I know you!"

"How are you doing, Omar?" Joanna answered as she gave him a hug.

The man named Omar nodded. "I'm good. You here for another tattoo?"

She shook her head. "Not today. I brought a friend to see you instead."

Mingus gave the man a nod, his head tilting slightly. He extended his hand. "Mingus Black. What's up, brother?"

"Omar, and any friend of this beauty queen is a friend of mine."

"She said you could hook me up."

"We got you covered here. Do you know what you're looking for?"

Mingus shrugged. "I think I want to tie two existing tattoos together."

"Let me see what we're working with."

Joanna moved to an empty chair and took a seat. She hadn't been prepared when Mingus suddenly pulled off his jacket and then removed his shirt, tossing them both in her direction. She hadn't expected him to be getting a tattoo, instead under the impression that they were there to ask questions and get answers. But she knew to follow his lead, wherever that might take her. She suddenly inhaled swiftly at the sight of him as he stripped down to expose bare flesh.

His chest was broad, pecs like two rounds of marbled wood beneath taut skin. He sported a near perfect six-pack, his abdominal wall a thing of sheer muscular beauty. He was definitely no stranger to tattoos, more than she'd expected adorned his skin. A full sleeve decorated the length of one arm. It was tribal in nature with bold, black coloration defining the image. An intricately detailed cross rested against his heart, a rosary dangling up and over his shoulder. There was also a spectacular winged dragon inked across his back and shoulders, and the phrase *Work hard, play harder* wove around his wrist like a bracelet.

Omar admired each of them, clearly impressed by the level of work. But it was the image of Mingus's parents on his right arm that got the artist excited. Someone had replicated a wedding portrait. "I only know one tattooist who can do this caliber of portrait work. Jon Bua did this, didn't he?"

Mingus nodded. "I met Jon when I was in South Africa. They said he was the best, so I had to see what he could do."

"That's some nice work! Seriously nice!"

"When were you in South Africa?" Joanna questioned, forgetting for a split second why they were there.

Mingus tossed her a look. "A few years ago," he answered before turning his attention back to the man, who was still studying him intently. "I think I want a stack of books representing the foundations of faith," he said, pointing to the open space near the crucifix. "The Bible, the Quran, maybe the Tanakh. I want to tie it to the cross and the rosary beads."

Omar nodded. "Why books?"

"I like what you did with Joanna's tattoo," he said. "The stack of books with the fluttering pages and the George Santayana quote is epic and clearly represents what she stands for. For me, books represent knowledge and knowledge is essential. It also speaks to my belief in a higher power. I want it to represent my faith walk, which hasn't always been easy."

Omar continued to stare at what would soon be his canvas. His fingers skated across Mingus's existing tattoo, following the line of the artwork already there. His mind was clearly racing, his artistry being manifested in the creative process. Finally he said, "We got this! Why don't you climb up here on the table and we can get to work."

Mingus took a seat where the man gestured, reclining against the table and making himself comfortable. He and Joanna watched as Omar prepped his worktable and slid on a pair of latex gloves. Omar began to draw his design by hand, laying out the detail in red pencil. Minutes later the sound of the tattoo machine hummed with the beat of the music playing over the sound system.

Joanna listened intently as Mingus and Omar discussed his tattoo, football and the legacy of Harley-Davidson. When Omar slipped on headphones, someone's dance tunes beating in his ear, Mingus talked to her instead. He was relaxed, despite the pain associated with the needles that were assailing his skin, and he talked more than she had ever heard him talk. She delighted in the stories he shared and when she interrupted with a question, he answered. Despite Omar's presence, it quickly felt as if they were the only two in the room.

She found herself discovering things about the man that she didn't know and the more she learned, the more intrigued she became. After leaving the police force, he had traveled extensively, spending a year in South Africa and many months in Turkey and Greece. He was nonchalant about the experience, saying only that it had been a transitional period to discover himself and what he wanted to do with his life. He wasn't boastful or arrogant, but there was no doubt he was appreciative of the opportunities that had ensued.

He'd taken risks others only dreamed of. He'd run with the bulls in Spain, bungee jumped off the Macau

Tower in China, para-glided through Switzerland and had swum with whale sharks in the Maldives. He admitted to being an adrenaline junkie and was unapologetic about putting himself in jeopardy for an experience. He had no regrets and was clearly enjoying his life.

Joanna was slightly jealous and she said so. "I've always wanted to go skydiving, but I've never been able to get up the nerve. I constantly worry about everything that could possibly happen. I wish I was as daring as you."

"And I don't see any point in worrying. I have enough people in my life who do that for me."

Joanna laughed. "So, is there anything left on your bucket list? Anything you haven't done and still want to do?"

"There are a few things." Before he could elaborate, his cell phone rang, an incoming call disrupting the conversation.

He eyed the screen and cussed, annoyance flooding his face as he answered. "Hey, what's up?"

There was a lengthy pause as he listened to the person on the other end.

"She's right here. She's fine. I had something I had to do, and I needed her to come with me. I also called her bail bondsman before we left and told him where she'd be."

There was another pause.

"Just smooth it over. Do what you do." Mingus shot her a look, clearly irritated as the conversation continued. "That's fine. Tell them to do a drive-by. We're sitting right here in the tattoo parlor talking to the owner."

There was another pause.

"Yeah, whatever." He disconnected the call.

Joanna shifted forward in her seat. "Are we in trouble?"

"You missed your curfew."

"I have a curfew?"

"Apparently someone at the monitoring center became concerned because you haven't moved in the last three hours and you're not pinging from your home base. They called in a device check, which meant they also called the attorney on record to verify your location. That was Ellington. He called to lecture."

"I'm so sorry."

"Why?"

She blinked. "Because I don't…well…it's… Because…" she stammered, unable to find the words to express what she thought she should be feeling.

"Exactly. You have no reason to be sorry. Someone got overzealous. They didn't check the logs or ask the right questions and just assumed you had to be doing something wrong."

"Are the police coming?"

"I doubt it."

Omar paused, looking from one to the other. He'd shifted his earphones off one ear, the conversation suddenly piquing his curiosity. "Something I need to know? 'Cause cops aren't a good look around here."

Mingus shook his head. "It's good, man."

Omar nodded, his head dropping as he refocused on the last of the work he was doing. The final hour passed by quickly and when he finally laid down his tattoo machine and snatched off his gloves, Joanna and Mingus were still lost in conversation, simply enjoying each other's company. He pointed Mingus to the full-length mirror in the corner of the room.

* * *

Rising from the table, Mingus moved to stare at his reflection. The image on his chest was more than he could
have ever anticipated. Omar had brilliantly married the
old with the new, the two tattoos looking like they'd been
done at the same time. He'd skillfully placed the books
Mingus had wanted behind the cross, integrating them
as if they had always been there. The detail was impeccable and striking. Mingus was happy with the result.

Joanna was grinning from ear to ear as she stared
with him. "It's wonderful!" she gushed as she moved
to his side to admire the handiwork. "It's so good!"

"Do you mind if I take a picture for my book?" Omar
asked, interrupting the moment.

Mingus eyed him with a raised brow. "Your book?"

Omar nodded. "My portfolio. I like to memorialize
my work. I also use the images to give new clients a
sense of the type of work I can do."

"It's a nice showpiece," Joanna said. "I even think I
have a photo or two in it."

"I think you do." Omar moved to the shelves on the
back wall and pulled down an oversize black photo
album. He passed it to Mingus. "Have a look. Then take
a moment to think about it while I go check if my next
client is here. You can let me know when I get back."

"Thanks," Mingus answered. He began to flip through
the pages as Joanna stood over his shoulder.

A few pages in was an image of Joanna's tattoo and
Joanna, a bright smile on her beautiful face. She looked
happy and carefree, her legs crossed as she showed off
the artwork on her thigh.

"I'd actually forgotten about that photo!" she said.
Heat tinted her cheeks.

"It's a great shot. You're very photogenic," Mingus responded, giving her warm smile.

Mingus stared for a split second then turned the page, flipping quickly through the other images.

Minutes later Omar returned with a digital camera in hand. "So, we're good?"

Mingus nodded. "We're good. But I'm going to pass, my man. I appreciate your work. I really do. You've got mad skills, but I want to keep this exclusive. I'd be a little pissed if I saw someone sporting the same tattoo. You know what I mean?"

"Hey, I understand. But I assure you, I don't do repeats. I don't rubberstamp my designs. No one can come in and get this tattoo, or the tattoo I did for your girl. I work hard to ensure they're all unique." He rested the camera on top of the portfolio.

"I'm sure," Mingus responded, his eyes narrowing ever so slightly. "But I'm good. My answer's no."

Omar nodded. "Let me wrap you up then," he said as he reached for a protective bandage and began to explain the aftercare instructions.

When he was done Mingus reached into his pocket for his wallet. He counted off a string of twenty-dollar bills, paying his bill in cash. Omar wished them both a good night then called for Leslie to bring in the next customer. As they passed the young woman in the narrow hallway, she winked at Mingus and told him not to be a stranger. She ignored Joanna completely.

A Chicago patrol car was parked in front of Joanna's home when the two returned. Mingus pulled into the driveway and shut down the engine.

"You go on inside," he said. "I'll see what he has to say."

"Are you sure?" Concern washed over her expression.

He gave her the faintest smile and pointed her toward the front door. Joanna watched as he sauntered down to the end of the driveway and met the officer who'd exited the vehicle. The two men stood in conversation as Joanna unlocked her front door. She turned in the doorway to stare. Minutes later the uniformed officer climbed back into his car and disappeared down the road. Mingus turned and moved toward the entrance.

"What did he say?" she asked.

"Nothing," Mingus said with a shrug. "He didn't say anything that you need to be concerned about."

She blew a soft sigh. "Are you going to come in?"

Mingus shook his head. "No. I have somewhere I need to be."

"Oh. Okay." Joanna crossed her arms over her chest, a hint of attitude rising. "So why didn't you ask Omar any questions about my tattoo? Isn't that why we were there? To get answers?"

"We got answers," Mingus said without elaborating. "But I need to run. I'll wait until you lock up."

"When will I see you again?"

He flicked a gentle finger beneath her chin, giving her the sweetest smile. "Sleep well, Joanna," Mingus responded, purposely not answering her question. "Now lock the door."

An hour later Mingus walked back into the tattoo parlor. The neon Open sign was no longer illuminated but the front door was still unlocked. Music still played loudly in the background but the sound of bodies in the building no longer echoed off the walls. There was no one at the reception desk to greet him, nor did he call out to announce his arrival. He made his way down the narrow hallway toward the booth at the back of the shop.

He wasn't surprised to find Leslie and Omar alone together. Leslie stood naked except for her high heels and was bent forward over the tattoo table. Omar's denim jeans were wrapped around his ankles, his pelvis thrusting back and forth against her buttocks. His one hand clutched the side of the table. The other was tangled in the length of the woman's hair as he pulled the silky strands with each push of his hips.

Leslie moaned and groaned like a porn star, the oohs and aahs easily meriting an Academy Award–winning performance. Omar spat profanity, dirty words tangling around his tongue. Neither noticed Mingus standing in the doorway, his arms crossed as he leaned back against the doorjamb. He cleared his throat and gave them both a slight wave of his hand when they jumped in surprise.

"Don't mind me," he said. "I'll wait."

"Yo, dude! What the hell?" Omar snapped.

Leslie let out a little scream, crossing her arms over her chest. She scrambled for her clothes, holding them up to hide herself.

"Did you forget something?" Omar asked.

"Some information," Mingus answered. "I forgot to ask you about your cousin, and that tattoo you did for her a few weeks ago."

"My cousin?"

"Alicia Calloway. You might know her as Alicia Champagne. She dances over at the Boys' Room. You gave her a tattoo identical to the tattoo you did on my friend."

Omar suddenly looked nervous. He grappled with his pants, adjusting himself as he pulled up the zipper. "You need to get out!" he yelled.

Mingus crossed the room in two swift steps. His hand was around Omar's neck, lifting the man off the ground. Before Omar knew what was happening Mingus slammed him hard against the table. Leslie gasped loudly, her eyes like two large saucers. She stood frozen, unsure if she should move. Mingus took a step back as he released the hold he had on the other man.

"I'm not going to ask you twice," Mingus said.

Omar looked like he was about to cry. His hand was shaking as he pressed his fingertips to the rising bruise around his neck. "Don't think I don't know who you are. I know your entire family. Damn dirty cops, the lot of you!"

Mingus shook his head. "Don't talk about my family."

"I know your father's the police commissioner. You all think—" Omar started. He clearly wasn't expecting the floor suddenly rising to slam him in his face. His knees buckled, his feet flying out from under him so quickly he probably didn't know how it happened. Blood was spewing from his nose, spattering down the front of his white T-shirt as he lay sprawled on the floor.

"Ouch!" Mingus exclaimed. "That was a nasty fall, Omar! I'd hate for it to happen again. That looks like it might be painful."

"Don't hurt him," Leslie said, beginning to beg. "Please, don't hurt him!"

"As long as someone gives me some answers, I'm sure Omar won't have any more accidents. Now, I really don't like repeating myself," Mingus said calmly, standing over the man. "So, where were we?" His gaze turned to the receptionist. "Maybe you can tell me, Leslie. Why would Omar give a stripper the exact same tattoo he gave another client?"

Omar was still shaking away the chaos that had filled his brain. Tears rained out of his eyes as his nose began to clot. He stood slowly, moving on shaky legs to his feet. "Look," he muttered, "it was no big deal. Her boy-friend paid me five thousand dollars to do it. Cash!" He and Leslie exchanged a look.

Not missing the goo-goo-eyed exchange, Mingus turned his attention back to Omar. "Whose boyfriend?"

"Alicia's boyfriend. His name's Rourke Something-or-other."

"Did he say why?"

"I didn't ask, man. It was good money and I didn't think it was a big deal."

"Did you take a photo of it for your book?"

Omar pointed to the cabinet where the portfolio had been returned. "Yeah," he said. "But not for my book. Just to keep."

Mingus gave Leslie another look. "See if you can find that photo for me, Leslie. I also want the picture of Ms. Barnes."

Still mostly naked and holding the skimpy shorts and tank top she'd been wearing, Leslie moved to the cabi-net and a stack of images stored on a top shelf. She lifted the image in question from the pile and then slipped the other from the plastic sleeve in the photo album. She moved back to hand both to Mingus.

"Thank you. Omar, I'm going to need you to make a formal statement about doing this second tattoo." Min-gus reached into his pocket and pulled out a business card. He tossed it in the man's direction. "First thing in the morning will be fine. I'll see you around ten o'clock."

Omar was still shaking. "I'm going to press charges! You can't do this!"

Mingus waved his index finger from side to side, stalling the other man's comment. "Leslie, how old are you?"

Leslie gave him a bug-eyed stare, her anxiety level seeming to rise substantially. "Why…how come…" she stammered.

"Because," Mingus said matter-of-factly, "I don't think you're eighteen years old yet. Which means Omar just committed a crime. Isn't that right, Omar?"

Omar suddenly looked sick. "She's legal! Tell him you're legal!"

Leslie rolled her eyes skyward, her attempts at modesty completely forgotten. "You can't prove anything," she quipped, one hand falling to her narrow hip.

"How many kids at Riptide knew about Ms. Barnes's tattoo, Leslie? Who'd you tell?"

She rolled her eyes a second time. "Everyone. She walks around the school all high and mighty, so why not?"

"And you showed them that picture?"

"Yeah! The jocks had a party and we passed it around. It was a good laugh."

"Tell him you're eighteen!" Omar yelled, singularly focused on his own situation.

"She could," Mingus said, "but she and I both know that's a lie, don't we, Leslie?"

Leslie moved to the door, her naked backside shimmying from side to side. "You don't scare me!"

Mingus laughed. "Maybe not, but the video I took

while you two were doing what you were doing should scare both of you. I would hate for that to fall into the wrong hands!"

"Video? You son of a…" Omar was suddenly shaking, his words catching in his throat.

Mingus gave him a look then turned back to his companion. "And I'm going to need a statement from you, too, Leslie. To corroborate Omar's statement. You can tell your father you just want to do your civic duty. He'll understand."

The girl's eyes widened yet again. She looked like a deer in headlights as she stared at him. "How do you know my father?"

"The congressman is a good friend of the family and I'm certain he would be very disappointed to see what you're up to in your spare time."

Leslie's demeanor suddenly turned contrite. "You can't tell him! Please, I'll do whatever you say. Just don't tell my father!"

"Then you just tell the truth. All you must do is tell the police what you know. It's that simple."

Omar tossed up his hands in frustration as Leslie stormed out, stringing a long line of profanity behind her.

"Ten o'clock," Mingus repeated, tossing Omar one last look. "And don't make me come look for you."

Chapter 8

When Mingus walked through the doors of his brother's office the next day, Ellington was right there to greet him.

"You assaulted a witness?" Ellington snapped before even saying good morning.

Mingus responded with a wry smirk. "Now why would I do something like that?"

"His face looks like someone used him for a punching bag."

"Is he going to press charges?"

"No. He says he fell. But that's not the point."

"Then we don't have a problem," Mingus answered. "Did he tell you about the tattoo?" He passed his brother the file folder he'd been holding, the two images he'd taken from Omar the previous night inside.

"He did. Have you found the other woman with the second tattoo?"

"Yeah, but I still don't know what her connection is to the boy, just that they're acquainted with each other. And I'll be honest, I doubt she's going to give up any information if she doesn't have to. Right now, she doesn't have any incentive to talk and as soon as she realizes we're on to her that tattoo might become fish."

"Fish?"

"Or dolphins. Or something. I don't know which."

Ellington stared at his brother, his eyes blinking away his confusion. He shook his head and changed the subject. "How's our client doing this morning?"

"She's fine."

"You are keeping it professional between the two of you, right?"

Mingus and his brother exchanged a look. He shrugged his broad shoulders but didn't bother to answer. He hadn't spoken to Joanna, only sending her a text message to say he had an early morning meeting. She had already responded, wanting to know if she would see him. Asking about his plans after and what if anything else he'd discovered. She was frustrated and anxious and there was little he could do to alleviate her angst.

For reasons he couldn't begin to explain he hadn't been able to get her off his mind. He had enjoyed the time they'd shared at the tattoo parlor. He had liked that, for a few minutes, what had been between them had been everything but professional. Any other time, any other place, had their circumstances been different, or had she been any other woman, he would not have cared about any business relationship. He would simply have allowed himself to enjoy her. But Joanna was his sister's friend and damn near family and that in itself made her off limits.

His attraction to Joanna was palpable. She excited him. He appreciated her spirit and found her determination admirable. She knew what she believed, and she allowed nothing to sway her from her principles. She was the calm before a storm and fire in the midst of rain. She was everything he imagined himself wanting in a woman. *If* he wanted something with a woman! But he didn't. He didn't do relationships and he wasn't interested in any happily-ever-after. Besides, she was a client and neither his brother, or his sister, had any plans to let him forget that.

"Please, Mingus, tell me you haven't crossed the line with that woman!"

Once again Mingus ignored his brother's question, changing the subject. "What about Ramos? He give you anything else helpful?"

"He's adamant that it was just a financial transaction. The girl and her boyfriend wanted that tattoo in the exact same place and they paid well for it. He insists he doesn't know why it was so important to them. But we have his deposition and if it goes to trial, he'll testify."

Mingus nodded. "I need to take off. I need to figure out what's next. I'll call you when I get something else."

Ellington slapped his brother on the back. "Be smart out there, please. We can't afford to take any risks that might come back to bite us."

"Speaking of..."

Ellington began to slowly shake his head. "Do I even want to hear this?"

"You're going to get a call from Congressman

Franks. His teenaged daughter wants to corroborate Omar's statement."

"His daughter?"

Mingus shrugged. "Yeah. She's responsible for them knowing Joanna had a tattoo and where it was. She worked for Omar and they had a relationship, of sorts. I'm sure she's nervous about that getting out and his ass going to jail. Apparently she lied about her age and he fell for it. Or so he says."

"She's underage?"

Mingus nodded, his brows raised ever so slightly.

"You know I'm obligated to report it, right?"

"That's why I'm dropping it in your lap. They'll both deny it I'm sure but do what you have to do as long as you get their statements to help Joanna."

"I swear, Mingus, you never make anything easy for me."

"I love you, too, big brother!"

Mingus was blasting an old Eminem CD as he maneuvered his car across town. He still wasn't sure where he was headed; part of him wanting to get lost and disappear for a few days and the other part needing to see Joanna. Despite his best efforts the woman had gotten under his skin. She was an itch he couldn't scratch, and he was beginning to think that taking on this case had not been a good idea. He was finding it difficult to concentrate, unable to focus long enough to figure out the pieces to the puzzle. Nothing made sense to him and, still being unsure about all the players, he couldn't begin to know how to twist and turn things into place.

He bobbed his head in time to the beat. The deep rhythm of the song "Mockingbird" vibrated through the space. He was desperate to lose himself in the music. To cloud his head with thoughts that didn't revolve around the stunning woman, and then he remembered he had a case to solve and that put Joanna Barnes right back in the center of his mind. Taking a deep breath, he engaged the car's Bluetooth and dialed her number.

Joanna was surprised when her new cell phone rang. She hadn't been expecting any calls, few people having her new number. The device rested on the kitchen counter in the same spot she'd laid it the day Mingus had given it to her. She was even more surprised and suddenly excited when she realized he was the person calling. She answered on the fourth ring.

"Hello?"

"Hey, Joanna, it's Mingus. Are you busy?"

"Mingus, hey! No, I'm not busy at all. I was hoping to hear from you."

"Do you feel like getting out of the house?"

"Yes," she said, responding quickly. Maybe a tad too quickly, she mused after the word had jumped out of her mouth. She should have at least paused to take a breath, she thought, sensing that she'd probably sounded too enthusiastic. Usually, Joanna was more disciplined when it came to the opposite sex. She paced herself in new relationships, artfully containing her enthusiasm until she'd fully assessed a situation. Careful not to show her hand until she was sure she, and whoever, were on the same page. With Mingus she found herself reacting instead of responding.

She took a deep inhale, releasing it slowly. Then she repeated herself. "Yes, I would love to get out of this house."

"Great! I should be there in ten minutes. I really need to go to the gym and I thought you might like to tag along. Working out relieves stress. At least, that's what they tell me."

Joanna giggled softly. "I don't know about all that," she said. "Personally, I'm not fond of sweating."

He laughed. "Trust me, it'll be good for you."

She paused before responding. "I do trust you," she answered. "I'll be ready when you get here."

The Chicago weather was stuck in that nanosphere between winter and summer. The days were beginning to warm too rapidly and cold lingered far too long in the late evening hours. Residents were dressed in layers and forecasters were regularly predicting afternoon thunderstorms with chances of hail.

The midday air felt like spring and Mingus drove with the windows down, allowing the last remnants of the day's cool breeze to ripple through the car. Joanna closed her eyes and enjoyed the draft of air that blew past. They were both relaxed, enjoying the moment as they caught up and he shared what he'd learned.

"I recognized Leslie from the yearbook in your bedroom," Mingus was saying. "She was a student at Riptide until her father transferred her to a private school last year. She admitted to showing everyone that picture of you and your new tattoo."

Joanna sat straighter in her seat. "She was a student at my high school?"

"Yeah, her sophomore year."

"And you recognized her from a yearbook picture?"

He shrugged. "Photographic memory," he said nonchalantly.

Joanna shook her head. "I don't remember her at all, but then I don't get a lot of freshman or sophomores in my advanced classes."

"Well, she remembered you. Said you walked around all high and mighty," he said with a slight smirk. "That's why she did it."

"Reason number 145 why teachers can't have a life."

"Unfortunately we still can't prove it wasn't you in those photographs, only that someone else has an identical tattoo."

"But you talked to the girl, too, right?"

He nodded. "Her name is Alicia Calloway. But I haven't been able to tie her to David Locklear. And we still don't have a reason for why someone would go to so much trouble to set you up."

Joanna turned to stare out the open window. The city sights were flying by as Mingus drove a touch too fast to get them to wherever it was they were going. Joanna still didn't know their destination.

"So what gym do you use?"

He smiled. "The one in my apartment."

Her eyebrows lifted. "We're going to your home?"

"Unless that makes you uncomfortable?"

She stammered, shaking her head as she suddenly felt slightly out of sorts. "N-no. I just wasn't expecting... I thought we...hell, I don't know what I thought."

"Sorry, I'm not a people person. I avoid public places whenever I can."

"That's not a good thing, Mingus."

He laughed. "Now you sound like my mother."

"Judge Black is a very wise woman."

Mingus cut an eye in her direction. "I forgot. You've actually met my mother."

"I have. In fact, I've gone shopping with your mother and your sisters a few times. The women in your family are very people-oriented."

He smiled. "We guys know better. Most people have been nothing but trouble and we avoid trouble at all costs. Keeping to myself just makes things easier for me," he said.

"That sounds like a story waiting to be told."

He chuckled softly. "Not really. The men in the Black family just know to avoid drama whenever possible. So we avoid women with drama, friends with drama, strangers with drama, and when we can, family with drama. We never risk bringing scandal and shame upon the Black family name. Ma and Pa Black would bust a blood vessel if we did!"

"Your parents sound like my parents!"

"Exactly!"

"So is that why you're a private investigator?"

"What do you mean?"

"You get the drama, get to fix the drama, and then you get to call it business."

Mingus gave her another look, pausing to reflect on her comment. "You ask a lot of questions, don't you?" he finally answered.

She shrugged, rolling her eyes skyward. "I'm just curious by nature. I'm also discovering that you may be on to something when it comes to drama and trouble."

He reached for her hand, squeezing her fingers. "Don't change who you are, Joanna. I like who you are."

She smiled. "I think you're pretty cool, too, Mingus Black. You just need to smile more. You have the prettiest smile and you're wasting it scowling all the time!"

Mingus laughed. "I smile!"

Laughter was abundant and continued until they reached the North Bissell Street property where Mingus lived. The four-bedroom duplex was located in a prime Lincoln Park neighborhood. The contemporary space featured hardwood floors throughout with coffered ceilings and custom built-ins. Packing boxes were stacked in every corner and the entire space was sparsely decorated. There were stools lined up at the kitchen counter and an oversize recliner in the living room. A massive big-screen television adorned one wall.

"Did you just move in?" Joanna questioned as she moved slowly through the living areas being nosy.

Mingus shrugged. "It's been two years but I'm still unpacking."

She shot him a look. Hilarity danced in her eyes as she continued to take it all in. "Two years?"

He shrugged his shoulders. "I've been waiting for Simone and Vaughan. They've been threatening to unpack me since I bought the place."

"If it's been two years, I'm thinking they might not be coming," Joanna said. She giggled softly.

Mingus gestured for her to follow him to the lower level. Joanna was surprised to find a fully equipped gym in the basement area of the home. There were treadmills, two elliptical machines, an oversize weight machine and a Peloton exercise bike. Free weights were lined on a rack against one wall. There were jump ropes, dumbbells, kettle balls and a punching bag hanging in one corner. It wasn't at all what Joanna had expected for a home gym, the space feeling like its own national fitness chain.

"Make yourself at home," Mingus said. "I need to change my clothes, so I'll be right back."

"Thank you," Joanna said as she watched him disappear up the stairs. Music suddenly rumbled out of speakers in the ceiling, Mingus having flipped a switch from somewhere on the main level. She stood for a moment, still taking it all in as she assessed her options. She finally selected one of the elliptical machines and climbed aboard. After entering her age and weight, she engaged the unit and began to pedal. Ten minutes later, when Mingus returned, she had begun to perspire, her heartbeat elevated.

Mingus gave her a slight smile and moved to the weight machine. He began instantly to work on chest presses. Joanna continued to pedal, her arms and legs in sync with the music. When she was finally gasping for air, Mingus had done a full rotation of his upper body and was running on the treadmill.

She stepped off the machine, her hands clutching her narrow hips as she sucked in air. Her breathing was labored as she struggled to catch her breath. Mingus slowed his pace on the treadmill, his run stalling to a fast walk.

"You okay over there?" he asked.

Joanna nodded her head. "I'm good. I'm really good. I didn't realize how much I needed that."

He nodded. "If you want to shower, just make yourself comfortable in either of the bathrooms. There are clean towels in the closet in the hallway."

"Thank you," she responded. "I can definitely use a shower."

Mingus pushed the stop button on his treadmill. "The master bedroom is on the main level upstairs and there are two other guest bathrooms on the third floor. You are welcome to use whichever one you want."

"Thank you," Joanna said as she moved toward the stairs. Behind her, she heard Mingus resume his run, pushing the treadmill to maximum capacity.

Curiosity moved her to peek inside the master bedroom, wanting to know where he rested his head at night. A king-size bed occupied most of the space and it hadn't been made. The pillows and covers were askew and falling to the floor. A family portrait rested on the one nightstand in the room and the dresser was littered with bottles of cologne. The room was painted a pale gray and an abstract painting in shades of black and gray with red accents adorned a wall. The decor was elegant and understated. He was a minimalist, everything simplified, nothing extravagant. She found herself wondering if he was as staid in bed as he was out of it.

Moving to the living room Joanna gathered her gym bag and purse and headed upstairs to the third level. There were two more bedrooms and two additional bathrooms on the upper floor. Minimal furniture and a multitude of boxes decorated both spaces. But it was the wall in the room that was clearly his office that captured her attention. It was where Mingus found her still staring an hour later when he came upstairs to check on her.

In the larger of the two bedrooms, Joanna had taken a seat in the center of the floor. She sat focused on the photos and notes Mingus had affixed to the drywall with pushpins and tape. Her legal issues were splayed out in review, a tapestry of half steps and missteps, turns and twists. Seeing it all in the photographic images and his notes written in black marker had her feeling slightly defeated. There was no straight line leading them to the answers they needed. Seeing it in black, white and color made her realize proving her innocence was going to be harder than she had imagined.

When Mingus found her, she had stopped crying and was still staring, desperate to discover the answers needed to make it all go away. He dropped to the floor by her side, saying nothing; it was clear that in that moment he didn't have the words to bring her the peace she needed. He wrapped his arms around her, pulling her close. Joanna rested her head on his shoulder, allowing herself to settle into the warmth of his body.

"We will figure it out," he said softly. "I promise."

An hour later, after that much-needed shower, Joanna sat at Mingus's kitchen counter, watching as he stir-fried vegetables and shrimp into a meal for two. She slowly sipped a glass of white wine, now feeling comfortable and completely relaxed. She realized that Mingus's commitment to her case was all about blind trust, believing that she was telling him the truth despite the evidence that said she wasn't. He hadn't jumped to any conclusions about her being a bad person having done bad things. He was trusting his own instincts, even when others were telling him he was wrong. But he didn't have any answers, either, and was no closer to the truth than when he'd originally taken the case. She appreciated that he was not giving up on her. She needed that more than she had realized.

For whatever reasons she had thought of the infamous Salem witch trials and the women that were persecuted and sentenced to death. She was feeling similarly attacked; that prompted an interesting conversation between them when she'd mentioned it to Mingus. The conversation had led to a discourse about angels and religion, and then his theory about the afterlife. The serious had transitioned to the nonsensical and the ease with which they were able to converse had her feeling all kinds of happy. She suddenly realized he was talking to her, pulling her from the thoughts she'd fallen into.

"Was that a yes?" Mingus was asking, his gaze narrowed. He was staring at her, eyeing her intently.

"I'm sorry," Joanna answered, "did you ask me something?"

"I wanted to know if you needed a refill. I also have beer, juice and milk. Although I don't think you really want to mix milk and wine."

"That's not true. I have a great recipe for a wine and milk smoothie and it's pretty good. It's actually vanilla almond milk, cocoa powder, sweet red wine and a spoonful of sugar."

"Why?"

"Why not?"

"I think I'll pass," Mingus said. He set two plates onto the counter and filled both with stir-fry.

"Don't knock it until you try it. I'll have to make it for you one day."

"Just don't warn me first," he said with a warm chuckle.

"This smells really good!" she exclaimed as Mingus pushed one of the plates in front of her.

He grinned. "You say that like you're surprised."

"You have been nothing but surprises," Joanna responded.

After checking that he'd turned off the stove, he moved around the counter to sit beside her. He blessed the food, whispering a short prayer over the meal, and then they both began to eat.

After the first few bites Joanna hummed her appreciation. "Bodyguard, personal trainer, now chef! What else are you good at, Mr. Black?"

"What's that saying—'jack of all trades, master of none'? I'm good at a lot of things!"

"Why are you still single? What's wrong with you?"

Mingus laughed. He wiped his mouth with a paper napkin. "You get right to the point, don't you?"

"I figure there's no point in beating around the bush since we're such good friends now."

He shrugged. "I guess I've been waiting for the right woman to say she wants the job."

"You do realize you have to let the right woman know the job's available, don't you?"

He laughed again. "I guess waiting for the right woman just took longer than I thought it would."

Joanna smiled. "Good thing I got here when I did," she said, her expression smug.

Mingus turned to stare, locking gazes with her and holding it for a good moment. He finally nodded his head but said nothing. Amusement danced between them and lingered long into the evening hours. He talked about his family and what it was like to grow up in a house of tree-huggers and do-gooders, with sisters who were bossy and determined and parents who set standards that sometimes felt unsurmountable. She shared stories about her parents and growing up an only child. How her fantasies about other people and other places were fueled by books at the public library and a library card that had been the key to her future.

At one point, someone's dance tune pulled them from their seats and they danced from the kitchen to the living room and back, releasing pent-up energy that felt like fireworks exploding. They shared a single pint of Ben & Jerry's Bourbon Pecan Pie ice cream with two spoons. He swore she took bigger bites and she proclaimed him testy because he had issues with sharing his treats.

They talked about everything and about nothing, enjoying the process of getting to know one another. For just a little while, neither spoke about the case or the ramifications if she were to be convicted. All she could focus on was him and the something that was clearly growing like a wildfire between them. That something had begun to take on a life of its own, blooming beautifully, tangling abundantly and feeling as they imagined heaven might feel.

When the dishes were washed and his kitchen cleaned, Mingus stole a quick glance to his wristwatch. "I need to get you home," he said. "It's getting late."

"Do I have to go?" Joanna asked, the look she gave him teasing.

Mingus gave her a slight smirk. "Yes, Joanna, you have to go. I have some work I need to get done and you are distraction."

"I hope I'm a good distraction?" Her voice dropped an octave, low and seductive, like the sweetest honey was wrapped around her words.

He smiled. "You have your moments."

She blew a soft sigh. "I'm actually surprised your cell phone hasn't been ringing off the hook. I would have thought they'd be looking for me by now."

"They won't. I called and registered my address with the monitoring company at the police department. They know this is one of the places you'll need to frequent. They know you're here."

"You think of everything, don't you?"

Mingus shrugged. He was still staring at her, the look in his eyes warm and endearing. "Are you okay with that?"

"As long as I can come back. I can come back, right?"

"My feelings would be hurt if you didn't."

Chapter 9

Joanna had wanted him to kiss her. She'd even thought about initiating that first touch herself, but then she'd chickened out. She still stood staring out her front window, wishing he would change his mind about where he was going and turn his car back around. Minutes passed and the street outside remained dark and empty, no sign of anyone, least of all Mingus, returning to indulge her sexual whims.

A low gust of warm breath blew over her lips as she finally closed the blinds. She checked the door one last time and then she engaged the alarm. For a split second she thought about calling him, but she knew he wouldn't appreciate the interruption, even if he did want to hear from her.

Moving through the house, she made her way to the master bathroom and began to fill the tub with hot water and her favorite lavender-scented bath beads. She needed to rest but feared sleep would not come easily. Despite the good time, it had been a long day. It had been productive because she and Mingus had managed to steal a few hours of quality time with each other. Unfettered time with no interruptions, no one pulling for their attention. For just a moment she'd felt normal, just a regular girl enjoying time with a boy who seemed to like her back. She hadn't wanted to go back to being the woman charged with a crime and thought to be a pariah in society.

She slipped out of her sweats, dropping her clothes to the floor. She slowly eased herself into the tub. Soapy bubbles teased her brown skin and tickled places she wished someone was there to touch. She lay back and savored the sensation of the water lapping against her sweetest spots. Truth be told, it had been a rough week and the simple pleasure of lounging in the bath felt indulgent and deserved.

She was missing Mingus, and it had barely been an hour since they were last together. An hour since he'd made her laugh and had her wondering what it might be like to feel his body pressed tightly against her own. She found it fascinating that she had never missed any man before Mingus Black. Even in previous relationships she had never minded any distance, remaining objective about the longevity of their entanglements. Never allowing her heart to become embroiled in their experiences because she wasn't willing to risk her heart on relationships she knew had no chance of lasting. Most had been good guys, decent and honest and only interested in a good time. She'd been singularly focused on her career and hadn't been ready for anything permanent. It had served them, and her well, relationships with no strings and no expectations.

Hours later her skin was wrinkled, her body water-logged. The bottle of wine she'd opened was empty and her bed was finally calling her name. Joanna grabbed a plush towel to dry the dampness from her skin. After slathering her body with cucumber moisturizer, she wrapped a silk scarf around her head, tying it into an oversize back bun. She slipped on a satin nightdress and then slid her body beneath the cool sheets.

Closing her eyes, she fell back into fantasy, thinking about the man who had committed himself to being her knight in shining armor. She drifted into the sweetest thoughts, whispering Mingus's name over and over again as she let her hands dance deliciously between her thighs. Her only regret was that Mingus wasn't there to dance with her.

Mingus couldn't say so, but he hadn't wanted to leave Joanna. He had enjoyed their day and hadn't been ready for their time together to end. She had him completely enamored, feeling like the effort it had taken to grab his attention had been minimal with even less needed to hold it. She was just that good.

She had flirted, subtly at first, then more boldly. He'd enjoyed every moment, even flirting shamelessly back. He had teased her and had enjoyed the easy back-and-forth banter that had ensued. She'd been fun, and he'd appreciated the levity she brought out in him. Enjoying the time they'd shared made what he now had to do even less desirable because all he could think about was what it might be like to kiss her luscious lips and never stop.

He'd been parked outside the Boys' Room for over an hour, tailing after Kyle Rourke and his gal pal Alicia "Champagne" Calloway. The first part of his evening found them roaming from storefront to storefront shaking down owners and employees. They worked low-income neighborhoods and proprietors of family-owned businesses. Twice he'd watched as Alicia and another young woman had visited some no-tell motel off Stony Island Avenue on the South Side. Kyle had waited in the parking lot for them to finish their business and return. Prostitution was a booming business for a pimp who had no skin in the game.

Men like Rourke gave the male sex a bad name. He was a parasite that exploited women for his own personal gain, caring nothing about the ramifications of his actions. He was one of dozens and Mingus, like the rest of his family, worked hard to get the lot of them off the streets.

He suddenly sat upright, watching as Rourke and the dancer exited the nightclub and returned to their car. She was angry about something, her body language saying she was ready for a fight. Rourke didn't seem fazed by the tantrum she was throwing, turning once to shout back. She said something that clearly struck a nerve and he rushed at her, his arm raised as if he intended to strike. But she held her ground and braced for the impact, never once flinching. The glare across her face made Mingus think that if Rourke threw a punch, he needed to be ready because Alicia fully intended to throw a punch back.

The exchange of words continued for another few minutes then, just like that, it was over. Alicia threw her arms around the man's neck and kissed him, a tongue-entwined exchange that would have made a porn star blush. The two climbed into his car, moving on to their next destination. Mingus sighed, his body settling back against the car seat. As they pulled out of the parking space, turning right toward downtown, he followed.

Surveillance lasted longer than Mingus would have liked. By the time the couple was done with their business, the early morning sun was just beginning to rise. Mingus sat in front of their Maplewood Avenue townhome until he was sure they were done, no one making any surprise trips back out.

As he headed toward his own home, he found himself once again thinking about Joanna and that twinkle in her eye that gave him pause. Wanting to see her happy made everything he found himself doing well worth it.

Chapter 10

The Black family home was located in the heart of Chicago's historic Gold Coast neighborhood. Characterized by timeless stone-and-brick architecture, it was situated on a large corner lot. The solid wood-and-glass front door was unlocked and Mingus entered without knocking. Stepping inside felt like entering the comfort and quiet of a family retreat. Laughter echoed through the interior as he called out in greeting.

"Hey! It's just me! Who's here?"

His mother's voice responded from the rear of the home. "We're back here in the kitchen, Mingus!"

Mingus moved through the home, past the walls papered in silk, the sparkling chandeliers, ornate wood moldings and fireplaces meticulously carved in stone. The windows were draped in sumptuous fabrics and every detail, from the coffered ceilings to the highly polished hardwood floors, reflected his parents' taste and wealth. His mother met him as he sauntered through the family room toward the kitchen.

The Honorable Judith Harmon Black was a tall woman, nearly as tall as her sons. She had picture-perfect features: high cheekbones, black eyes like dark ice and a buttermilk complexion that needed little if any makeup. A hint of blush to her cheeks complemented her fair skin and her lush silver-gray hair fell in thick waves past her shoulders. She wore a red-silk dress, low black heels and her requisite pearls. The sight of the family matriarch made him smile, her own bright grin reaching to kiss his cheeks.

"Hello, baby!" she said as she wrapped him in a warm hug. "I wasn't sure we were going to see you today."

"You really need to answer your phone, son!" Jerome Black's deep baritone voice vibrated across the room. He sat at the kitchen table with Ellington and Davis. Parker and Armstrong stood at the kitchen counter, filling plates with food.

He and his brothers had inherited their father's good looks as well as his height and his athletic frame. Their patriarch was a distinguished man with salt-and-pepper hair, a rich, dark complexion and a full beard and mustache.

Jerome Black was also in a mood, clearly not happy with his son. "I left three messages for you. What's the problem that you can't call me back?"

Mingus and his mother exchanged a quick look.

"I can't help you," she said. "You ignore my calls, too."

"He ignores all of us," Vaughan added as she stepped

into the room behind him. She reached up to kiss her brother's cheek. "Hey, big brother!"

Mingus wrapped her in a big bear hug and kissed her forehead. "What's up?"

"We should be asking you that. What's up with you?"

He shrugged his shoulders.

"Yeah, what's up with you?" Ellington interjected. "And where's Ms. Barnes?"

Simone suddenly peered around the corner from the family room, moving into the space. "What do you mean 'where's Ms. Barnes'? What's wrong with Joanna?"

"Where do you want me to start?" Ellington quipped. "Yesterday she spent the entire day at your brother's house. Almost twelve hours. Ask me how I know."

Mingus rolled his eyes skyward. "Shut up, Ellington!" he snapped, annoyance rising swiftly. He had expected an interrogation but had hoped they'd let him in the door to enjoy his meal first. His family could be a bit much on a good day. He was grateful that he was in a good mood.

The women chimed in simultaneously. "Why is Joanna at your house?" Simone questioned.

Vaughan looked surprised. "A woman is staying at Mingus's house?"

"Who are we talking about?" Judith asked, her gaze sweeping over her children.

His brothers laughed heartily.

Simone shook her head. "My friend Joanna Barnes. You remember her, Mom."

Their mother nodded. "The teacher! Yes, I do! I really like that young woman. I hate that she is going through such a difficult time right now."

"Isn't she in jail or something?" Vaughan probed.

"She was arrested," Armstrong added, "for sexual misconduct. But she's out on bond."

"The charges are extremely serious," Jerome Black stated matter-of-factly.

"She didn't do it," Simone snapped.

"And why is she staying at your home, Mingus?" Davis queried.

Mingus suddenly felt like a circus side show, his family staring as they waited for him to answer. He shook his head.

"Sorry, Dad," he said, moving to the table to shake hands with his father. "But I did try to call you back. I called last night but it went right to voice mail."

"That's because your father forgot to charge his cell phone," Judith interjected. "He never charges that thing!"

"It's why we have a house phone," her husband responded. "If you really wanted to reach me, you could have called there. No excuses!"

Ellington shifted in his seat. "So, are you going to explain yourself?"

"We are not about to have this conversation," Mingus answered. "What I don't have to do is explain what I do on my time and who I do it with."

Ellington tossed up his hands in frustration. He yelled, "She's a client!"

"She's a friend!" Mingus snapped back. "Now, let it go!"

Simone shot both of her brothers a look. "I swear, if you two numbskulls screw this case up, I'm going to kill both of you."

Suddenly they were all arguing like toddlers in a

sandbox in dispute over some toy they all wanted. It was controlled chaos with chatter that was loud and disruptive.

"Enough!" Jerome's raised voice brought the entire conversation to a complete halt. His annoyance painted his expression as he glared at each of them.

Looks skated back and forth between them, each waiting to see who was going to jump first. No one said anything as the brothers went back to their meals and Simone exited the room. Vaughan followed her sister, their footsteps echoing up the stairs to an upper bedroom.

Mingus grabbed an empty plate and moved to the stove. His mother had fried pork chops and he helped himself to two. He added candied yams, mac and cheese, and a soft dinner roll to the mix, then sat, taking the empty seat between his father and Parker.

"Everyone good?" Judith asked. She held a pitcher of iced tea in her hand, moving to refill her husband's glass.

The men all nodded.

The matriarch rested her eyes on each of them, stopping when she reached Mingus. She called his name. "Mingus?"

Mingus glanced up to meet the look his mother was giving him. "Yes, ma'am?"

"Right now, I need to go up and help your sisters. But make sure you and I talk before you leave this house this afternoon, is that understood?"

He swallowed the bite of macaroni he'd taken. "Yes, ma'am."

No one else spoke, the men eating in silence after Judith exited the room. Their father's booming voice had always been the barometer for what they could and could not do and him shouting that something was enough easily brought any disagreement to an abrupt end. It had been that way since Mingus had been a small boy, little about their family dynamics changing since. His parents commanded obedience, despite each of their children being grown and independent, and had earned their respect. Not complying wasn't even a consideration for any of them.

It was only when their father rose to get them each a slice of the chocolate pound cake resting on a plate on the counter that any of them spoke.

"So how is this case going?" Jerome asked.

Ellington shrugged. "We're a long way from getting the charges dismissed. The prosecutor has offered a plea deal, but it's been declined."

"She didn't do it," Mingus muttered, knowing he sounded like his sister.

Ellington nodded. "I don't want to believe the charges are true, either, but, you have to admit, some of the evidence is damning."

Jerome nodded. "Obviously this family has a personal connection to the case. Simone's friendship with the young woman and now your relationship with her, Mingus, calls all of our actions into question."

"It's not like that—" Mingus started.

"Maybe not," Jerome interjected. "But what we want to ensure is that it doesn't look like any of us is affording her special favor because of her relationship with this family and your connections to the police department."

Parker nodded. "You need to let my officers do their jobs, Mingus. She's on an ankle monitor for a reason. If they come to the house to check, you need to let them. Don't tell them it's okay for them to not do their jobs and to ask me if they have any issues. Because they do check, and then I have to jump on their asses because they screwed up."

"He wasn't going to find anything, and she didn't need the interrogation."

"He needed to do his job," Parker said matter-of-factly.

Ellington added to the conversation. "I just need you to not make things harder than they need to be. Like when you circumvent me with the monitoring company, you make things difficult. You can't just add addresses you want her to visit without telling me, because when they call and I don't know what they're talking about, it makes us all look like we're aiding and abetting some wrongdoing. If I had to stand before a judge and explain it, I couldn't."

Mingus sat back in his seat. He blew a heavy sigh, a gust of hot air blowing past his full lips. He folded his hands in his lap and nodded. He was being scolded and although it was something he was used to, his brothers and his father giving him a hard time never sat well with him. It also didn't change that he would always do what he thought he needed to do, whether they agreed with his decisions or not.

"I remember Joanna," Davis said, shifting the conversation. "I thought she was really cute. I tried to ask her out but of course your sister blocked that! She said I was too young!"

Jerome laughed. "My girls can do that well!"

"At least Simone's good for something!" Mingus exclaimed. For a split second he thought about what might have been, had their sister not been there to stall his baby brother's advances. Would Davis and Joanna have been able to develop a romantic relationship? Would he have not been interested because his brother got there first? He was glad he would never need to know the answers.

Armstrong said. "I've seen pictures, but I don't think I've ever met her in person."

"Mingus was abroad, and you were studying for your detective's badge when she used to come to the house on the regular. I know she was at a few Sunday dinners," Ellington noted. "And she's definitely beautiful, there's no denying that. But I've seen how she looks at Mingus. I don't think anyone else would stand a chance with her."

"It's not like that!" Mingus repeated. "Really, we're just friends. I'm just doing whatever I need to do to help her get through this. I'm doing my damn job!"

His brothers all exchanged a look and then burst out laughing. Mingus shook his head, knowing there was the faintest smirk pulling across his face.

Jerome tapped him on the shoulder. "Just know that if you need to talk, I'm here. Anytime."

"We're all here if you need us," Parker and Armstrong echoed.

"Not me!" Davis chimed in. "Hell, I can barely handle my own love life, so I know I can't tell anyone else what to do with theirs!"

Laughter rippled with a vengeance through the home.

Mingus found his mother in her office, her attention focused on her computer screen. She looked up as he entered the room, pulling her reading glasses from her face and resting them on the desktop.

"Did you get enough to eat?"

"I did. The food was good. Thank you."

A smile shimmered in the older woman's gaze. "The next time you should bring Joanna. I'd love to see her again."

"Is it that obvious?" His mother knowing him better than anyone else, he wasn't but so surprised by her question. Despite his efforts to keep his emotions in check and his feelings to himself, she could read him like an open book and often did.

"It's obvious that you care about her and, under the circumstances, that's understandable. But she's a family friend and we don't turn our backs on our friends. Especially when they need us most."

Mingus nodded. He moved to the wing-backed chair in front of the desk and sat. "I like her, Mom. I like her a lot. But I don't know if I can help her. I don't know if I'm going to be able to prove her innocence."

Judith sighed. "You'll do what you need to do," she said after a moment of pause. "Just remember to trust your instincts."

"No lecture? I was sure I was going to get a lengthy lecture."

"Not from me. You have always danced to your own beat, Mingus. There's no reason for you to stop now, son! And you definitely don't need your mommy to tell you what to do."

He smiled. "Like that's ever stopped you."

Judith fanned her hand at him, the lilt in her laugh painting the room a warm shade of happy. "I give advice when it's needed. Whether you take it or not is on you."

"I promise I'll try to do better about answering my phone and returning everyone's calls."

She rolled her eyes skyward. "No, you won't. Don't even tell that lie. You'll answer when it suits you and respond when you have no other choice."

Mingus laughed. "I said *try!*"

His mother laughed with him. "If nothing else, I do know my children."

Mingus moved to stand but his mother gestured for him to remain seated a moment longer.

"I also need a favor from you, baby."

"Yes, ma'am? What do you need?"

His mother passed him an envelope. It was sealed, and his name was written in his mother's signature purple ink across the front. He met her eyes as she explained.

"I need you to find someone for me. All the information I have is there. Once you find him, I just need an address."

Mingus nodded. "Him?"

His mother gave him a look, her expression stoic and unreadable. "It's all there."

"Okay, I'll get right on it."

She shook her head. "Finish Joanna's case first. This can wait. It's not a priority."

"Yes, ma'am!"

"And one more thing!" Judith said as he stood, moving to make his exit.

"Yes?"

"I'd appreciate it if you don't say anything to your father or your siblings. I need you to keep this just between us."

Mingus stared and his mother stared back. Theirs

was a silent conversation, nothing explained and even less questioned. There was an understanding that what she asked was important to her and anything important to his mother was important to him. If she needed his discretion, he would afford it to her without reservation. That she trusted him enough to ask for his help was all he needed to comply. There was nothing he would not do for his mother. Finally he moved around the large oak desk to kiss her cheek and made his exit.

Chapter 11

"There's a school board meeting tonight!"

Joanna made the announcement like she was proclaiming the second coming of Christ. Her exuberance was telling, filling the room with an air of optimism. She shot Mingus a look. He knew his expression lacked the enthusiasm she had hoped for, so she repeated herself. "The school board, they're meeting tonight. We really need to go! I think it might help my case."

Mingus shifted his gaze to eye her. It had barely been two weeks since her arrest and they were no closer to solving the case. She was staring at him, her hands clasping the curves of her hips. She was stunning. She'd been working out for almost an hour and perspiration rained down her face. Her body temperature was raised a few degrees, her skin tinged a warm shade of pink beneath her dark brown tones. She wore shorts and a sports bra, exposing just enough flesh for him to ap-

preciate her toned form. She'd forgotten her headband
and her hair was unkempt, framing her face delight-
fully. She made him smile even when he struggled to
maintain his composure. He had never let his guard
down with any woman and with Joanna he found himself opening up and being vulnerable in ways that surprised him.

He shifted his eyes back to the television as he spoke.
"That might not be a good idea, Joanna. Why would
you want to put yourself through that?"

She spoke emphatically. "I'm not going to hide, Mingus. I didn't do anything wrong. If they're going to talk
about me, they're going to have to do it to my face."

He didn't say anything, his stare focused on a CNN
news story that played on the flat-panel television on the
gym wall. Mingus didn't bother to respond because he
knew her mind was already made up and there would be
no dissuading her. He had much respect for her resolve
and was whole-heartedly impressed by her gumption.
So he simply nodded.

Understanding swept between them, filling the room
like a warm breeze. Mingus increased the speed on his
treadmill as Joanna engaged the elliptical machine, re-
suming her workout. Neither had anything else to say.

The rest of the afternoon went by swiftly. They both
retreated to separate corners in his home, Mingus behind the closed door to his office and Joanna curling up
on the recliner in the living room with a book.

He had other cases to catch up on and a staff of employees who hadn't seen his face since the beginning of
the week. His secretary, a retired insurance agent who
sometimes worked from home, had been holding down
the office without him, but he had investigators who

need to run things past him for his approval. He needed to be on the phone for a while without distraction. Joanna needed time to herself to relax and not worry.

They had established an easy balance with one another. It was comfortable and together they were discovering that sometimes it was just about being in the other's presence, no conversation needed. They were learning each other's idiosyncrasies, quirks and aversions. Feeling each other out and discovering what made them tick. It was a game of give-and-take and it simply worked the way they needed it to work. It required effort he'd never before considered putting forth with any other woman.

Behind his closed door, Mingus sat staring at the wall. For two nights he had followed the stripper and her pimp, neither one leading him to anything he could use. He knew it was only a matter of time before they would have to show their hand or he would lose his window of opportunity to connect them to the case. He had no doubts Alicia was ready to rid herself of that tattoo, but that piece of body art also put Joanna in pictures she hadn't taken. One photo of Alicia and David in the schoolyard wasn't enough to prove anything. Mingus still had to place Alicia in bed doing the dirty deed with the boy. Whoever had staged that photo opportunity had gone to great lengths to completely obscure Alicia's face to ensure the tattoo was the only identifiable factor that could connect Joanna Barnes to David Locklear. But who would do such a thing, and why go to such an extreme? What was their payoff?

Mingus still needed to find a motive. He believed her accuser held most of the answers he needed, but the prosecution had tightened a circle around the young man, making it near impossible for Mingus to get to him without jeopardizing Joanna's defense.

He cursed, frustration furrowing his brow as he continued to try to connect the dots in his head and have it all make sense. None of his what-ifs thus far seemed plausible, one dead end after another. Although he had reservations about the school board meeting, he was beginning to think Joanna was on to something. Maybe, just maybe, the clues they needed would be there. If not, he wasn't sure they had any other options available to them.

Joanna rested her cell phone against the chair arm. She'd spoken to Simone and then to Angel; both of her friends had been offering advice and support. Simone had focused her comments and questions on what was going on with her friend and her brother. She'd been able to make Joanna laugh, her sisterly advice including a long list of Mingus's eccentricities.

"Don't say I didn't warn you," Simone said with a soft chuckle.

Joanna laughed. "Mingus has been very sweet. I think you just like to give him a hard time."

"He has moments! But he's still a man."

"Simone Black, all men are not bad."

"I'd disagree, but we don't have time for that debate. I need to leave for the courthouse in a few minutes. I really just wanted to check that you were all right."

Joanna chuckled. "Have you called Dr. Reilly since he's been back?"

"Dr. Who?"

"You know who I'm talking about," Joanna said, referring to Dr. Paul Reilly, Simone's ex-boyfriend. The good doctor had stolen Simone's heart and was still holding tightly to it. But she was stubborn and determined to have the last word in a relationship in which neither was talking. The two women had polished off many bottles of wine together, crying their woes over the men who had come and gone in their lives. Dr. Reilly had been at the top of Simone's woe list.

"He left me, remember? I have absolutely nothing to say to that man."

"He was altruistic. He wanted to save the world. His making the decision to do mission work in Africa doesn't mean he left you. Besides, if I remember correctly, Dr. Reilly asked you to go with him."

"I don't remember that, but we're not talking about me right now. We're talking about you and my brother."

"No, we're not talking about your brother!"

Simone suddenly gasped, an epiphany ringing through the line. "You two did it, didn't you!" she squealed. "You slept with my brother!"

Joanna laughed. "We did not, I swear! I did not sleep with Mingus. He's just been a stand-up guy when I needed a friend." She was grateful Simone could not see the heat that colored her cheeks, a wave of embarrassment sweeping through her as she found herself suddenly thinking about it.

"I was just checking! But seriously, Mingus is a great guy. You could do worse. Besides, I have hated most of the women he's dated. You would be perfect for him. I absolutely adore you!"

"I adore you, too. And I appreciate you checking on me."

"Come to Sunday dinner. My parents would love to see you. I'll make sure Mingus brings you."

"I'll let you know. I wouldn't want to intrude."

"You would never be an intrusion."

"Thank you, Simone. You don't know how much you mean to me!"

"Yes, I do! Now, you take of yourself. I'm here if you need me but you still make sure my brother does right by you. Or else!"

"I'll pass on the message."

"I mean it, Joanna, call me if you need me. Love you."

"Love you, too, my friend!"

After disconnecting the call, Joanna had dialed Angel, the woman answering on the first ring. She'd been anxious to catch her friend up on the gossip, hopeful that Joanna might be able to spill her own tea.

"It's been crazy around here," Angel gushed. "Marion's been strutting around like she won the lottery and Principal Donato constantly looks like she's on the verge of a nervous breakdown."

"Who's teaching my classes?"

"They brought in a substitute. Some guy who constantly smells like cheese. The kids have been brutal to him."

"I miss them!" Joanna exclaimed, a moment of melancholy piercing her spirit. She was suddenly reminded of just how much she her students and teaching meant to her. She'd always found much comfort in the day to day responsibilities of her classroom.

"The little bastards are still annoying. But they miss you, too. And most don't think you did it."

"I didn't do it," Joanna said emphatically.

"Most of us know that. But you always have a few crabs in the barrel trying to pull everyone down with them. How is that investigator friend of yours? Girl, that man is too fine! If nothing else, tell me he's been a pleasant distraction!"

Joanna laughed. "He's good. He's been working hard to prove I'm innocent."

"He could work for me anytime! Is he married?"

"Down, girl!" She hesitated briefly before she added, "He's unavailable." The words slipped past her lips before she could catch them. Angel fawning over Mingus had Joanna in her feelings, a wave of jealousy doing sprints in her tummy. It felt natural to claim the man, even if she didn't just come out and voice he was hers. Saying he was unavailable was enough to get the message across, that no one else could have him.

Angel laughed. "Damn, I always miss out on the good ones. He even had Marion salivating and you know it takes a lot to get that ice queen to melt!"

Joanna laughed again. "Are you going to the school board meeting tonight?"

"Unfortunately! The teachers' union wants as many teachers there as they can get."

"What's on the agenda?"

"Are you sure you want to know?"

"I asked."

"You…and the future of the school. Apparently, Riptide has moved farther up the closing list."

Joanna cussed. "This really is unbelievable."

"Don't worry about it. You'll be surprised by how many people have your back."

"I'm sure I will be." She sighed heavily. "Well, save me a seat."

"You're coming?"

"I think so. I really think I need to be there."

"You want to go grab drinks after?"

"No promises. Let's see how things go."

"I can't wait to see you. I've really been worried. Then when I couldn't reach you, it had me feeling some kind of way."

"I really appreciate it. But I'm good. Definitely better!"

"Does that man have something to do with that?"

Joanna giggled. "Goodbye, Angel. We'll talk when I see you!"

"You are so wrong! You know I want details, right?"

"Girl, 'bye!"

"Hugs, bestie!"

Joanna was replaying both conversations over in her head. Denying that there was anything between them had been well fine and good in that moment. But she couldn't continue to lie to herself about the growing connection between her and Mingus. Something was definitely brewing between them and everything about the evolution of it felt good and right. But if she were honest, she wasn't sure if they could ever have a future together. She couldn't help but wonder if she might always just be a client he felt responsible for.

The flirtation and banter they shared passed the time. The levity between them kept her from being a basket case. But she had to question if the fibers of their relationship were enough to weave the two of them into something permanent. Could he be her happily-ever-after? Was she his? In all honesty Joanna wasn't certain of anything, least of all if Mingus was interested in more from her.

Doubt was beginning to fester, and it had her slightly shell shocked when Mingus bounded down the steps calling her name. Something clearly had him unsettled and his agitation in turn put her on edge. He clutched a stack of papers in his hand as he stormed into the room.

"What's wrong?"

Mingus pulled the coffee table directly in front of the recliner and sat on it. Both his hands rested on the chair's arms, knocking her cell phone to the floor as he leaned forward, his face just inches from hers. "How did those photos get sent to Locklear from your phone?"

"Excuse me?"

His voice was raised. His face had turned a deep shade of red as he fumed with emotion. "You heard me! How did the porn get sent from your cell phone?"

"I don't know… I didn't…"

He yelled again, his voice rising another two octaves. "You have to know! They were sent from your phone, Joanna. How did it happen if you didn't do it?"

"I told you I don't know! They weren't sent from my phone!"

"Ellington just called. He faxed over the police forensics report and it says positively that there is a digital footprint showing those photos were on your cell phone. They can also trace the transmission of images from your phone to David Locklear's phone. All dated and time-stamped."

"That's not possible!" Joanna was incredulous. "There has to be some mistake!" She began to shake, her eyes skipping back and forth as she tried to make sense of what he was saying. None of it made any sense to her and she couldn't begin to fathom why Mingus would think that she could be capable of such a thing. Him questioning her, judging her, suddenly had her feeling broken and scared.

She took the documents Mingus suddenly extended toward her. After reading the results, she felt like another nail had been hammered into her coffin. "This can't be right!" she cried. "It can't!"

"Unfortunately, that's not what the report says. And someone has already leaked it to the press. You just led the five o'clock news!" Mingus flung the papers in frustration, the documents flying across the room.

"Stop yelling at me!" she snapped. "I told you I don't know anything about those damn pictures! I didn't send them. That hasn't changed just because you're screaming at me. I didn't do it!"

Mingus took a deep breath and held it. Tears had risen to her eyes and she was still shaking. He suddenly realized he must seem like a madman, the way he had come at her. He stepped back, releasing the grip he'd had on the chair. A moment passed between them as he reached for the cell phone that had fallen to the floor. He rested the device on the table.

He was much calmer when he next spoke but there was still an edge of tension in his voice. "Ellington is going to ask for a second review, but this company is top notch. The law firm has used them before and he has always trusted them. They don't make mistakes."

A tear rained from Joanna's eye and she wiped it away with the back of her hand. "Is this ever going to end? What is it going to take to prove I didn't do this?"

Mingus took another deep breath. "Look, I know you didn't send that kid any pictures. I believe you. I really do. But we really need to figure out how he made that happen. You have to know something!"

Joanna hung her head and dropped her face into her hands, leaning forward to stall the quiver of nausea rising in her midsection. She suddenly felt Mingus's hand gently caressing the length of her back. His touch was warm, his fingertips burning hot, but she couldn't even begin to enjoy the wealth of it. She shrugged him off, sitting back up to stare.

Mingus found the look she gave him disconcerting. Clearly a wall of friction had risen between them, bricks of discord, grouted with distrust, piling up a mile high.

She stood. Her tone was terse. "I need to go home and get ready for the board meeting."

He nodded. "I'll take you."

She shook her head. "No. I'll call for an Uber."

"Joanna, that not necessary. I can—"

"I need some time to myself. I'll be fine."

The air between them was tense. Mingus exhaled. "Okay. I'll pick you up at six thirty for the board meeting."

"No. I can drive myself."

"Don't do this, Joanna. You don't have to—"

"No! *You* don't," she said, voice rising slightly as she pointed her finger at him. "You don't get to scream at me and then pretend like everything's okay between us. You either believe me or you don't, but you're not going to treat me badly while you try to figure out where you stand. That's *not* going to happen."

"I didn't mean to yell at you," Mingus said, feeling contrite. "I just…well…" He shrugged, unable to explain himself. It hurt his heart to suddenly have her angry with him.

"Whatever… I have to go." And then, just like that, Joanna picked up her cell phone, turned and stormed out of his home.

* * *

The Uber driver hadn't known how to deal with her. All he had done was ask about her day and the floodgates had opened. She had cried like a toddler one moment then ranted like a lunatic the next. Between Mingus's home and her own she had alternated between sad and distraught. By the time they reached her front door she looked disheveled and completely lost. Her eyes were red, swollen, and her mascara was running. She was one hot mess and the Uber driver was clearly conflicted with what to do.

As the car pulled into her driveway they were greeted by the local news crew, the anchorman calling out her name. He was throwing questions like confetti, wanting her to make a statement about the photos and pornography charges. Pulling her hoodie up and over her head, she thanked the driver as she exited the car and hurried from the vehicle to her front door.

By the time she made it inside, it was all Joanna could take. She suddenly felt all alone, desperation and loathing consuming her. She wanted to rage but had nowhere to direct her fury. Mostly she was missing Mingus, wishing things could be different between them. Wishing they had met at another time, under better circumstances, when the weight of her problems wasn't so oppressing. She missed him and missing him hurt like nothing she'd ever felt before. She hadn't expected to feel so lost or so angry that he would have doubts about her. She had trusted him instead of keeping him at arm's length. He'd become her anchor thorough this storm and she'd become dependent on him to help her through the dangerous undercurrent. Walking away from him had felt brutal and she couldn't begin to know if they could recover from it. What if this was the end and they couldn't recover from it? Thinking things might not ever be good between them ever again had her missing him something fierce. Joanna dropped to the tiled floor and sobbed.

Mingus flung his cell phone to the bed. He'd lost count of the number of times he'd called her, leaving as many messages for her to call him back. She was angry, and hurt, and he understood it. He was equally as frustrated and irate.

He had taken his feelings out on her, despite his efforts to not react so abysmally. He owed her an apology, and an explanation, but he didn't have the words to express how completely worthless he felt. He had no answers, not one solution to make this all go away. Mingus wanted nothing more than to be able to give Joanna her life back, so she could return to a level of normalcy. So she could feel that all was right in her world again.

He could only imagine how all of this was playing out in her head. He didn't even want to fathom the level of hurt she was feeling. How could he make her understand the hell he was going through being unable to stop her pain? How useless he felt when all he wanted was to protect her? The feelings were foreign to him, which made expressing the emotion even harder. The words hadn't been there and so he had yelled instead, screaming at her like a crazed banshee. He couldn't fault her for walking away.

He stood in reflection, weighing his options, pondering what he needed to do next. His feelings for Joanna had become an albatross around his neck, breaking every one of his professional rules. It was the elephant in the room waggling its trunk for attention. He was falling for her and unable to stop himself from tumbling into the rabbit hole. Now, as he stood thinking about her, he wasn't sure he wanted to stop, believing that for the first time he might be able to fall and land on his feet instead of crashing and burning at the bottom of a black hole.

As he stripped out of his clothes and headed for the shower, the realization that things had changed definitively suddenly came to him. He and Joanna were suddenly broken before they'd even been able to proclaim themselves together. It had only taken a split second for the universe to turn them upside down and now she was furious with him. But she couldn't be as angry as he was with himself. He'd put doubt where none had existed, and he reasoned that now she didn't trust him. He needed to fix this and for the first time, he wasn't certain he could.

What if this was the end for them, before they'd even enjoyed a beginning? What if she refused him, wanting nothing to do with him? What if she didn't imagine them together, fighting a good fight? What if all his worries were for nothing and Joanna wasn't concerned for him at all? His list of what ifs was suddenly miles long and for the first time, Mingus was feeling insecurities he'd never before known. The wealth of emotion was overwhelming and cut deep to the quick of everything he'd ever thought about himself.

Standing in the spray of hot water he pondered the ramifications of everything that had happened. He thought about Joanna and made lists in his head of things he wanted for his life. Suddenly he realized he wasn't willing to lose her. He refused to let her go, even though he wasn't even sure if he had her. He prayed it wasn't too late. Suddenly the decision of what he needed to do was easier than he would have ever imagined. He hurried to finish his shower and get dressed.

Chapter 12

Joanna was pacing her living room floor when the doorbell rang. She'd worn a dull path along the hardwood floors, moving from her bedroom to the kitchen and back. She was dressed and ready to head to the board meeting, but fear had reared its ugly head, holding her hostage where she stood.

When the bell rang a second time, someone leaning persistently against the buzzer, she moved slowly to see who it was. Admittedly she was fearful of being ambushed. The media and protesters at the end of her driveway were like vultures ready to pick her to pieces. They were intent on being ugly and she didn't put anything past the lot of them. Although she'd braced herself for anything, she wasn't at all prepared to find Mingus on the other side of the door.

He stood imposingly, his hands clasped behind his back. He wore a navy meticulously tailored wool-and-

silk-blend suit, paired with a white, collarless dress shirt
and black leather dress shoes. He looked quite dashing
and his presence suddenly had her gasping for air. The
shock that washed over her expression hit like a sledge-
hammer and moved Mingus to laugh.

"Do I look that bad?" he asked.

Joanna shook her head. "No, you actually look that
good."

He smiled. "May I come in?"

She hesitated. "Why are you here, Mingus?"

"I am here to take you to the school board meeting. You really didn't think I would let you go alone,
did you?"

"You really don't have to—" Joanna started before
he interrupted.

"No, I don't. But I want to. And about what happened. It won't happen again."

"If that was supposed to be an apology, it really
sucked!" She finally gestured for him to step into the
foyer, closing the door behind him.

He smiled. "You're right. It was bad. Let me try again.
I can do better. I came here prepared to beg." He ges-
tured with his head toward the living room sofa. "May
I sit down?"

Joanna shook her head. "No, you can't." She crossed
her arms over her chest, the look she gave him defiant.

Mingus gave her a slight nod, his smile widening. "I
want to apologize. I didn't mean to hurt you, Joanna.
And I certainly shouldn't have yelled at you the way
I did. It was disrespectful and was not a reflection of
how I feel about you."

"I really thought you knew me, Mingus. I swear on
everything important to me that I did not take any pho-

tographs or send any nude pictures with my phone. But you made me feel…"

Mingus took a step toward her, resting his hands on her shoulders. "I really am sorry. If I could begin to explain to you what I was feeling, I would. I just didn't know how to handle the emotion and I took my frustrations out on you. I was wrong."

"You hurt my feelings."

"Baby, I swear on my life it will never happen again."

Joanna stood staring into his eyes, a wave of emotion flooding through her spirit. Whether she was ready to admit it or not, she needed him. No matter how much she might have wanted to protest, she wanted him. And she was finding it very difficult to still be angry after he had just called her *baby*.

Mingus persisted. "Will you forgive me?"

Joanna turned, reaching for her purse and jacket. She spun back to face him, tears misting her eyes. "I'll think about it," she said as their gazes connected.

Mingus smiled. "Will you do me one more favor?" he asked, his brows raised.

She felt herself falling headfirst into the seductive look he was giving her. "What's that?"

Mingus stepped forward, meeting her toe to toe. He eased an arm around her waist and gently pulled her to him. She gasped, air catching in her throat, and her body began to quiver from his touch. He eased his other hand to the back of her head, his fingers entwining in the length of her hair. "Think about this, too," he whispered and then his kissed her, capturing her mouth beneath his own.

* * *

The silence on the car ride to the public hearing at the Chicago Board of Education building on Madison Street was jaw-dropping. Mingus maneuvered his car through traffic, his expression smug as he stole occasional glances in her direction. Joanna stared out the passenger-side window, still lost in the heat of Mingus's touch. That kiss had left her shaking, her knees quivering and her heart racing. She couldn't *not* think about it if she wanted to.

His kiss had been everything she'd imagined and more. It was summer rain in a blue sky, fudge cake with scoops of praline ice cream, balloons floating against a backdrop of clouds, small puppies, bubbles in a spa bath and fireworks over Lake Michigan. It had left her completely satiated and famished for more. Closing her eyes and kissing him back had been as natural as breathing. And there was no denying that she had kissed him back. She hadn't been able to speak since, no words coming that would explain the wealth of emotion flowing like a tidal wave through her spirit.

They paused at a red light. Mingus checked his mirrors and the flow of traffic as he waited for his turn to proceed through the intersection. Joanna suddenly reached out her hand for his, entwining his fingers between her own.

"I'm still mad at you," Joanna said.

"I know. I'm still mad at myself. I just felt like I was failing you. You need results and I'm not coming up with anything concrete. I want to fix this and suddenly I didn't know if I could. I felt like I was being outwitted. Like someone's playing this game better than I am, but it's not a game. They're playing with your life and I don't plan to let them beat either one of us."

"From day one you believed me. Most didn't and, to be honest, I don't know that anyone else does. But not once have you looked at me like I'm lying or that I'm crazy. This afternoon, you yelling at me felt like doubt, and I couldn't handle you doubting me. It broke my heart."

Mingus squeezed her fingers, still stalled at the light, a line of cars beginning to pull in behind him. "I don't doubt you, baby. But we need to figure this out and, frankly, we're running out of time."

The honking of a car horn yanked his attention back to the road. He pulled into the intersection and turned left. Minutes later he slid into a parking spot and shut down the car engine. Joanna was still staring out the window.

"Are you okay?" he asked.

Joanna nodded and gave him her sweetest smile. "Yeah. I was just thinking that I really like it when you call me 'baby.'"

The garden level boardroom of the Board of Education was beginning to fill quickly. The evening's meeting was a public forum, allowing comment from educators, parents and members of the community about the issues on the agenda. Speaker registration had started an hour earlier and the public comment segment of the hearing would conclude after the last person who had signed to speak had been given an opportunity to voice their concerns.

Joanna knew the comment segment could easily go on longer than the scheduled two-hour meeting if public sentiment was running high. This night didn't feel like it was going to be an exception. She and Mingus took seats toward the back, but with unobstructed views of the seven board members who sat on a semi-round dais at the front of the room.

It didn't take long before someone recognized her, hushed comments and blatant stares welcoming her presence. People were whispering, some pointing, others sneering as they eyed her with visible disgust. She was feeling self-conscious and ready to make an exit when Mingus draped an arm over her shoulder. His touch was calming and she lifted her chin a little higher and pulled her shoulders back with his quiet encouragement.

Angel suddenly slid into the seat beside her, wrapping Joanna in a warm hug. "You look great!"

"Thank you! I have missed you!"

Angel waved a hand at Mingus. "How are you?"

He nodded his head. "Fine, thank you. It's good to see you again."

"So, what's new since I've been gone?" Joanna asked.

"The same story, different day. One of those little demons stole my wallet this week. I left the room for five minutes and he took it right out of my desk drawer."

Mingus suddenly leaned into the conversation. "You don't lock those desks?" he questioned.

Joanna shrugged. "We do. Most of the time. But occasionally, depending on the class, a few of us have been known to not bother."

"It's usually not a problem," Angel interjected. "I can count on one hand the number of students I wouldn't trust. This one surprised me. Apparently he did it on a dare."

Mingus nodded slowly. Joanna sensed that he was

filing the information away. She made a mental note to ask him about it later.

Valentina Donato was suddenly standing beside them. She greeted Joanna and Mingus politely, extending her hand to shake his. "How are you, Joanna?"

Joanna gave her a slight smile and responded, "I'm doing very well, thank you for asking."

"Hopefully this will all be over soon and we can get you back into the classroom. You've been missed."

"Thank you. I'm confident that I'll be vindicated and my name cleared," she said, hoping her tone sounded as sure.

Valentina smiled, her thin lips lifting ever so slightly. "I'll keep you in my prayers, Joanna," she said as she turned to find a seat on the other side of the room.

"Well, that wasn't chilly at all," Angel quipped. "Her sincerity is just so heartwarming!"

Joanna giggled, her eyes rolling skyward. "Give her a break, Angel. At least she spoke. That's more than I can say for the rest of these hypocrites." She nodded toward a science teacher, the coach and Marion Talley, who stood off to the side huddled in conversation.

"Every one of them is hateful," Angel whispered. "And devious. You can't trust the lot of them."

Minutes later John Talley, the Board of Education president, called the meeting to order. The board members dealt with a flurry of paperwork and administrative details as the standing-room-only crowd waited with bated breath for the community comment portion of the agenda. There was a brief discussion on teacher tenure and they tabled a vote on expanding the roles of special coordinators in the elementary schools. It was boring at best and Mingus tuned the noise out as he stared around the room, studying the crowd.

Many were circling like sharks in infested waters, churning around in a murky blood bath. Because of her tenure and the board's relationship with the teachers' union, Joanna's termination was not automatic or final until she was found guilty of the charges, either by admission or trial. The union had challenged her employment status, pending the trial results since she had not admitted guilt. They were fighting on her behalf for continued paid leave. The board could opt to table that discussion, as well, but it was clear the community wasn't going to walk away without its opinions being heard. It seemed to be the only issue of concern to most of them.

Mingus shifted his focus, tuning in to the board president, who had mentioned Riptide High School and its current climate. John Talley was a small man, stout and round with a sizeable beer gut. His wore a sweater vest over a short-sleeved white dress shirt and khaki slacks that pulled awkwardly though his thighs and legs. Balding, he'd become adept at coming over the remaining strands of hair on his head, his sandy-blond locks covering the growing bald spots.

"We will be calling a special meeting to discuss the school's future," Talley was saying. "We've received a generous offer to purchase the building and land and in light of the school administration's current legal issues, as well as the continued accreditation issues, I for one believe that we should consider cutting our losses."

One board member bristled with indignation. "The school is a community fixture. Why is this even a discussion?"

Another board member spoke. "Because we know

that the budget isn't going to allow us to keep all of our schools open. It's just a fact of the current economy. If not Riptide, then one of our other schools will eventually have to close. Either way, the decision is not going to be easy and families are not going to be happy."

One of the female members interjected, raising her hand for attention. "I want to know more about the offer. Is that something that will have to be presented to the community for their input?"

John Talley shrugged. "I think it's something the board should consider and address prior to any public discussions. I will say that we do have Frank Sumpter here with us tonight. Mr. Sumpter is a lawyer for Kaufman and Associates, the legal firm representing the Tower Group. The Tower Group is the company wanting to buy the land and building where Riptide High School sits. I'm sure he'd be willing to give us a brief statement."

Another on the board, a man with a head of reddish-blond hair and a ruddy complexion, shook his head. "That's a bit presumptuous, I think. We've had no discussions about which schools we will be closing. I think we should table this issue for a special meeting."

"That's not true. It's all we've been discussing for the last six months. If you had been here, you would've known that!" another interjected.

There was a brief heated exchange between the two men before John Talley regained order. He tapped his gavel against the table. "Clearly we're not going to get anywhere with this tonight."

One of the women raised her hand. "I make a motion to table the discussion until a later date when we can invite Attorney Sumpter back to speak with us."

"I second that motion," said the man who'd been accused of not attending meetings.

"Then we'll move on," John Talley snapped. He shot a look across the room, shrugging his shoulders slightly.

Mingus followed where he looked and suddenly sat forward in his seat. Standing with John's wife, Marion, toward the back on the other side was the stranger he'd seen with Kyle Rourke that night in the strip club. Once again, the man was meticulously dressed in an expensive suit, but this time looking more at ease with his surroundings. Mingus suddenly had questions, wondering why lawyer Frank Sumpter was in bed with a small-time criminal and with the Talleys. What did they all have in common? And what did it have to do with Joanna?

Joanna's palm lightly grazed his back, the look she gave him questioning. He gave her a slight smile and sat back. At the front of the room Talley had shifted the discussion to the petition submitted by the teachers' union on Joanna's behalf. Tension suddenly bristled through the room like an electrical current gone awry. Mingus felt her body tense as she leaned into his side.

"Is this not a personnel issue?" a board member asked. "And should it not be private?"

"I agree," said the guy who'd been accused of being absent.

"The vote and the board's decision will be private," Talley said, "but the issues surrounding Ms. Barnes's suspension are of major concern to the community and the general consensus of all is that we should address those concerns. There has been a violation of public trust created by the alleged abuse of a student at Riptide High School, and all the events that have followed have led to diminished confidence. It's become a distraction from our primary focus of preparing students for higher education and eventual success. It's my understanding that the union, as well as Ms. Barnes, are in agreement."

Joanna's eyes were suddenly blinking rapidly. She didn't recall having that conversation with anyone from the teachers' union. She made a mental note to discuss that with Ellington when she saw him next.

Mingus leaned to whisper in her ear. "Breathe…"

The two exchanged a look as she took a deep breath.

Principal Donato was the first person to step to the podium, adjusting the microphone before she spoke.

"Good evening! My name is Valentina Donato and I am the principal at Riptide High School. But I am here tonight to also speak as a parent and member of the community who supports Joanna Barnes. As principal, I hired Ms. Barnes to come teach at Riptide High School. I still believe that was a wise decision. She came to Riptide and immediately meshed with the community. She distinguished herself. She is an outstanding person, someone who has worked with me very closely, and who I feel very strongly about. She has served as a constant to staff and students during difficult times. As a parent, my experience with Joanna is that she is consistent and fair in her discipline with both students and teachers. Honest, stable and dependable are words that come to mind when I think of Joanna.

"Her dedication to the school and love of the students is without question. She is part of the fabric of our school and our community. To have that ripped from us, when the allegations against her have yet to be substantiated, is truly unconscionable. I hope the board will consider her past performance records and her admonishments of her innocence in their decision. Thank you."

Principal Donato's statement was met with applause as she returned to her seat.

Angel muttered under her breath, "Well, now! I guess I'm eating a little crow tonight!"

Joanna smiled, nodding her head as she wiped a tear from her eye.

A parent at the high school was called next to the podium. "Thank you. First, I'd like to thank the board members for this opportunity. Although I can appreciate Principal Donato supporting one of her own, I fear that the moral fabric of our society is being taken to task. What message do we send our children to allow a predator to remain in the classroom and on the public payroll?"

The next five speakers espoused personal and religious opinions about child abuse, personal experiences and public safety within the classroom. Two additional persons extolled Joanna's résumé, insisting that her exemplary career path be a factor in any decision. They exalted her academic degrees in education leadership and management. Others questioned her integrity and professionalism. It was a mixed bag of opinions serving only to assuage public trepidation about what they did and did not know about the case and the charges.

The president of the local chapter of the NAACP was the last to speak on Joanna's behalf. "At a time when we need more minority role models in our public school system, this is not the time to perform a career assassination on one of the best minority teachers we have," he said to applause and hecklings. "We will stand with Joanna Barnes, believing her innocent until proven guilty," he said of the NAACP, "and not hope, but demand that her termination be rescinded."

As the distinguished gentleman walked off, he paused for a moment to shake hands with members of the crowd. It was only then that Joanna and Mingus both saw her parents, her mother expressing her gratitude to the man for the kind words he had spoken on her daughter's behalf. Joanna hadn't spoken to either since the day she'd been arrested and the argument with her mother had sent her parents storming out of her home.

Three hours had passed from the first comment to the last, some forty-plus persons having expressed an opinion or a concern. When John Talley declared the meeting concluded, slamming his gavel against the table, a loud rumble filled the room, the noise level rising exponentially.

Mingus leaned over to whisper into her ear a second time. "Go talk to your parents. I'll be right back to get you." Then he kissed her cheek, stood and followed the crowd toward the exit doors.

Angel grinned. "So are you two a *thing* now?"

Amusement danced in Joanna's heart as she gave her friend a slight shrug. "We're still getting to know each other," she said. "I don't know if you can call us a thing, yet."

"Well you two are definitely something," Angel said with a soft giggle. "And I like it. Whatever it is, I like it a lot."

Joanna shook her head and laughed with her friend. "Let it go, Angel! Mingus and I are just friends."

"Friends with benefits, I hope!"

Joanna gave her a look. "I hope so, too!"

Both women came to their feet, easing into the aisle. They slipped past people going in the opposite direction, trying to reach her parents, who were still standing at the front of the room. The trek was made challenging by people stopping to express their support and the one or two who felt it necessary to give her a piece of their mind. When she finally made it to the front of the room, Joanna's father greeted her with a heavy bear hug, squeezing her so tightly that Joanna could barely breathe.

"I need air, Daddy," she gasped as she hugged him back.

Her father laughed. "I just needed to make sure my baby girl was okay. You are okay?"

Joanna nodded. "I'm really good," she said.

"We been worried about you. You should've called us."

"I'm sorry, but it's been a rough week."

"That's no excuse, Joanna," her father admonished. "You really need to do better."

"Yes, sir. I really am sorry."

Behind her, Angel waved. "Hi, Mr. Barnes! How are you, sir?"

"Doing as well as can be expected, Ms. Graves. How have you been?"

"Very well, sir."

"And your parents? We haven't seen them in a while. I do hope they are well?"

"Yes, sir, they are doing exceptionally well. Traveling a lot. They're on an Alaskan cruise as we speak!"

"That's some good news! Please tell them hello from me the next time you speak with them."

Joanna's mother suddenly pushed her way to her husband's side. She greeted both women politely, reaching to kiss Joanna's cheek. "I wasn't sure we were going to see you here," she said.

"I wasn't sure I was going to come," Joanna responded.

"It's good you did. You cannot let these people bully you into hiding. You haven't done anything wrong. You hold your head up."

"So now you believe me?" Joanna responded, a hint of attitude in her tone.

"Don't start, Joanna," her father snapped. "Your mother is trying."

"I'm sorry. I didn't mean that," she said, contrition spinning with her words.

Her mother gave her a nod and wrapped her arms around her daughter's shoulders. "Apology accepted. And I hope you can forgive me, as well. I wasn't doubting you the other day, but I did not do a good job of explaining myself. I just hope you know that I love you."

"I do, and I love you, too."

Mrs. Barnes turned and gave Angel a look. "Ms. Graves, who is that handsome young man I saw you and Joanna sitting with?"

Angel's eyes widened as she shot Joanna a look. "He's a friend of Joanna's, Mrs. Barnes. His name's Mingus Black."

For a second Joanna's mother looked stunned. "Joanna, that's the same young man we met at your house the other night?"

Joanna shook her head. "Yes, Mother."

"The private investigator working for the law firm? Simone's brother?"

"One and the same."

"Oh, my goodness! Doesn't he clean up nicely!"

"You say that like there was something wrong with the way he was dressed before."

Her mother continued. "Not at all. He just looks so nice in a suit!"

"I'm sure he'll appreciate the compliment. I'll be sure to pass it on," Joanna said as she rolled her eyes skyward.

"So why is he here?" Mrs. Barnes questioned.

"I guess he's doing what everyone else here is doing, Mother. There are no restrictions on community concerns," she said snidely.

The Barnes matriarch's gaze narrowed as she looked from her daughter to Angel and back. "Well, at least he comes from a good family," she muttered.

Joanna nodded. "Because that's definitely important." Her words dripped with sarcasm.

Her mother bristled ever so slightly. "I really don't want to fight with you, Joanna."

"I wasn't trying to pick a fight, Mother. I really wasn't. It's just that sometimes—"

Mr. Barnes interjected. "I think you two should just hug and wish each other good-night and we can pick this conversation up at dinner next week."

"I'm not sure…" Joanna started.

"It's not optional," her father stated. "I expect to see you at dinner in the next five to seven days. You decide which day."

"Yes, sir."

"Ms. Graves, as always, it's been a pleasure. Please do take care and we hope to see you again soon." Mr. Barnes shook the woman's hand.

"I could always come for dinner, too," Angel joked.

"Not funny," Joanna muttered. "You are so not funny, Angel."

Angel laughed. "Just trying to lighten the mood!"

Mr. Barnes winked at the two women and gave his daughter one last hug. Mrs. Barnes reached out to adjust the collar of Joanna's jacket, brushing her shoulder gently as if to move a shard of lint. She gave her child one last kiss and a hug before making her exit. The couple headed toward the door together.

"She never quits," Joanna said, tossing up her hands. "If it's not one thing, it's another."

"You can be a little hard on her," Angel interjected. "But that's just my opinion."

Joanna sighed. "I really don't mean to be such a pain. But she's been pushing my buttons since I was sixteen."

"I won't say your mother's ways aren't a little funny sometimes, but she loves you and she's being the best mother she knows how to be. You need to give her some slack. Just a little."

"You know she's going to find a million and one things wrong with Mingus, right?"

Angel laughed. "Hell, she wouldn't be your mother if she didn't!"

Mingus followed the lawyer into the men's restroom. He and the other man both stood at the urinals pretending to ignore each other and everyone else in the room. Mingus moved to the sink to wash his hands first. Frank Sumpter followed just minutes later, both men heading out the door at the same time.

Back out in the hallway John Talley stood waiting for Sumpter to return. His eager expression was almost comical. Mingus moved off to the side, pretending to be waiting for someone else to join him. He pretended to scroll through his cell phone, angling his body just enough to put both men in his view. He stood eavesdropping on their conversation, the two stepping behind a half wall to obscure them from view.

"It's almost a done deal," John said enthusiastically.

"Whatever you do, it needs to happen soon," Sumpter responded.

"All the board members received a copy of the proposal. I'm calling a special meeting for us to discuss it next week."

"There's over one hundred million dollars on the line here. We need that property," Sumpter said, his voice dropping an octave.

"You'll get it! I assure you. You have nothing to worry about."

"I'm not the one who needs to be worried. If you want your money, then you make this happen. Screw this up and there will be hell to pay for all of us."

Sumpter adjusted his suit jacket, buttoning the single button closed, then he turned and disappeared out the door. Talley looked around, seeming uneasy, then he, too, turned back toward the conference room.

Mingus waited until they were both out of earshot and then pulled his cell phone from his pocket and placed a call to his office. When his secretary answered, he barked out orders. "Get me everything you can on the Tower Group. I also need a complete dossier on a man associated with their firm. His name is Frank Sumpter. And I needed it yesterday."

Chapter 13

Something between them had shifted and even in the silence, which had previously been only slightly awkward and very comfortable, both Mingus and Joanna could feel it. There was a current of energy that wafted like a cool breeze between them. It was energizing and draining, honest and deceptive, heated and calming. They allowed themselves to relax in it one minute and sat uneasy in the midst of it the next.

Both had questions but neither was interested in shifting the mood. The balance they'd established had been regained and no one wanted to upset the cart and turn things over. For the moment everything between them felt good and neither Mingus nor Joanna saw any reason to ruin it.

"Dinner? Are you hungry?" Mingus asked.

"I could actually eat," Joanna answered. "I was too nervous to eat anything earlier."

"Is there anything in particular that you have a taste for?"

Joanna shook her head no. "I'm easy," she said. "We could grab a Happy Meal from McDonald's and I'd be good with it."

"I don't do Happy Meals," Mingus said with a soft chuckle. "I need a real meal."

Joanna smiled. "What's your favorite food?"

"Meat."

She laughed. "Just meat, not a particular meat? You're not a chicken man?"

"I like great food and I like it simple. It doesn't need to be fancy or have a lot of stuff with it. Grill me a steak, fry me some chicken, give me a burger and I am a happy camper. I loved your spaghetti because it was simple. Just pasta and meat sauce."

"Well, I'm not picky, so you choose. Whatever you have a taste for, I am good with."

Mingus nodded. He made a sharp right turn and then a quick left. It took less than ten minutes for him to pull up to what appeared to be a deserted street. There was a row of abandoned buildings and a few parked cars lined the street. Exiting, Mingus rounded the front of the vehicle to the passenger side and opened the door. He extended his hand to help her out, leading her to the door of an old brick structure, Passing through the entrance, they headed down a flight of well-worn steps to a second door. The ornate entrance was painted a vibrant shade of glossy red with a heavy gold knocker. Three knocks and Mingus waited for someone on the other side to open the door and let them in. A doorman looked Mingus up and down before allowing him entry.

"What's up?" Mingus said as he and the man slapped

palms and gave each other a fist bump. "My brother around?"

"Nah, man! Haven't seen him around here tonight. You need him?"

Mingus shook his head. "No. I'm good."

The man gave Joanna a nod. "Good evening, ma'am."

Joanna gave him a smile back. "How are you?"

He nodded and then pointed them toward a third door at the end of a short corridor.

Mingus pressed a warm palm to the small of her back and guided her through the entrance. As the third door closed behind them, Joanna stared in awe. The space was a complete surprise. The clublike atmosphere was unexpected, the lighting was low and slightly seductive. The oak-paneled walls were polished to a high shine and looked like an expensive old library. Tables were neatly arranged around a dance floor and there was a full bar against a side wall. An eclectic mix of adults filled the room, everyone seeming to be having a good time. The staff greeted Mingus warmly, calling him by name. Mingus guided her to a rear table, pulling out a chair for her and then taking a seat for himself.

"This is so cool! What is this place?" Joanna asked as she settled in her seat.

"Welcome to Peace Row," Mingus answered. "It's a membership only establishment for law enforcement officers. My brother the cop owns it. He designed it specifically for other cops to give them their own space to hang out and relax."

"And nepotism gets you through the door?"

Mingus laughed. "Nepotism and my former police badge."

"I keep forgetting you used to be a police officer. You never did tell me why you left the force."

Mingus shrugged, pushing his shoulders toward the ceiling. "It was no specific reason, just a culmination of bad experiences. I didn't always follow orders and there were times when I needed to do things a little underhandedly to catch the bad guys. It was easier to leave the police force than risk doing something that would sully my family name."

"Your family is very important to you, aren't they?"

"They are. They're everything."

"I don't have any siblings, but I get it. I just wish my relationship with my mother wasn't so contentious. It's like the minute we're in a room together things go left."

"How much of that has to do with you?"

Before Joanna could answer a waitress dressed in black slacks and a black turtleneck moved to the table and dropped a bottle of Corona with a wedge of lime to the tabletop. "Good evening, Mr. Black! How are you tonight?"

"I'm very well, Brenda. How about you?"

"I'm good, sir. Thank you for asking." She shifted her gaze to Joanna. "What would you like to drink, ma'am?"

"Can I get a shot of Hennessy, please?"

The young woman nodded. "I'll bring that right over," she said as she turned toward the bar.

"Thank you."

Joanna settled in her seat. The atmosphere was completely relaxing. The waitress delivered her order and promptly excused herself. Joanna savored the first sip and blew a sigh of relief. "So, tell me, where did you disappear to after the meeting?"

Mingus swallowed a sip of his beverage. "The lawyer from the Tower Group—"

She interrupted. "The one that didn't get to speak?"

He nodded. "Yes. I recognized him from the strip club and I wanted to see who he talked to before he left."

"Anyone interesting?"

"John Talley."

"Is that strange? I mean, I talked to a lot of people, most of them I didn't know. John's the board president and he probably talked to a lot of people."

"Maybe not," Mingus said with a shrug, "but you never know." He took another sip of his beer, resting the bottle against the table.

"Tell me about your business. I realize I don't know much about how you operate."

"There's not much to tell. People bring me their problems, and my team and I try to solve them. We investigate cases, do surveillance and gather facts that are usually admissible in court."

"Is my case unusual or different from the kinds of cases you usually work on?"

"Not at all. We'll work anything from civil to criminal. I've handled child custody, domestic cases, fraud, missing persons, wiretaps, surveillance and forensics."

"You said you had a team?"

He nodded. "There's my secretary and I have six agents who do investigative work for me. They all have specialized talents and we've had a decent success rate."

"Just decent?"

Mingus laughed and chugged back his beer.

Joanna relaxed with her drink, shifting her attention to the evening's entertainment. There was a lovely young woman backed up by a trio playing on the stage.

The piano player, a bassist and a drummer were covering a medley of jazz hits. The music was seductive and engaging, and a quiet reverie had settled over the whole room.

Mingus waved the waitress back over and ordered a cornucopia of dishes for them to savor: a platter of fried chicken, chopped barbecue, macaroni and cheese, green beans seasoned with bacon, candied yams and homemade biscuits.

It was more food than either of them could've eaten and every forkful was delicious. Joanna ate until she was stuffed, her tummy bulging. Mingus was equally full.

"I would order the peach cobbler for dessert, but I don't think I could eat it," he said.

"I know I couldn't eat another bite," Joanna said.

He gestured again for the waitress. "Let's take it home," he said. "We might get hungry later."

Joanna smiled.

On the ride home Joanna couldn't stop talking. She talked about her mother and her father. She asked about Mingus's parents, curious about the longevity of their relationship. She told him about teaching and how she had hoped to one day open her own school. She shared her dreams and her disappointments.

Mingus was thoroughly amused, listening intently and sharing his own aspirations and dreams. They laughed and there was a harmony of sorts that echoed through the space.

At the front door of her home, he hesitated.

"Aren't you coming in?" she questioned.

"I don't know if I should, Joanna."

"Do you want to?"

He nodded, suddenly feeling like a teenager on his first date.

Joanna laughed. "Then come in."

He paused a second time.

"What's wrong?"

"I don't want us to do something we're going to regret."

"I think we're past that point of no return," she said. She licked her lips slowly as her eyes locked with his. "But if you're really concerned, I'll understand."

"You've had a lot to drink. I don't know if you're thinking clearly."

"Trust me, I'm not drunk. I am fully aware of what I'm doing. I'm talking too much because I'm nervous. I'm sweating because I'm excited. And I'm not planning to hold you hostage or do anything crazy, Mingus. I promise." She turned and stepped over the threshold, tossing him one last look over her shoulder.

Mingus met the look she was giving him and trailed after her. Joanna kicked off her shoes in the entrance and he followed suit, turning to lock the door behind them. She moved into the kitchen and rested the bag of dessert on the counter. Mingus watched with bated breath as she turned to him and moved slowly in his direction.

"I want dessert," Joanna stated, meeting his gaze evenly. She moved against him.

"Dessert? I don't…"

"Yes, you do," she said in a soft whisper.

Mingus felt his pulse quickening, his body responding to the soft whisper of her breath on his skin. "Oh… dessert!" he managed to blurt out.

She laughed and nuzzled her face into his neck, pressing a damp kiss against his skin.

Mingus slipped a large hand beneath her blouse. His fingers tapped gently against her skin. "I like dessert," he said.

Joanna arched her back ever so slightly as she felt his fingers gently running over her flesh. Mingus dropped his mouth to hers and kissed her hungrily. His lips danced against her lips, tasting the remnants of sugared yams. Tracing his tongue along her profile, up her neck to her ear, gently licking and biting the lobe, he could hear the desire in Joanna's breathing and he was instantly hard, every muscle below his waist tightening. He turned back to her lips, inviting her tongue to dance with his as he kissed her.

Time seemed to come to a standstill and it was surreal. Both had imagined the moment, fantasized about it, and in that moment, it was more than either imagined. Her lace bra suddenly became undone, her hardened nipples like rock candy protrusions pressing for attention.

Mingus pulled at her top, the buttons flying as he snatched the fabric, tearing it from her and tossing it to the floor. She reciprocated, the buttons of his dress shirt hitting the hardwood floor like small pebbles. His hands trailed down the length of her back, exploring every square inch of flesh. The bra slid from her shoulders, tangling in the crook of her arms, her hands sliding across his broad back and shoulders as her mouth continued to taste his.

Standing in the center of her kitchen, he stripped her naked. His kisses trailed a damp path from her head to her toes, following where his fingers led. He pulled her closer, her breasts pressed against his chest. His desire was rampant, his heart beating like a drum line in his chest. It took everything in him to contain the wealth of emotion exploding through every nerve ending. He had never wanted anyone, or anything, more than he wanted her. He wanted to claim her and make her his, to ensure no one and nothing could ever come between them. He needed to feel himself settled in her soft folds, to savor his hard lines enveloped in her silky lining. He was territorial, and in that moment every part of him belonged to her and no one else.

Mingus suddenly swept her up in his arms, moving swiftly toward her bedroom. As he laid her across the bed, he snatched the bedclothes away, sending them flying to the other side of the room. He covered her body with his own, his lips finding their way to her breasts to suckle one and then the other. Joanna moaned, a soft purr that sounded like the whisper of a prayer to his ears. Her hips lifted against him, her own need growing with a vengeance.

Mingus pulled himself from her and the bed, tearing at his clothes until he stood in all his glory. He was decadent and delicious, a visual treat of pure, unadulterated pleasure. Taut abs, thick thighs and an erection that stretched full and abundant teased her sensibilities.

Joanna rose onto her forearms just enough to stare in appreciation. The sight of him took her breath away. She begged him back to her with her eyes, her stare like a call to arms. Mingus crawled between her parted legs and kissed his way forward. By the time he captured her mouth again she was bathed in perspiration, every raw nerve begging for release.

After fumbling with a condom retrieved from her dresser drawer, Mingus sheathed himself quickly and entered her slowly. They took delight in not rushing, wanting every second of their time together to last forever. He stared into her eyes, pleasure exploding in his dark orbs. Joanna gasped, his name spilling past her lips as she welcomed him home.

He loved her slowly, and completely, like she had never been loved before. He loved her over and over again, not stopping until the wee hours of the morning. As he curled his body around hers, a hint of sunlight beginning to peek through her window blinds, he fell asleep loving her with every ounce of his being.

When Joanna finally woke, the midday sun was sitting high in a cloudless sky. The afternoon news was playing on the bedroom television, the volume turned low. She rolled, searching out the heat from Mingus's body, only to find the bed empty. She jumped, startled. Waking up alone suddenly felt unnatural, the anticipation of waking next to Mingus having consumed her. She called out his name but got no answer.

Rising from the bed, she headed into the bathroom first and then made her way to the kitchen. Amusement crossed her face as she retrieved her clothes, garments trailing from the hallway to the refrigerator. Her lace bra was even hanging from a cabinet near the stove. Mingus had left her a note on the kitchen table, which she read once and then a second time. Beside the note on the table was a key to his home. Joanna moved to the refrigerator and poured herself a glass of orange juice. It was going to be a good day, she thought, and then her telephone rang.

"Hello?"

"Joanna, hello! It's Ellington Black. Do you have a moment to talk?"

"Ellington, hey! I do. How are you?"

"Unfortunately, I'm calling with bad news."

"Let me sit down for this," she said. "I keep saying that it can't get any worse, but clearly it can."

"Well, it's nothing we didn't expect. David Locklear and his parents have filed a civil suit against you and the school. The school has indicated that they will file to have the cases separated and your liability excluded from theirs."

"A civil suit? So how much are they asking for?"

"Ten million dollars," Ellington stated.

Joanna choked, beginning to cough as orange juice spewed across her kitchen table. "Ten million dollars? Are they crazy?"

"Clearly they're taking advantage of the situation."

"Can they actually sue me before I'm convicted? What happens when I'm found innocent?"

"They can sue you for anything, but it doesn't mean they have a case or that they'll win. And, of course, if there's no credibility with the legal case, we will be able to get the civil suit dismissed."

"Unbelievable. This is absolutely unbelievable."

"I wanted you to hear it from me personally because I'm sure once the media gets its hands on the filing, it'll be featured in the news. It also means they'll have access to the details of your case, including the photographs."

"Can we ask for the document to be sealed? Is that a thing?"

"That's definitely a thing," he said. "We can definitely petition the court and ask for that to happen."

"Please! My reputation has already taken a hit, but if the media gets their hands on those photographs, they will follow me around even after I prove I didn't do it."

"I understand, and we will do everything in our power to make sure that doesn't happen."

"Thank you, Ellington. I really appreciate everything you're doing."

"You are very welcome, Joanna. And we're going to do everything we can to make this go away."

"You have a good afternoon," she said and then she disconnected the line.

Joanna sat for a good half hour, staring into space. She knew that everyone was doing everything in their power to help her, but she was desperate to help herself. She needed answers and she wasn't going to get them waiting around for other people to ask the questions that needed to be asked. Rising, she headed to the bedroom and the shower, needing to get dressed. If she didn't hurry, school would be out and she would lose her window of opportunity.

Chapter 14

Mingus had risen on just a few hours of sleep, wanting to get to the office. Joanna had been sleeping soundly, snoring softly as she rested on her side. He wished he could stay under the covers with her, his body wrapped around hers, but there was work that needed to be done. He had pressed a gentle kiss to her shoulder before pulling the covers over her body and tiptoeing out of the room. Putting Frank Sumpter's name to the face had Mingus wanting to know more about the man and what he was up to.

No one was in the office when he arrived. But the reports he'd requested were sitting on his desk, front and center. He made himself a hot cup of coffee and settled down to read. A few hours later, Mingus was back in his home office, connecting the dots with what he already knew.

Frank Sumpter's résumé read like a how-to manual

for self-made success. He'd been orphaned as a child and raised in foster care by the state of Michigan. He'd put himself through college working multiple jobs and eventually landed an internship with a local law firm that had helped him through law school.

Mingus learned that Sumpter's relationship with the Talley family went back to the schoolyard. John Talley and Frank Sumpter had both spent time in the same group home as children. Their little clique had also included one Kyle Rourke. School reports reflected a host of devious behavior revolving around one or more of them. The trio was eventually busted in high school for shoplifting, an incident that had been the catalyst for their separation. Frank had aged out of the foster care system. John Talley had been placed in the custody of an aunt who'd moved to Chicago from Texas and Kyle had gone to live with a single father raising four other foster children. Nothing in the records told Mingus when or how the three had reconnected.

The Tower Group was something of an anomaly. It was a shell organization for multiple real-estate holdings and investment companies. Ownership was vague at best and management turned over frequently. Mingus knew he would have to dig a little deeper if he wanted to know more. He did learn the Tower Group was purchasing large acreage of property around Chicago. Two massive skyscraper projects bearing its name were currently under construction. The land it wanted from the purchase of the school would give them a third. Hundreds of thousands of dollars were being pumped into the Tower Group and their investments. He was going to have to call in more than a few favors to follow the money trail.

His cell phone suddenly ringing was the first distraction he'd had all day. He was disappointed to see the call was from his brother, having hoped that Joanna had started her day with him on her mind. He answered the call with a hint of attitude in his tone.

"Yeah, what's up?"

"Good morning to you, too," Ellington responded.

"Sorry, I just have a lot on my mind. How are you?"

"Frustrated. Where are we on the Barnes case?"

"Frustrated," Mingus answered. "But I think I've got a new lead," he said, filling his brother in on the school board meeting and what he'd learned about the new players.

"So you think the Tower Group has something to do with this? You're reaching a bit, aren't you?"

"I may be, but at this point we don't have anything to lose."

"I don't know how much longer we have before I'm going to need to consider advising her to take the plea deal."

"Don't you dare!" Mingus snapped. "She's not taking a plea deal. Joanna is not guilty."

Ellington snapped back, "Then give me something I can use to clear her name. Because right now, what we do have will get her a maximum sentence at Metropolitan Correctional Center."

Mingus released the breath of hot air he'd been holding. "I hear you," he said finally.

"You are keeping things professional between you two, aren't you?"

"What do you mean?"

"Mingus, you know exactly what I mean. Let's not play games. If there is something going on between you two, don't let it be a surprise that throws another crimp in this case. Please. I don't know if we can take another hit."

"Do you really want to know?"

"Not really. But as her attorney, I will need to know if it could potentially impact the credibility of anything you discover."

"It won't."

There was a moment of pause. Ellington broke the silence. "She must be pretty damn special. You have never mixed business with pleasure. That's not like you."

"No, I always left that for you and Armstrong."

"Armstrong maybe, not me!"

Mingus laughed. "Not to worry, big brother. I'm not purposely trying to make you job harder."

"So is she coming to family dinner any time soon?"

Mingus laughed again. "Soon!"

"Keep me updated, please. I really could use some good news!"

"Before you go, I need a favor."

"What's up? What do you need?"

"I need to visit the school again during class. Tell them I need to see Joanna's classroom specifically."

"You do understand you can't talk to any of the students, correct? In case that's what you had planned. Not without a parent or guardian present."

"Just get me in."

Ellington sighed. "I'll take care of it," he said before hanging up the phone.

Chapter 15

Principal Donato did not look happy, but she greeted him warmly. "Mr. Black. I'm surprised to see you again."

"I appreciate you taking time to see me."

"How can we help you?"

"I need to see Joanna Barnes's classroom. I won't interrupt the students. Something Ms. Graves told me at the board meeting has me curious."

The principal looked confused. "And what exactly did she tell you?"

"A student stole her wallet?"

"Oh, that!" Principal Donato waved a dismissive hand. "We typically don't have a problem with theft. I'm not sure why she even made that an issue."

"She didn't. She said she didn't lock her desk."

"All the teachers know that there is a risk if they do not secure their desks."

"My father used to say that a locked door only keeps an honest man honest."

"I'm not sure what that has to do with Ms. Barnes's case."

"It doesn't have anything to do with the case, but I would still like to see her room."

Principal Donato sighed. "I really want to cooperate but…"

"I won't speak to any of the students about Ms. Barnes or the case. I promise."

The woman still looked unsure.

Mingus gave her a smile. "Five minutes, not a minute longer. Please."

"Follow me," she said finally.

"Thank you."

Mingus followed the woman, who hurried in the direction of the second building. She pointed two students to classes they were seemingly intent on cutting, waiting until the classroom doors were closed behind them.

"How long have you had cameras?" Mingus asked, eyeing the CCTV cameras for the first time. The black-domed units were placed inconspicuously through the hallway.

The woman looked up. "Just over a year now. They've actually cut down on some of our theft issues."

"I don't remember seeing cameras in the other hallway when I visited Mrs. Graves's classroom. Were there any there?"

The woman shook her head. "There are a few buildings that aren't on the system yet. This section was the first because of its proximity to the gym. Students tend to sneak down the back stairwell and out the gym to leave early. Ms. Graves's classroom is in the new wing.

We anticipate those cameras being in place by the end of the month."

At the classroom door Mingus paused, noticing the camera perched on the ceiling in front of the room across the hall. He glanced up and down the length of corridor, noting the placement of the other units, as well.

Principal Donato knocked on the door and pulled it open. The substitute teacher in charge had clearly lost control of the classroom, the students loud and rowdy. He looked like he was ready to cry, or snap, whichever would bring him relief fast. He was surprised by the visit, the administrator's presence adding to his anxiety.

"Principal Donato, the students were just reading to themselves," he said, trying to explain the melee. "Is there a problem?"

"No, Mr. Lawrence. I apologize for the interruption. This won't take but a minute."

Mingus had moved to the back of the room, his eyes skating back and forth. The students were eyeing him curiously, most settling in their seats to be nosy.

"Principal Donato, who's the new guy?"

"Who is the new guy?" one of the girls purred.

There was a round of giggles and a few catcalls. Mingus winked at the girl as he moved to the front of the room. He moved behind the desk, staring first to the row of desks in front and then to the door. From the teacher's seat, he had a clear view of the camera in the hallway.

"Yo, dude! You speak or what?"

"Mr. Morrow, that will be enough!" Principal Donato chastised.

"Enough, Mr. Morrow!" the teacher named Mr. Lawrence echoed.

Mingus smiled as he shook his head. He moved to

open the desk drawer, pulling it open easily. An insulated lunch bag with a floral motif rested in the bottom.

"Um, that's mine," Mr. Lawrence said, pointing with his index finger. "It's what's left of my lunch. Tuna salad and carrots."

Mingus closed the drawer and straightened. "Please excuse the interruption," he said to the teacher.

"Um, no problem…don't worry…"

Mingus moved to the door, Principal Donato close on his heels.

"What was that all about, Mr. Black?"

He extended his hand. "Thank you. Someone will be in touch."

"Will this help her?" she asked as he hurried down the hallway.

Mingus didn't bother to respond.

Mingus sat in the student parking lot waiting for the bell to ring. He had taken a call from another client, able to resolve a problem quickly. As he dialed his brother's office he noticed that there was more activity in the lot than he would have imagined for the time of day. Many students were leaving earlier than the two forty-five buzzer. Ellington's secretary connected him almost immediately.

"Twice in one day! To what do I owe the honor?"

"You need to get a warrant for the security video outside of Joanna's classroom."

"There's video?"

"Yeah, that's what I said."

"And what am I looking for?"

"Someone stealing Joanna's cell phone from her purse."

"That sounds like a lot of video we'll need to go through."

"Start the day after Omar did that second tattoo. Something tells me if I'm right it won't take you long to find it."

"Do you think it was caught on video?"

"If I'm right, we will know when those photos got on her phone and who did it. One more piece to the puzzle!"

"You think you can just get me a confession from all this? An admission of wrongdoing, maybe? Right now, you're giving me a ton of circumstantial evidence that I'm going to have to tie together to convince a jury."

"Trust me, I'm working on it."

A commotion across the way drew Mingus's attention. A crowd of students had gathered around a Mercedes Benz SL 450 sports coupe that had pulled into an empty parking spot. The top was down, allowing the afternoon sun to shine down on the driver and his female companion. The vehicle was a work of art in metallic candy-apple red, with black leather interior and 19-inch multispoke wheels. The car was a showpiece and clearly making an impression.

Ellington called his brother's name. "Mingus, you still there?"

"Yeah, sorry about that. Question for you, did David Locklear receive a settlement from the city or the school district that we don't know about?"

"Of course not, why do you ask?"

"Because the kid just pulled up in a one-hundred-thousand-dollar car. Now, unless the family hit the lottery, or his single parent who's been living paycheck to paycheck found herself a magic genie, it smells like a payoff to me."

"You're kidding me, right?"

"No lie, man! I'll send you pictures," Mingus said, snapping a quick shot with his cell phone. "The ride is sweet!"

The two men continued talking as Mingus watched what was going on across the way. David Locklear was clearly enjoying the attention. His friends were having a good time snapping selfies and taking photos of one another. The kids were being kids and for everything that was wrong about it, there was also something very right.

He saw Joanna before she saw him. The woman was stomping purposely across the parking lot toward the crowd.

"Damn it! What the hell is she doing?"

"What is who doing?" Ellington asked.

Mingus started his engine, pulling the vehicle out of the parking spot. He hurried to intercept Joanna before she made it to her destination. "Yo, Ellington, we might have a situation. If you can, meet me in Parker's office in thirty minutes."

"Are you going to tell me what's going on?"

"I'm sure you'll know soon enough," Mingus said, "but I've got it handled. I'll see you in a few." As he disconnected the line he pulled up in front of Joanna, bringing the car to an abrupt halt. He leaned across the seat and pushed open the passenger-side door. "Get in, Joanna! Now!"

Her determined expression fell. She looked from Mingus to the crowd of students and back. The fatality of her actions suddenly slapped her broadside as police sirens rang loudly through the air.

* * *

"I just wanted to talk to him," Joanna insisted. She was pacing the floor in the police station. "He's lying, and no one is asking him why!"

Mingus shook his head. "Did you really think he was going to just give you an answer because you asked nicely?"

"Who said I was planning to be nice?"

Mingus was amused and fighting to not let it show. They had pulled out of the school's parking lot just as three police cars were pulling in. Her ankle monitor had signaled an alert the moment she'd stepped on school property, violating her bond. Two turns and three stoplights later Mingus was guiding her into the West Harrison Street police department. He had walked her straight to his brother's corner office. Lieutenant Parker Black had not been happy to see either of them, especially when Mingus explained the situation. Now it was proving to be more of a challenge than he'd anticipated to keep Joanna from being arrested.

"Baby, I don't know if I can fix this. They're not happy with you right now."

"I didn't ask you to fix it, Mingus. I know what I did. You should have just let me talk to him. At least if I had been able to look him in the eye it would have been well worth me going to jail."

"Look, I understand you're frustrated. I'm frustrated. But you need to trust the process. You need to trust me."

Joanna turned to stare at him. "I do trust you, Mingus. And I understand you have to do things a certain way, but it just feels—"

Before she could finish her statement, the door swung open, Parker moving through the entrance. Ellington followed on his heels and a female officer behind him. Their expressions were stoic, neither man looking happy.

Parker started, "Joanna Barnes, please put your hands behind your back."

Joanna's eyes widened. "Why? What...?" She shot Mingus and then Ellington a look.

Ellington shrugged.

Tears suddenly burned hot behind her lashes as she complied, the other woman snapping handcuffs around her wrists. The officer grabbed her by her elbow and guided her out of the room. Parker closed the office door after them.

"What the hell?" Mingus snapped. "If I'd known you were going to arrest her, I wouldn't have brought her here. She had a lapse in judgment! She didn't do anything wrong."

Ellington shook his head. "She didn't do anything wrong because you were there to stop her. What would have happened if you hadn't been there? I keep telling you two, the prosecution is jumping at the bit to take her down and you two are helping to make their case."

Mingus crossed his arms over his chest, attitude swelling through his large frame. "So what now?"

"Technically she did violate her bond. If she were going before a judge, they would decide if she'd remain incarcerated until her trial," Ellington said, shooting Parker a look. "And I'll be honest, with so much public attention on this case, I doubt we'd be able to keep her out of jail."

Mingus looked confused. "*If she were going*? She isn't going to get a hearing? You're not going to contest this?"

"We've determined that there's a defect in her monitor," Parker said. "Since she was just *passing by* the school, en route to the police station, the unit should not have registered an alert. They'll send someone down to change it out later today."

Mingus gave his brothers a look, his gaze shifting back and forth between them.

"I'm giving your girl a break," Parker said. "And you can thank Ellington, because I wasn't feeling so generous."

"The fact that you brought her directly here helped us make that case," Ellington added. "But I'm sure that's why you did it. We're no fools, little brother."

"Look, it's like I said, she had a brief lapse in judgment."

"Well, she's going to cool off in a cell downstairs for a while. I think she needs to think about the consequences of her actions. You can come pick her up around seven o'clock, before the shift change," Parker said as he moved to his desk and sat.

Ellington and Mingus dropped into the seats that faced him.

"That's a violation of her rights, isn't it? Holding her illegally?" Mingus asked.

"You really don't want to go there!" Ellington interjected. "She really is just a signature away from being legitimately incarcerated. We won't be able to help her if she does it again. Just say thank you."

"But I can't just leave her!" Mingus ran his hand over his head. He felt desperate, needing to fix the mess he felt like he'd made. He knew her frustration. He knew it better than anyone else. She'd been desperate to do something that would prove her innocence. He couldn't help but wonder if he'd been more open about what he knew, if he'd shared more of his tactics with her, if she would have been less inclined to strike out on her own.

His brother snapped him back to attention. "You don't have a choice. I had to answer for what she did. They only agreed not to pursue charges because Parker said he would hold her in custody until the issue with her ankle monitor could be resolved. It was either that or we argue it out before a judge."

"Why were you at the school?" Parker questioned.

"Following up on a gut feeling," Mingus responded. He turned to Ellington. "Did you request the video?"

"My office is filing the request as we speak. I'll get a judge to sign it before the day is out."

Mingus shifted forward in his seat. "I need another favor," he said, the comment directed at Parker.

"Are you *trying* to get my badge pulled?"

"Hear me out. Your detectives believe this case is a slam dunk. The evidence points to her guilt, I get that. But they haven't done their due diligence. They don't know everything I know. I need David Locklear interrogated again. And I need to be there."

Parker threw up his hands. "So now you know better than my men do?"

"I know Joanna's not guilty. And I know that boy is lying." Mingus spent the next few minutes updating his brother on everything he'd found: from the stripper and her tattoo to the triad working for the Tower Group. "If the school's videotapes show what I think they're going to show, then we're on the right track to make this go away," he concluded.

"You do realize if I interfere, it's going to trigger a

red flag for Internal Affairs, right? I'm sure after today they'll already be looking at me sideways."

Mingus shrugged. "I need to be there, and I need Danni to do the interrogation," he said, referring to his brother Armstrong's wife-to-be, a detective with the Vice unit.

"So we're just going to step on everyone's toes and completely undermine two veteran investigators?"

"Go big or go home," Mingus quipped.

Parker shook his head slowly. He took a moment to ponder the request. "Find something on those tapes," he said finally. "Then come back to me and ask for a favor."

Joanna wiped the moisture from her eyes. She'd really messed up this time, she thought. Getting to David Locklear had sounded like a good idea until she'd pulled her car into the school parking lot. Even as she had crossed the lot toward where he was standing, she'd been firmly committed to having her say. Mingus stalling her in her tracks had knocked her confidence. The wind had swept her sails into a tangled mess and, just like that, she'd realized how big her mistake had been.

Mingus couldn't fix this, but she'd held out hope that they might let her slide. As a guard had slid the cell door closed, her hope was dashed. They had made it crystal clear that a violation of her bond would mean incarceration until her trial. Knowing that she might be looking at an extended period of time behind bars had her in her feelings.

The other woman in the cell was watching Joanna closely. Her gaze was narrowed, her stare unnerving. She was middle-aged with a portly frame, thick black hair swept into an updo and just a hint of makeup.

Dressed casually in khaki slacks, a white tank top and a plaid bomber jacket paired with red Timberland boots, she sat on the opposite bunk, seemingly unconcerned with her situation.

"You look familiar. Weren't you on the television?" the woman suddenly asked.

"I really don't want any problems," Joanna responded.

"Yeah. Yeah! You're that teacher! What are you in for now? More kiddie porn?"

"I didn't have anything to do with kiddie porn." Joanna rolled her eyes.

"Yeah, whatever. I'm innocent, too!" The woman laughed. "My name's Gloria."

"Joanna."

"So, really, Joanna, what did they get you for?"

Joanna held up her foot and shook the ankle monitor from side to side. "Bond violation. I went somewhere I wasn't supposed to be."

"Yeah, those things can be a bitch. Had me one once. That was the longest six months of my life!"

"So, what did you do?"

Gloria shrugged, leaning back against the wall as she crossed her arms and legs. "Hooked up with the wrong man! I met this great guy when I was in New Jersey. We hit it off, were having a good time together, and he convinced me to drive down to Florida with him for the weekend. We got stopped on the way back and they found kilos of meth in the trunk. The car was registered in my name and he lied and said he didn't know anything about it. Now I'm looking at a drug trafficking charge."

"Oh my God! That's crazy!"

"I should've known better, but I thought he was a good guy. He had some shady friends down in Florida, but he was treating me well and I thought he liked me. I should have known not to trust a man!"

"I am so sorry."

The woman shrugged. "Hey, crap happens!"

"How can you be so nonchalant about it? My charges aren't nearly as serious and I'm a nervous wreck."

"I've been here before. All you can do is keep your head down, do your time and hope for the best."

Joanna sighed. "I guess so."

"You got kids?"

Joanna shook her head. "No."

"It's harder if you have kids. Not being able to see your children grow up. My daughter was six the first time I got locked up. She was eight when I got out. Losing those two years hurt us both."

"I'm sorry."

"No reason for you to apologize. I know what I did and why I did it. I hate that I got caught, but crap happens!"

"So why did you go to jail the first time?"

"I like to eat. And I needed to feed my baby girl. I worked for this nonprofit and I started helping myself to some of the donations to supplement my minimum wage. I got a little greedy and it caught up with me. I served time for an embezzlement charge."

"You're not scared about this new charge? Drug trafficking is a big deal, isn't it?"

"Hell yeah, I'm scared! I just hope I get a good public defender."

The two women continued chatting for over an hour. Joanna appreciated the other woman's perspective about their situation. She didn't feel quite so alone. When an officer returned, calling Gloria by name and unlocking the cage door to let her out, Joanna was a little sad to see her go.

She was beginning to wonder why she hadn't heard anything from Ellington or Mingus. She wasn't sure if she was allowed one phone call, or if she would be seeing a judge before the day ended. Every time she asked a passing officer, she was ignored. She was beginning to feel abandoned, even though she knew she wasn't. She had no doubt Mingus was doing whatever he needed to get her out, but she hated that she had made being able to do so such a chore.

Joanna lay her body against the cot, pulling her knees to her chest. The wool blanket scratched her arm and the pillow was thin. All she could do, she thought, was go to her happy place and think about what made her happy. Thinking about Mingus had her wishing they were back in her home, in her bed, still making love. Their night together had been as near perfect as either could have imagined. Now she was missing him and thinking that her impatience, and her impulsiveness, had clearly been a mistake.

Chapter 16

Even though he didn't often say it out loud, Mingus appreciated that when he bent the rules, he had family members who were willing to help him bend them back. He knew Joanna was not going to be happy with their decision, and that she might not forgive him for her current situation, but she was safe. Her safety was his primary concern.

He stepped through the storefront entrance of the Wicker Park neighborhood restaurant. His father had insisted on meeting him at Schwa, a fine-dining establishment with a renowned chef whose artistry with the food fully engaged the senses. They typically serviced an exclusive clientele, patrons waiting weeks for a reservation, but the Chicago police commissioner always seemed to be able to snag a table when he wanted one.

Commissioner Black was seated near the window.

He was holding court, in conversation with the young waitress, who was giggling at the attention. His father gave him a nod as he took his seat. "My prodigal son, I was surprised when you called me."

"It's good to see you, too, Dad."

Mingus gave the waitress a smile as his father waved her away.

She returned moments later, resting two shots of bourbon on the table, announcing the chef was preparing their meals. Mingus knew to expect the unexpected. The meal would be twelve courses of freshly prepared decadence, the two table settings putting them back some two hundred dollars each. He would enjoy each plate. He always did, but a burger and fries from 25 Degrees would have served him just as well.

His father always chose Schwa when he wanted Mingus to remember the finer things in life, like he would forget his family's affluence if he didn't partake in reminders so ultra-extravagant. Dinner at Schwa was supposed to be an example of what one could achieve with hard work, commitment and dedication. Mingus always showed up to remind the patriarch that he had raised them all to be more pragmatic, abstemious and thrifty. That his hard work didn't necessitate unnecessary accolades and honors. It had become a *thing* with them and something the two shared at least once every other month.

The patriarch had a *thing* with each of his children. He and Armstrong shared their love of the prestigious Union League Club of Chicago. Parker and their father both collected Winchester rifles, spending hours together searching for the beloved antiques. Jerome traveled with his daughter's annually, surprising them with vacations to destinations that only they shared. The city of Paris had been the first trip for both girls, celebrating their sixteenth birthdays.

He and Mingus dined extravagantly, both considering themselves connoisseurs of great cuisine. The two men had an affinity for good food and always challenged each other with conversation.

"Parker told me about the situation with your friend. Your brother is taking a lot of risk to help you."

"I like to think Parker is doing what's right, even when the system is set up against Joanna, wanting to see her fail."

Jerome's gaze narrowed ever so slightly. "Well, you and I always do see things differently. I guess I shouldn't have expected anything to change."

"I disagree. I think you and I see things exactly the same. You're just willing to accept things I'm not."

Jerome shook his head, his annoyance visible. "So, what can I do for you, son? I'm sure you weren't calling just to enjoy my engaging repertoire."

"What can you tell me about the Tower Group?"

His father bristled ever so slightly. "What do you want to know?"

"Who are they laundering money for?"

There was an awkward pause. Jerome sat back in his seat. "Why don't you start by telling me what you do know?"

Mingus sat forward, folding his hands together on top of the table. He'd been digging since the organization had come on his radar. Following the paper trail, he'd discovered his parents had invested a substantial amount of money in two of the Chicago skyscraper projects. On the surface it seemed to be a typical real-estate venture. But it was tied to moneyed speculators with questionable backgrounds that gave rise to suspicion. "I know you have a substantial investment in the company," he said.

"I do, but it's completely aboveboard."

"That's questionable."

"Are you saying it isn't?"

"I'm saying I have questions. I also know that anything tied to the Balducci family is never on the up-and-up."

One of the oldest crime families in Chicago history, the Balducci family was notorious. His father and the Balducci patriarch, Alexander Balducci, had a long-time friendship that many didn't understand. For years the two had walked on opposite sides of the law. Even their children had history of going toe-to-toe with fatal outcomes. His brother Armstrong had gone up against Alexander's sons and both had lost; one his freedom and the other his life. But through it all, Jerome had continued a relationship with the man that others would have publicly distanced themselves from.

"Until you can show me there's something illicit about my investment, then it shouldn't be a problem. Whether people want to admit it or not, the Balduccis have done a lot of good in this town."

"Is that before or after the drugs and prostitution? Is there anything they're not trafficking illegally?"

"Don't be a smart-ass," Jerome snapped.

The chef delivered the next course himself, interrupting the conversation. He'd plated a fried fish tray of walleye, morels, malt vinegar, fava and blackberries. Mingus sat back, offering little to the conversation, as the young man and his father chatted about the food.

From the first bite to the last, the dish was exceptionally good.

They both fell into silence as they savored the meal. His father was watching him intently and Mingus knew he was carefully choosing his words before he spoke.

"If there is anything untoward about the investments with the Tower Group or how it's operating the business, I don't know it. I haven't been given any reasons to believe they're not what they say they are."

"What about the third project they're trying to get off the ground?"

"It'll be much like the other two. Investors have been assured of a sizeable return on their investments. Personally, your mother and I have netted a gain of fifteen percent on the first project and twenty-three on the second. We could potentially earn over thirty on the next one. And for the record, I took the deal to Alexander. He didn't bring it to me. His company didn't come on board until the second building. But the Tower Group has been a part of my portfolio since before building one was even under consideration. I helped secure that financing. There's a minimum buy-in for investors and Balducci's pockets are deep enough that he didn't blink. Plus, it was a good deal."

"What's the minimum?"

"One million."

Mingus blinked as he let that settle. He continued. "The proposed location for the third skyscraper… Do you know why they want that property?"

His father shrugged. "Look, prime real estate of any kind is a hot commodity. The right building site and investors can make millions on these projects. The wrong site can mean the difference between ten million and one hundred million."

"Do you know a man named Frank Sumpter?"

"We've met, and I've talked to him briefly. He is spearheading building three. I know that securing financing was a challenge for him at first, but he seems to have gotten it done."

"Is there a public record of the investors somewhere?"

"Now, Mingus, you know how that works. People know what we want them to know."

"Do you know who the investors are? Even the ones who don't want to be known?"

His father gave him a look, suddenly tight-lipped. He turned his attention back to the food on his plate, polishing off the last bite of his fish. He dropped his fork to his plate and wiped his napkin over his lips. "So, let me ask you a question, son. What does all of this have to do with your new girlfriend?"

Mingus shrugged. "I'm not sure yet. But I plan to find out."

Jerome studied him briefly. "I'll text you that list."

Mingus nodded. "Thanks, Dad."

Their conversation continued over *unagi* with sweet watermelon and *togarashi*. Dessert was cheesecake made with Humboldt Fog cheese and adorned with a glaze of fermented apricot and edible nasturtium flowers. The food combined a complicated mix of flavors and textures to satisfy and bring patrons to a happy ending. It felt much like the relationship between Mingus and his father and Mingus and Joanna—complicated and textured, and joyous in all it offered.

Joanna's nerves were completely frayed. She had no idea of the time, simply aware that it had been far too

long without someone, anyone, coming for her. She had
begun to fear that Ellington wasn't able to get her in
front of a judge and that she would have to spend the
night behind bars. Suddenly the thought of losing her
freedom was very real. She was scared to death, realizing that this might very well be her future if proof of
her innocence was never found.

When Lieutenant Black signaled for the jailer to open
the gate she was shaking as though she were cold. Just
the sight of him brought her immense relief.

"Is there anything I can get for you, Joanna?"

She shook her head, wrapping her arms tightly around
her torso. "No, I just really want to go home. Have you
heard from Ellington?"

"Why don't we go up to my office?" he said as he
guided her down the corridor of concrete walls. "There's
an agent here from the monitoring company who needs
to take off your ankle bracelet."

Joanna's stomach fell. Panic cramped her limbs and
she suddenly felt like she might vomit. It was a struggle
to maintain her composure, but she didn't want Mingus's brother to see her cry. Her bottom lip quivered
and she blinked rapidly to stall the threat of water wanting to rain from her eyes. If they were removing her
monitor, then most certainly her bail had been revoked,
she thought.

Inside his office, Parker gestured for her to take a
seat. He sat in the other chair, turning his body to face
her. "I'm glad we have a few minutes to talk," he said.

"I'm so sorry," Joanna said. "I really didn't mean to
be so much trouble."

Parker shook his head. "I understand you're in a very
difficult position right now. I also know my brother

wants to do everything he can to help you. You and Mingus are just getting to know each other, but he has a reputation for being reckless. So it really doesn't help either one of you when you're behaving just as impulsively."

"You're right, I know it. But I felt like I needed to do something."

"From this point forward, I need you to do what the state of Michigan has ordered you to do. Nothing more, nothing less. You are fully aware of your restrictions and boundaries, so don't violate them. Stay away from the school. Stay away from Mr. Locklear. And just trust your legal team to do what you are paying them to do."

Joanna nodded her head again. "So what happens now?"

"Because there is a defect in your ankle bracelet, you were held for your own safety. They are going to replace that monitor with a new one. Once the new one is in place, Mingus should be here to take you home."

Understanding suddenly washed over her and she gasped. "That's why your brother brought me directly here to the station. He was giving me an alibi!"

"Mingus was breaking the law. He could've been charged with aiding and abetting. Like I said, my brother can be reckless. And you violated your bond. You also violated your restraining order. The next time, you being impulsive could very well keep you in that jail cell."

"I swear, it won't happen again."

"It better not."

"Thank you! I really appreciate all your help."

"Like I told Mingus, thank Ellington. If it had been

left up to me, the two of you would have been sharing a jail cell together."

The two exchanged a look. Joanna didn't bother to respond.

Minutes later she sported a new ankle monitor pulled right out of the box. The technician was still muttering about the old device seeming perfectly fine. Mingus walked through the door just as the other man was walking out. She had never been happier to see anyone in her entire life. Leaping from her seat, she threw herself into his arms, her tears finally falling against his shoulder.

Mingus held her tightly. She was shaking, and her distress pulled at his heartstrings. "Shh…it's okay, baby…everything's okay…shh…" he muttered into her ear.

Minutes passed before she finally pulled herself from him. He cupped his palm around her face, lifting her chin to kiss her lips. Silk glided against silk, his touch like a faint whisper of warm breath. She had missed his touch, in that moment, realizing how much she needed the security of it.

She hugged him a second time. "Can we go home?" she whispered.

Mingus looked to Parker, who nodded his head.

"Check in with your attorney in the morning, please. And the two of you, stay the hell out of my precinct!"

"Thanks, bro!"

Parker gave them both a slight smile. "I'll see you two on Sunday," he said, wishing them both a good night.

Joanna looked confused as she shifted her stare from one man to the other. "Sunday?"

Mingus sighed. "Mandatory family dinner."

Parker winked at her. "Welcome to the family, Joanna!"

Joanna didn't have the energy to be mad. Her short incarceration was the result of her own bad decision. She was grateful that Mingus's brothers had cared enough to want to teach her a lesson. Despite her assurances that she was well, Mingus was still concerned for her.

"Mingus, I'm fine," she said for the umpteenth time. "Really, you need to stop worrying. It's not like your brother put me in a maximum-security prison. It was a local jail cell. We both know it could have been worse. I could still be there."

Mingus nodded. He climbed in beside her on the lounger, her body shifting until she was reclined against his lap, his arms wrapped warmly around her. He kissed her, nuzzling his face into her hair.

After leaving the station she'd insisted on going to her house first to pick up an overnight bag. From there they'd gone to Piece Brewery & Pizzeria on North Street to get her a white pizza with clams, garlic and bacon. Standing in line to place her order, she'd become acutely aware of people staring, recognizing her from her fifteen minutes in the spotlight. They'd whispered, some speaking loudly enough for her to hear; most remarks were rude, a few even cruel.

She'd felt her anxiety level rising tenfold. "I should have just gone home," she'd whispered. "This wasn't a good idea." She'd turned to face him, leaning her forehead against his chest.

Mingus had pressed a kiss to the top of her head.

Before he could respond an older woman had stepped up to them, hand on her hips, venom spewing from her mouth like water from a faucet. "I can't believe you would show your face in public! You're disgusting. Sleeping with young boys. God should strike you dead for what you've done to that poor child! They have a special place in hell for women like you!"

Mingus had stepped between Joanna and the woman. His gaze narrowed, he'd shaken his head from side to side. Voice low, even as he'd spoken, his tone was edged in barbed wire. "Step off!" he'd snapped, his hardened expression speaking volumes.

The woman had persisted. "Someone needs to tell her about herself."

"Should I tell you about yourself?" Mingus had questioned. "Because we can discuss your bad behavior. You're rude, nasty and judgmental, and for you to invoke God's name while you spew hatred speaks volumes about your Christian spirit. Now, step…off…and if you even look in her direction again, you may come to regret it!"

The woman had gasped, her hand clutching imaginary pearls around her neck. She'd turned and stormed out of the building just as the woman behind the counter called him by name. "Your pizza is on the house tonight, Mr. Black. What can we get for you two?" she'd asked, giving Joanna an apologetic smile.

With pizza in hand, they'd returned to his place. Once there she had gone straight to the shower to rinse the afternoon's experience down the drain.

Hours later, when she was feeling better, she took a sip of the white wine Mingus had poured for her. "So how badly did I mess things up?"

Mingus shook his head. "You didn't mess anything

up." He updated her about finding the cameras at the school and requesting the footage.

"I forgot all about those cameras. Do you really think you'll find something?"

"We can't afford not to find something, baby."

Joanna blew a soft sigh. She reached to place her glass on the coffee table then turned to kiss his lips. The sweet connection reminded her of the Creamsicles she'd loved as a little girl, the candied orange strips he'd been eating all evening painting his mouth with sugary goodness.

"Are you ready for bed?" she asked when they finally pulled away from each other. "Because I'm ready for bed."

Mingus smiled, the bend of his mouth dimpling the slightest hollows in his chiseled cheeks. "Lead the way, my lady!"

They made love for hours. Sometimes slow and methodic and then fast and frantic. It was a night of exploration with easy caresses and sweet murmurings. Fingers tracing the dimples in her thighs, the scar on his calf, the deep well of his belly button and the piercing in hers. Her private tattoo was no longer private, Mingus using his tongue to trace the three fluttering butterflies inked over her pubis. He lay sprawled on his back as Joanna teased and taunted him, pleasuring him with her hands, her mouth and body. Again and again and again. When sleep finally came, both rested well.

Chapter 17

Mingus stared down at her, Joanna's slumbering frame curled around a pillow in the center of his bed. She was naked, her dark brown skin glowing beneath the dim moonlight that shone through the window. She was stunningly beautiful as she snored softly, lost deeply in slumber.

He had woken from a bad dream and hadn't been able to fall back to sleep. After tossing and turning for longer than he had hoped, he'd slid from beneath the covers and was headed up to his office to see what work he could get done. But he couldn't resist taking the moment to simply watch her.

Taking a deep inhale of air as he stepped into a pair of track shorts, he pulled the comforter up and over her body and smiled as she snuggled down closer around the pillow. He tiptoed out of the room and headed up the flight of stairs to stare at the wall of pushpins and photos.

For the next hour he replayed the details of the case over in his head. *David Locklear, student, accuses teacher of sexual misconduct.* Supports allegations with pictures, purported to be images of the teacher in a compromising position. The student had yet to recant or deviate from his story. Thus far Mingus had enough evidence to cast doubt on the photographs, but not enough to explain how they'd found their way onto the teacher's cell phone. Explaining the how was crucial to clearing her name.

And there was still the why. Why had the student picked teacher Joanna Barnes to lie about? How was a high-profile, real-estate investor connected to a low-profile pimp and a school board administrator, beyond their latent, quasi-familial relationship courtesy of the state? Were there other players and what was the payoff? What would they gain? Mingus still had more questions than he had answers.

His cell phone vibrated for his attention, announcing an incoming text message. As promised, his father had sent him a lengthy list of names associated with the Tower Group real-estate project. Some he recognized, movers and shakers in the Chicago community. It included his parents, the Balducci family, the current mayor, two former senators and a nationally recognized, former pro football player with ties to the area. But two names stood out and Mingus realized he had yet another question that he needed to ask. Where had Marion and John Talley gotten the money to buy in to a multimillion-dollar real-estate project?

Mingus hadn't expected to receive the school video recordings as quickly as he did. The delivery had come to his office some twenty-four hours after Ellington had petitioned the courts. He also hadn't expected to receive what he'd wanted on a USB flash drive. Two of them. In all honesty he had been expecting stacks of old videotapes, unlabeled and randomly tossed into a box. Tapes that would have taken twenty people and ten days to weed through. Anything to put another roadblock in his way. But the school's IT department had proficiently copied the requested footage, some eight months of data for the current school year, and had included a detailed manifest of dates, times and camera locations. He'd been pleasantly surprised.

Three hours later he was still watching students pass by the camera outside Joanna's classroom door. Three hours, twenty-six minutes and twelve seconds. Three-plus hours of students being loud and offensive interspersed with periods of quiet, just an occasional straggler wandering the hallways. Then there were the glimpses of Joanna. Joanna coming and going. Joanna and her students. Joanna and other teachers. Each time he saw her he couldn't help but smile. Joanna looked happy. Joy gleamed on her face and she laughed. There was an air of authority about her. Sometimes she chastised a student, other times she celebrated a student's success. What he saw on those glimpses of memory was the Joanna he prayed he would see again. The Joanna who hadn't lost a significant part of the woman she was.

Mingus's instincts had served him well. At the four-hour-and-sixteen-minute mark, he found what he had hoped to discover. He grabbed his cell phone and dialed, waiting for Joanna to answer his call.

"Hey, baby!"

"Hi! Is everything okay? Where are you?"

"At the office."

"On your way back, I hope!"

"I need you to think back. The date would have been March 3. Something was happening at the school that took you away from your classroom for an extended period. Can you remember what that was?"

"March 3?"

"Yes. You locked your room door and didn't return for almost three hours."

"Hold on. Let me check my calendar."

There was a lengthy pause before she spoke again. "Hey, you still there?"

"Waiting patiently!"

"We had an academic pep rally."

"What the hell is that?"

Joanna laughed. "It's what we do right before we go into state testing. We bring all the kids into the gymnasium and try to get them motivated. They play skill-building games, there's the teachers' talent show, and the principal buys pizza for lunch."

"Pizza for the whole school?"

"Everyone! It's one of the highlights of the year. The kids really get into it and since she's been doing it, our student test scores have been at a record high."

"Thank you. That's all I need to know."

"Is it a good thing?"

"Baby, I can't wait to tell you how good!"

"I could use some good news."

"I'll be here for a little while longer and then I'm headed straight home. Be naked when I get there so we can celebrate!"

Joanna laughed. "Really, Mingus? Naked?"

"Oh! Did I say that out loud?" He laughed with her.

"Just hurry back to me, please!"

"With bells on, baby!"

"I love you," Joanna said with another deep chuckle as she disconnected the line.

Mingus stood, still holding the phone, her words echoing in his head. Dropping the device back to the desk, he took a deep breath. "I love you, too," he muttered to himself. "Joanna Barnes, I love you, too!"

Ellington waved his brother into the office, holding up an index finger as he concluded a telephone call. He didn't look happy, clearly irritated by something, and Mingus found himself whispering a prayer that it had nothing to do with Joanna's case. He had news that would move the case two steps forward, so they couldn't afford to get pushed five steps back. He took a seat, listening as his brother castigated the party on the other end for their unprofessional conduct. He blew a sigh of relief.

When Ellington disconnected the call, he gave Mingus a questioning look. "I really need good news. If you don't have any, then this will have to wait until tomorrow. Maybe even next week."

"How about news that will blow this case wide open?"

Ellington's eyes widened. "Wha'cha got?"

Mingus moved around the desk and inserted the flash drive into the USB port on his brother's computer. The two watched as images of Riptide High School's hallway appeared on the screen. Mingus pushed the play button. Ellington cut an eye at him, not yet impressed. One minute in, a portly woman in a too small pantsuit that clung tightly to her hips and ass, paused in front of Joanna's classroom door. She tossed a look over her right shoulder and then her left, appearing to be waiting for someone. She stole a glance at her wristwatch, her foot tapping against the floor. Just seconds later a male student came bounding toward her. Words were exchanged as she shook a finger in his face.

Taking a set of keys from her pocket, she proceeded to unlock the classroom door. The student slumped back against the wall, his arms crossed over his chest as he seemed to be watching out for anyone coming. Mingus zoomed in on the doorway. He could clearly see the desk and the woman rumbling inside a bottom drawer, appearing to remove something from inside. The boy turned as if he'd been called then pulled a cell phone from his back pocket.

Mingus and Ellington watched as the two stood in the doorway, the woman with one phone and the student with another, appearing to be texting and scrolling over their screens. The woman was grinning broadly, something the kid said moving them both to laugh. The exchange lasted for exactly twelve minutes before the woman moved back into the room and the desk drawer, returning the phone to where she'd found it. Exiting, she relocked the door and then she and the student parted, going in opposite directions. Mingus pushed the pause button.

"Tell me, please, what did I just see?" his brother asked.

"You just witnessed Marion Talley, a teacher at Riptide High School, enter the classroom of one Joanna Barnes. You saw her rifle through Joanna's desk and remove her cell phone. Then you saw that teacher and that student, David Locklear, transmit pornography from his device to hers and back."

"How do we know what information they were exchanging? If any at all."

Mingus pointed to the date and time stamp in the lower right corner of the video. "The date and times match the date and times of the transmissions as detailed in the forensics report."

"Where was Joanna? And the other students and teachers?"

"Some pep rally thing."

Ellington sat back in his chair. "Locklear has testified that he was getting a bathroom blow job during some pep rally."

"Not this pep rally and not from Joanna. There are cameras in the gym and Joanna was there the entire time."

"And we're sure that's what was happening?"

"It only makes sense. Why was Marion Talley in Joanna's desk and why did she remove Joanna's phone from her purse? Plus, when you read the forensics report, the timing is exact. And something else. The report indicates the images appeared on Locklear's phone twice. The duplicate images could have been transmitted or they were already there first and then sent to Joanna's phone. Texted back to his phone and then deleted from hers."

"The prosecution is going to challenge that. I have no doubts they'll spin it and the two were doing something totally different."

"Maybe, but we can show David Locklear had possession of her phone when she was not aware and without her permission. We can also connect him to Marion Talley."

Ellington nodded slowly, pondering the information.

"Why don't I give you the icing on this cake?" Mingus said. He pushed the play button a second time and used the mouse to select another day of video.

He crossed his arms over his chest as he and his brother watched once again.

The camera angle captured a flight of stairs and a small alcove that looked out onto the ball field. Although the manifest detailed the location, Mingus still wasn't sure where in the school this was, but he knew it wouldn't be hard to find out. He and Ellington watched for three minutes. David Locklear descended the steps, pausing in front of the window. He was followed by a young woman who was talking rapidly. Suddenly the two were engaged in a tight liplock, the boy's hands like automobile windshield wipers on fast speed. Locklear suddenly spun the girl against the window as he grabbed her leg and slid it along his side until it was wrapped around his back. The two spun a second time and Mingus hit Pause. He pointed to the screen.

"Look familiar?"

Ellington grinned. "That infamous tattoo."

"Crystal clear and as pretty as you please!" he said. He pushed the play button again.

The make-out session lasted another six minutes. When it was done and finished, the girl's skirt was pushed high around her waist and Locklear's pants hung low on his hips and ass. Locklear was grinning as he pulled up his pants and adjusted his clothes. The girl didn't appear to be equally pleased. She pulled down her skirt and rebuttoned her blouse. She then bent forward to retrieve something from the floor. It was just as she moved to straighten that Mingus hit the pause button one more time, the girl's face in perfect view.

"Please, make my day," Ellington said.

"Meet Alicia 'Champagne' Calloway, professional prostitute."

Ellington threw his arms straight up. "That feels like a touchdown to me!"

Mingus nodded. He disengaged the flash drive, returned it to the envelope and rested it on his brother's desk. He moved back to his seat and watched as Ellington picked up his phone. His brother dialed and waited for it to be answered on the other end.

"Lieutenant Black, please. This is Attorney Black calling." There was a pause. Then he said, "Thank you."

Ellington engaged the speaker, Parker's voice echoing through the room as he answered the call.

"Is this business or personal?"

"Definitely business. I'm here with Mingus."

"What now? He and his woman in trouble again?"

"Better than that. He needs that favor you promised."

"I promised a favor?"

"I believe you agreed to another police interrogation of David Locklear."

"You found something on those videotapes?"

"Of course! I'm good at what I do!"

Mingus shook his head. "And I'm better!"

Parker laughed. "Sounds like I need to hear this story over a beer!"

The words had slipped past Joanna's lips before she could catch them. They had surprised her as much as she imagined they had surprised him. It was after she had ended the call that she realized how true the comment had been. She loved him. Had fallen in love with him. For the first time she couldn't begin to imagine a life without him.

Knowing the words had come naturally, without practice or worry, made the moment even sweeter. She'd spoken from her heart, the gesture as organic as breathing. Any other time, any other man, and she might have been concerned about his reaction. Did he feel the same way? What would he think about her saying the words aloud? But something told her Mingus Black had accepted her pronouncement as easily as she had spoken it. Even if he hadn't said it back.

It had been a few hours since they had last spoken. He had called her a second time to say that he was grabbing a drink with his brothers. His tone had been cheerful and celebratory. Clearly he'd been in a good mood. That meant good news and she was excited to hear what he had discovered.

Joanna broke down the last cardboard box, adding it to the pile that rested by the back door. It had contained a number of trophies and awards that Mingus had earned over the years. After dusting and polishing each one, she had carried them up to his office and had arranged them throughout his bookshelves. With her hands on her hips, she stepped back to admire her handiwork.

It had taken most of the day to unpack the moving boxes that had cluttered the living spaces. Joanna had started the task the moment she had awakened and was excited to be done before he arrived home. With all his personal possessions now in their proper places, Mingus's new house looked like a home.

She had taken a quick break to run to the market, stocking up on toiletries for the bathrooms. She had added the ingredients for dinner and now a dish of her mother's vegetable lasagna sat warming in the oven. When they were ready to eat, thick slices of crusty bread and tumblers of lemonade would complete the meal.

Her cell phone ringing pulled at her attention. She had left the device in the bedroom on the upper level. By the time she made it up the flight of stairs the ringing had stopped. Mingus had called a third time, leaving a message that he was on his way home. Joanna stole a quick glance at the digital clock on the nightstand. She fathomed that she had just enough time for quick shower before he would be coming through the door.

Despite the good time he and his brothers had shared, Mingus was glad to be home. He came to an abrupt halt as he stepped through the door. The stereo was playing, someone's country song wafting through the background. The lights were low, candles strategically lit around the room. Shadows reflected against the walls, flickers of light dancing.

A medley of vanilla and berries scented the air. The aroma made him instantly hungry. He peeked into the kitchen to find two place settings at the ready. Fresh flowers were posed in a crystal vase with two elongated candles decorating the countertop. The oven temperature was set on warm and when he peered inside he was delighted to find a meal ready and waiting. No one had ever had dinner ready and waiting for him before. *I could get used to this*, he thought.

He moved from the kitchen to the living room. The stack of boxes that had been there when he'd left that morning were gone. The contents of each had been un-packed and placed around the home. Everything about the room felt different. For the first time, Mingus felt like the space was actually his and not a bed-and-breakfast he visited on the regular.

"Joanna?" He called out her name. When she didn't answer, he climbed the stairs to see if she was in his office.

The surprises kept coming. His files had been neatly organized, his desk meticulously arranged. She had brought order to the chaos. He tossed a glance toward the case wall. He had no doubts that it would soon be coming down. He called out for her a second time, moving swiftly back down the stairwell.

"Joanna! You here?"

"In the master bedroom!" she finally answered, her smooth, alto voice ringing warmly through the home.

Mingus moved swiftly down the hallway, flinging open the bedroom door. Joanna lay sprawled across the master bed. She was propped up on one elbow, her head resting in the palm of her hand. Her body was extended and her legs were crossed at the ankles. Her other arm lay casually down the length of her body. She was completely naked.

Mingus grinned, appreciation flooding his face. "It must be my birthday because it's definitely Christmas come early!"

Joanna laughed. "See what happens when you make a wish!"

Mingus traced his tongue over his top lip and then bit down against his bottom lip. He suddenly found himself fantasizing about what he wanted to do to her. Her dark, smoldering eyes dazzled, drawing him in like a spider to a web. She was intoxicating and he was suddenly drunk with wanting.

Joanna crooked her finger and gestured for him to come to her. "What's taking you so long?" she asked. "It's not nice to keep a girl waiting."

Mingus's grin widened. "Well, I certainly don't want to do that."

He moved slowly in her direction, casually dropping his clothes with each step toward her. The protrusion between his legs hardened, swelling magnificently for her attention. He palmed the bulge with both hands. The gesture made Joanna smile and she grinned from ear to ear. Reaching the foot of the bed, Mingus teased the bottom of her foot with his fingers.

Joanna laughed, the wealth of it vibrating throughout the room. She sat upright, shifting her body toward him, reaching her hand out to touch him. The feel of his flesh against her palm was so incredible that he didn't want her to ever let him go. She stroked him slowly, her eyes darting back and forth between his face and his manhood. Her ministrations had him panting softly as he throbbed beneath her palm. Mingus suddenly leaned in to kiss her.

His lips were soft and warm, and she opened her mouth to welcome his tongue inside. Their mouths wrestled in a delightful game of give-and-take. His mouth left a damp trail from her lips to her cheeks, against her eyes and at the tip of her nose.

Mingus climbed onto the bed and hovered for a brief moment above her. "I love you, too, Joanna!" he said. Then he plunged his body down sweetly against hers.

Chapter 18

Detective Danni Winstead hugged her fiancé's three brothers, Parker, Ellington and Mingus greeting her warmly. Danni had been engaged to their brother Armstrong for only a few months and the wedding was just weeks away. The two had met a year earlier when Danni had been assigned to a special task force headed by Detective Armstrong Black to take down a sex trafficking ring. Together they had beaten the bad guys and found love in the process.

"Gentlemen, good morning! How are you all doing?"

Mingus hugged her warmly. "Detective! It's always a pleasure to see you."

"I bet you say that to all the pretty women," she teased.

"He's only saying it to one woman now," Parker interjected.

Ellington laughed. "Another one bites the dust, Danni. Mingus has given up his playa card!"

Mingus shook his head. "You all really need to leave me alone."

Danni laughed with them. "So what's going on? I hear you have a special job for me. What do you guys need?"

Parker gestured for her to take a seat at the conference table, taking a moment for them to all get settled. It had been less than forty-eight hours since Mingus had made the discovery on the school tapes and had called in his favor. They were all anxious to move the case forward another step.

"We need you to handle an interrogation," Parker said. "This one's a bit sensitive and Mingus felt you would be the best person for the job. Not that Mingus gives any orders around here," he said, cutting an eye in his brother's direction.

Mingus shrugged and grinned. "I don't know what you're talking about. All I ever do is stay in my lane."

"Well," Parker continued, "why don't you give Danni an update?"

For the next few minutes Mingus shared the details of the case. What they knew, what they were sure they could prove, and what they could cast doubt on. "We know the young man has lied," Mingus concluded. "We're still not sure why, but I think if you can work him the right way, he might break and tell us the truth."

Danni nodded. "I'll do what I can, but I don't think I'll have any problems getting you what you need."

There was a knock on the conference room door and then it swung open, Parker's secretary announcing David Locklear's arrival.

"Thank you," Parker said, "please put him in the interrogation room."

"Yes, Lieutenant."

"How old did you say he is?" Danni asked.

"He just turned seventeen," Mingus said.

"I just need a few minutes to prepare."

Mingus grinned. "Take whatever time you need."

A few minutes later David Locklear, his mother and their attorney sat around a table in the small room. Parker, Ellington and Mingus stood on the other side of the two-way mirror, unable to be seen. Mingus stood with his back against the wall and his arms crossed. He hoped he'd been able to convey just how important this interview was; Joanna's freedom depended on its failure or its success.

When Danni entered the interrogation room, she had pulled her hair back into a ponytail and had traded her tailored blazer for a floral-embroidered sweater. She gave David and his mother a bright smile as she shook hands with their lawyer.

David sat forward in his seat, smiling back. His smile was cocky, his arrogance visible. He was amused when others had expected him to be unsettled. On the other side of the wall, watching, the brothers realized Danni had put the three visitors instantly at ease, her appearance nonthreatening.

"Good morning! I'm Detective Black. I appreciate you coming in to speak with me. I apologize for the delay, but someone parked the prettiest red car in my spot!"

"That was your spot? My bad!" David said with a slight shrug, his smug smile showcasing a mouthful of braces. He swept a hand through his thick hair, leaving the lush strands in place.

"Dude, that's your ride? It's seriously nice. That must have cost you a grip!"

"I got it like that!" David boasted. He winked at her and Danni giggled.

"Detective, I'm sure you didn't call us down here to discuss my client's transportation issues," the attorney said, clearly annoyed.

"Of course not! We've come into some new evidence that we need to ask David about."

The lawyer postured. "I'm not sure what we can tell you that hasn't already been said to the other detectives. My client has suffered immensely."

Danni gave the man a look. "I'm sure." She shifted her attention back to his client.

"David, we were made to understand that you and your teacher engaged in sexual activity during school hours, is that correct?"

"Yeah. We did it during school and after."

Danni nodded and gave him a slight smile. "Can you tell us again specifically where these encounters occurred?"

"Sometimes in the bathroom. And we had this special place near the gymnasium where we used to go."

"Is that the little spot, sort of tucked away at the bottom of the stairs that looks out over the football field?"

"Yeah! You seen it? It's cool, right? Not everyone knows it's there."

"It's disgusting," the mother snapped, chiming in for the first time. "They should hang that woman from the rafters for what she did!"

Danni nodded her agreement but she didn't verbally

reply. Instead she opened the file folder she'd entered the room with, flipping through the pages as though she were searching for something. She dragged a finger down a list and stopped midway.

"That's great!" she exclaimed. "They do have cameras installed there. We'll be able to view the video."

"Video?" David suddenly sat forward.

His attorney echoed the sentiment. "What video?"

"For security purposes, the school installed video cameras in strategic locations. You know with all the trauma in our schools these past few years, you just can't be too safe." Danni gave them both another bright smile.

"Well, you got them pictures, so you don't need video, do you? 'Cause I'm not sure we're on them cameras. In fact, I'm sure we're probably not." The boy's voice was suddenly shaky, his comfort seeming to diminish ever so slightly.

"Well, there's an issue with the photographs. Because none of them show your teacher's face, it casts doubt on their validity. The video will just help us reinforce our case against her."

"I'm sure any video will corroborate what my client claims."

"Oh, most certainly! I have no doubts. I just have a few more questions for you, Mr. Locklear."

David sat back in his seat, his arms folded defiantly. He shrugged.

She gave him another smile. "Now I understand your teacher has a number of tattoos. Are you able to describe them all for us?"

David shot the lawyer a look. "Well, there's the one on her thigh. It's in them photos."

"And the others?"

The young man hesitated. "She got flowers and stuff."

"But you two did have sex, is that correct? So, you won't have any problems identifying any she may have in her private areas? And I only ask because we've be made aware of a specific tattoo that the defense will probably want you to detail."

David suddenly looked nervous. His eyes flickered back and forth as if he were trying to decide what he needed to do or not do. "What if I can't remember?"

"That would not be good. You filed a civil suit against her, correct? I'm sure if her defense can poke any holes in your story that they'll probably throw your case right out."

The attorney bristled. "I think we've had enough."

"You okay, David?" his mother asked, noticing his sudden discomfort.

David fanned a dismissive hand in her direction.

"I just have a few more questions," Danni persisted. "Please! If you can just bear with me a little longer."

"Make it quick. I got to get to school," David snapped.

"Real quick. Because we really want to nail this woman for taking advantage of you. I know you want to make her pay, right?"

David shrugged. "What do you mean 'pay'? Don't the school's insurance pay?"

"They'll pay what the school owes in any civil suit, but she'll have to cough up any money she owes out of her own pocket. But we're concerned with the criminal charges. We want to see her incarcerated for what she did. That's a minimum of twenty-five years."

"Twenty-five years?"

"Maybe even more, but she deserves it, right?"

David seemed to drop into reflection, his face twisted. "She's not a bad person," he muttered under his breath.

"Don't you dare defend that whore!" his mother snapped.

"I'm curious, David, we see you received a sizeable deposit recently. Can you explain where you got that money?"

"We're done here!" David's lawyer stood, gesturing for the Locklear family to follow.

"Too personal? Please forgive me. I take things too far sometimes. I was just wondering how you paid for that pretty car and...well...it's not important."

Danni moved onto her feet. As she lifted the folder into her hands, one photograph slid from inside. A picture of Kyle Rourke and Alicia Calloway fell face-up on the table. She didn't rush to grab it, allowing David to notice and recognize the couple. The color suddenly drained from his face.

"Look at me!" Danni exclaimed. "I'm just so clumsy!" she said, retrieving the image and tucking it back into the folder. "Well, I think we're done here, unless you have something we need to discuss?"

David shrugged. "I...well... I need to talk to my attorney for a minute."

"Of course!" Danni moved to the door. "Let me know if you have anything you need to tell me," she said as she exited the room and closed the door after herself. She flicked off the two-way mirror, impairing their view on the other side to afford David and his attorney their privacy.

* * *

Mingus nodded. "She shook him! That boy is peeing in his pants right now. Nice job!" he exclaimed as Danni moved into the viewing room with the men.

"He's rattled, but I'm not sure it's enough. I didn't want to push too hard because the attorney was ready to run. He knows you're on to him, though."

"We'll know soon enough if it worked or not." Mingus gave the woman a pat on her back. "Really nice work! If you ever get tired of this police kick, there's always a position for you with my firm."

Danni laughed. "I'll keep it under advisement," she said.

Ellington leaned over to give her a hug. He reached out to shake his brother's hand. "I have to be in court on a case in thirty minutes. Keep me posted if anything changes, please." He turned to Parker. "You really should try to convince him to come back to the department. I'm just saying!"

Parker chuckled, shaking his brother's hand. "So should you!"

Danni took a quick glance at her watch. "I am going to go back in and check on our victim," she said.

Parker and Mingus exchanged a look as she exited the room.

Danni returned almost immediately. "They're gone. They just got up and left."

Mingus rolled his head back, stretching his arms over his head. He said, "No worries, one of my guys is tailing him. He won't get far."

The phone in the room suddenly rang, drawing their attention. Parker answered, pulling the receiver into his hand. "Lieutenant Black speaking."

The man paused as he listened to the party on the other end. When he disconnected, he gave them all a look.

"What's wrong?" Mingus asked, the question washing over his expression.

"That was the prosecutor. David Locklear's attorney just called and apparently he and his client are headed over to their offices to make an official statement."

"Fingers crossed," Mingus said as he and Danni high-fived each other.

When Joanna looked up from the grocery list she was making, the two newscasters on the television were shaking their heads. Her picture flashing across the television screen had drawn her attention. She grabbed the remote and turned up the volume.

"*In a stunning development, the Chicago District Attorney's office announced this afternoon that it would likely be dismissing all charges against high school history teacher Joanna Barnes. Barnes, an educator at Riptide High School, was accused of having an inappropriate sexual relationship with a seventeen-year-old male student. According to District Attorney Michael Tambour, Barnes has been cleared of all rape allegations and the student has now admitted to lying about an affair. There's no word yet whether or not charges will be filed against the student for filing a false report or if Barnes will be returning to her teaching position at the high school. For more on this story and others, join us for the six o'clock news with Joe Kody and Valeria Peyton.*"

Joanna was stunned. The announcement was a complete shock. She jumped from her seat to find her cell phone. She was shaking by the time she found the device wedged between a loaf of bread and the sugar canister on the kitchen counter. She had twelve missed calls from Mingus and almost as many from Ellington. She called Mingus back first.

He answered on the first ring. "Where are you?"

"I'm still at your place."

"Don't leave. You should wait a minute before you leave for your house. It's a media feeding frenzy in your driveway."

"Is it really over? Are they really dropping the charges?"

"David Locklear admitted he lied. Right now, he's still down at the station being held for additional questioning. I'm not sure what they're going to do about charging him."

"Unbelievable! Has he said why? Did he give an explanation?"

"No, baby, I'm sorry. He hasn't told us anything useful yet."

"Well, at least it's over. Now people will know the truth."

Mingus nodded into the receiver. "I have to run, but I'll call you as soon as I'm finished here. But call Ellington, okay?"

"I will. As soon as we hang up."

"Love you!"

"I love you, too!"

Joanna's conversation with Ellington was short and sweet. He extended his congratulations but advised her to sit tight until her paperwork was processed. He was also demanding a formal apology and a complete retraction of the allegations from the Chicago police department, the school board and the DA's office. He also needed to arrange for the monitor to be removed and her bail money to be refunded.

"There will be a press conference tomorrow to clear up any misunderstandings. There's been so much negative press, I want to make sure you get an opportunity to finally see a positive spin on your side of the story."

"Do I have to be there?"

"Only if you're comfortable. Don't you want to finally get a say?"

"Only if I can give everyone who didn't believe me a resounding middle finger wave!"

Ellington laughed. "Okay, it's official. My brother is a bad influence on you because that is something he would say."

Joanna laughed with him.

"Have you thought about whether or not you want to return to your job, Joanna? Because if you do, I need to negotiate the terms of your return. You're owed something for your pain and suffering."

"I haven't even thought about it. I'm still shocked!"

"Well, you don't have to make a decision right now. We can even revisit it next week sometime and decide then."

"Thank you for all your help, Ellington. If it weren't for you and Mingus…"

"I have to give all the credit to Mingus. But he's not done yet. He's still pursuing a lead to figure out why this happened and who might be responsible for putting David Locklear up to doing what he did. Trust me, he has no plans to let this go."

"I'm just glad it's over and that I can have my life back."

"We're all happy for you, Joanna!"

* * *

Mingus had given strict orders for the surveillance detail to stay on David Locklear once he left police custody. He wanted to know where he went and who the kid saw and talked to. He wasn't naive enough to think this was over. David Locklear's admission that he had lied wasn't going to sit well with someone. Mingus needed to know who, imagining that this put a serious crimp in someone's plans for Joanna.

He'd provided Danni and her crew over at Vice with enough information to shut down Rourke. Danni had promised to pick him and Alicia up for questioning. He had no doubts that if anyone could get any answers from the dynamic duo, she could. If nothing else, he'd acquired enough dirt on the pimp's operations to take him off the streets for a few months. Mingus vowed to make it hard for the man to make a comeback if ever he tried.

Bob Marley was vibrating out of the club's speakers. One of the dancers was doing a sensuous side-to-side gyration to "Redemption Song." Her performance was equally awkward and mesmerizing, the entire room focused on her song choice and her assets. The man at the door had pointed Mingus in with a nod and he had taken a seat at a table near the door.

Just a few hours earlier the Vice squad had arrested Alicia after she'd propositioned an undercover police officer. Mingus had sat back and watched as she'd been handcuffed and taken away. Rourke had watched, as well, sitting low in the driver's seat of his Ford Crown Vic until the cops were finished and everyone on the corner had gone back to business as usual. Rourke had driven straight to the nightclub then, Mingus following.

Now he was throwing back shots like his life depended on it. He'd made two calls, one before entering the club and the other since he'd been sitting on the bar stool. Both had left him in a mood, more animated than usual, as he snarled at everyone in his path.

Frank Sumpter arrived first. He still looked like a fish out of water, but he didn't seem as nervous to be there like that first time. His conversation with Rourke was brief, Sumpter appearing to hiss at his friend between clenched teeth. John Talley arrived as Sumpter was preparing to leave. Their conversation was even more contentious. But few in the club noticed, all eyes lost on the beauty sliding down a pole to the beat of Marley's "Kinky Reggae."

Knowing how to follow the money trail had been the first lesson Mingus had learned as a private investigator. Tapping into his father's connections, he had discovered that the operating budget for the Tower Group had dried up substantially since Sumpter had been hired. Mingus found the man's name was tied to a few shell companies, multiple off-shore accounts, a half-dozen trusts and a homestead in Florida.

The business was faltering and Sumpter wasn't delivering as well as his predecessors, despite all the checks with the many zeros written by men like Mingus's father, who had found significant success with the first two projects.

When Sumpter stormed out, leaving his two friends behind, Mingus followed, no longer bothering to maintain his cover. Sumpter needed to know he was being watched. Mingus didn't want him to be comfortable with his situation. He wanted him unnerved. As the man drove off, Mingus climbed into his car and followed. Six blocks and four turns later, Mingus veered off in the opposite direction, leaving the man to wonder.

Chapter 19

Joanna had left him a text message that she'd gone back to her house to meet her parents. Their mood was congratulatory, everyone wanting to wish her well. When Mingus arrived, his father, Ellington, Simone, Danni, Armstrong and Angel were already there, as well. The party-like atmosphere made him smile.

"It's about time," Simone scolded. "We were beginning to think you were going to miss all the fun!"

Mingus gave her an eye-roll as he kissed Joanna's cheek. Mr. Barnes stepped forward to shake his hand. "We're told you're responsible for this good news. I want to thank you. You literally saved my daughter's life."

"Your daughter is very special to me, sir."

Her father studied him intently. "She's very special to her mother and me, as well, son."

Behind him, Joanna's mother eyed both men with

interest, clearly enjoying how her husband was sizing up their daughter's friend. She winked at her only child then reached for her glass and took a sip of her wine. Joanna waited for the matriarch to say something, but she didn't, holding her tongue.

"So what's wrong with your mother?" Angel asked.

"I was going to ask the same thing," said Simone.

Joanna shrugged. "Beats me," she whispered back. "But don't say anything. I don't want us to jinx it!"

Joanna's parents shook hands with Mingus one last time and then excused themselves, wishing everyone a good night.

Mingus eased his way over to his father's side. "Did you get my message?"

The patriarch nodded. "I did. There will be a surprise IRS audit of the Tower Group in the morning."

"I'm sorry."

"Nothing for you to be sorry about, son. You didn't mismanage that company. We've never had a problem until recently. And we would not have known about the problem if you hadn't brought it to our attention."

"I hate that you might have lost your money."

"It won't be the first time, and I doubt that it will be the last. It's the risk you sometimes take. It's only money. Hopefully we are early enough in the project to be able to recoup any losses and still move forward."

Mingus gave his father a smile. "Does Mom know yet?"

His father laughed. "In due time. No point in opening that can of worms before it's necessary. Let's just see what the audit turns up first."

Armstrong suddenly joined the conversation. "Hey, how are you two doing?"

Mingus gave his brother a nod. "No complaints here."

"I understand your investigation has ruffled a few feathers." Armstrong and his father exchanged a look.

Mingus shook his head and shrugged. "Really? I hadn't heard."

"The original detectives on the case didn't take kindly to you undermining their case."

"The original detectives didn't have a case. They had a witch hunt."

"Maybe, but the word is out that Internal Affairs may have some questions."

Mingus shrugged his shoulders a second time. "I don't answer to Internal Affairs, so I really don't care what they may have."

"Let it go," Jerome interjected. "Internal Affairs doesn't have a case. A few officers got their feelings hurt, felt like their toes had been stepped on, and now they want to make some noise. You boys got the job done."

"With a little help," Armstrong boasted as he pulled Danni into his arms and kissed her cheek. "I hear my girl did a great job."

"Your girl did a fantastic job," Mingus said. "She's got great instincts. I'm trying to get her to come work with me."

Danni laughed. "I really like my job, Mingus. I don't know that I'm interested in making a move right now. Once I get through this wedding, I might change my mind. You never know."

"Speaking of," Armstrong interjected, "you never returned your reply card. You are coming to my wedding, aren't you?"

"Of course, he's coming to your wedding!" Simone

said. "Why would your brother not come to your wedding?"

Mingus shook his head. "Sorry about that, but I think I lost that little card thing in that mess on my desk. That and I have had a lot on my mind lately."

"I actually found it," Joanna said with a light laugh. "I put it in the little box with the Urgent label that you have."

"And we hope to see you there, as well, Joanna," Danni added.

Joanna smiled as Mingus reached for her hand and kissed the back of her fingers.

"She'll be there, too! She's my plus one!"

After one last round of drinks, family and friends wished them both a good night. The house was suddenly quiet and Joanna began clearing away the dirty dishes and putting them into the dishwasher. As she stood at the counter, staring out into space, Mingus eased his body up to hers and wrapped his arms around her torso. He pulled her back against his broad chest.

"You okay?" He pressed a damp kiss to the curve of her neck.

"I am. I just thought I would get this major epiphany and things would be different. But they really aren't. Does that make sense?"

"It does. You've endured a trauma. Now you have to recover. It's going to take some time before things feel normal again."

"Your brother asked me about doing a press conference tomorrow, but I don't think I want to."

"Then don't do it. You don't owe anyone anything, Joanna."

"He also asked if I wanted to go back to my job. I

never imagined myself doing anything else but teaching, but I'm not sure I can go back to a classroom right now."

"Baby, take all the time you need to do what you need to do for you. You're on no one else's schedule." He hugged her closer.

"What about you? Do you just go on to a new case now?"

"I'm still working this case. I still don't know why Locklear lied about you. And there're some leads I still have to follow up on. I'm not done with it just yet!"

"Well, if there's anything I can do to help, you know I'm here for you just like you were here for me."

"I do."

Mingus helped her clear away the last of the dishes. When they were done, he moved into the living room and sat. Minutes later, Joanna joined him.

The sound of gunshots pulled Mingus from a sound sleep. Three rounds echoed loudly in the late-night air. Tangled in a cotton blanket, he rolled forward off the sofa. His heart was racing as his eyes darted back and forth, searching for Joanna. At the end of the hallway, the bedroom door flung open, her own sleep-filled stare wide with fright.

"Mingus!"

"Stay down!" he called out as he pulled at the covers she'd apparently draped over his body while he slumbered. He paused, listening intently, for sounds and movement.

Joanna dropped to the floor, meeting his stare. Fear danced in her eyes, resolve in his. He held up a hand then pulled his index finger to his lips, stalling her next comment. She held her breath and waited for him to advise her, unsure what she needed to do next.

Mingus moved swiftly to the back of the couch and the sofa table where he'd hidden his weapon. He wrapped his hand around the polymer grip of his Glock 26 and disengaged the safety. He moved to the front door and peered through the sidelights. A woman suddenly screamed and a dog barked excitedly. Flinging the door open, Mingus moved outside, his weapon raised as he searched out any potential threat.

At the sight of him, with his gun in hand, Joanna's neighbor screamed again; the older woman was out walking her poodle past the home. The piercing shriek vibrated through the air. She yanked her dog's leash, pulling the animal hurriedly as she tore down the street. Joanna rushed out the door behind Mingus, her gaze sweeping across the landscape.

Both saw a boy's body lying facedown in the middle of the driveway. Blood pooled on the ground beneath him, his bright white Jordan sneakers spattered red. He clutched a torn piece of notebook paper in his hand.

Still moving cautiously Mingus bent to check the body for a pulse. He and Joanna exchanged a look as he shook his head. He stood, sliding his gun into the back waistband of his pants. He pulled his phone from his pocket and dialed for backup. Sirens sounded in the distance, drawing closer with each passing second. Joanna started to cry, gasping for air as she tightened her arms around her body. David Locklear was dead.

Mingus had answered all the questions he intended to answer. Detectives had been hammering at him and

Joanna for hours. The same questions being repeated once, twice, multiple times.

"Why was David Locklear there?"

"Was Joanna still involved with the young man?"

"Did he know about the relationship between Joanna and the boy?"

"Did you see the shooting?"

"Who else might have seen the shooting?"

"Did you touch the body?"

"Did David say anything before he was shot?"

"Did Joanna invite him?"

"Do you have a permit for this gun?"

"What is your relationship to Ms. Barnes?"

There was nothing more they could tell them that hadn't already been said a dozen times over. His brother Parker could see that he and Joanna both had reached their limits. Joanna was curled up in a small ball in the corner of the sofa. Tears still rained down her face. It was a fifth officer asking her again about the alleged sexual relationship with the teenager that was the last straw. Mingus pushed past everyone in his way to get to where she lay broken.

"Enough!" he snapped, sounding like his father. "We've both told you everything we know. If you want us to answer any more questions, we'll do it down at the station tomorrow with our lawyer."

The officer hovering over Joanna bristled, a hint of anger intense in his bright blue eyes. "It'll be enough when we say—" he started.

Parker stepped forward, shutting the officer down and sending him out the door. He turned to Mingus, his tone professional. "You and Ms. Barnes are free to

go. If we have any further questions, we'll be in touch."
The two men exchanged a look.

Mingus whispered into Joanna's ear, "Go throw some clothes into a bag. We can't stay here."

Joanna nodded. He held her hand and pulled her to her feet, moving with her down the hallway to the bedroom. After she was safely inside, behind the closed door, he moved back to stand beside his brother.

"You got anything that can help us catch the shooter?" Parker asked, his voice dropping to a loud whisper.

Mingus shrugged. "Not sure. I had one of my guys tailing him, but we haven't spoken. I waved him off before your guys got here."

"Let me know what he tells you. And I mean it, Mingus." Parker cut his eye toward his brother.

The two exchanged another look but Mingus didn't bother to reply. He moved back down the hallway to the bedroom. Inside, Joanna was sitting on the edge of the bed, still visibly shaken.

"Who would do this, Mingus? He was just a kid!"

Mingus shook his head. "We'll figure it out. But right now, let's just get out of here. Did you pack?"

Joanna pointed to her overnight bag. She stood and slipped on her shoes. She stepped into his arms as he reached for her, holding her tightly in a warm embrace. Understanding swept between them. Even in the midst of chaos, they would be each other's haven.

Chapter 20

Joanna found Mingus in his home office the next morning. He had risen early and had been on the phone for over an hour asking questions about David Locklear. He'd spoken to his brothers, the coroner's office and two of his investigators. She dropped into the chair that sat at the corner of the desk and waited for his attention.

"Good morning," he said as he disconnected his last call. "How'd you sleep?"

"Not well," she answered. "I think I'm still in shock. Have they found out anything yet?"

Mingus sighed. "No."

There was an awkward pause that passed between them. Joanna shifted forward in the seat. She twisted her hands nervously together. Mingus sensed a rise of anxiety beginning to bubble within her. He knew she had questions that he would debate whether to answer.

"Last night they asked if we had touched the body."

He stared but said nothing.

She continued. "There was a piece of paper in his hand and then it was gone." She met his stare. "What was it, Mingus? What did it say?"

Mingus took a deep breath. He pulled open the desk drawer, extracting the paper in question, and he passed it to her.

Joanna's hand shook as she took it, the wide-ruled composition paper stained with dirt and blood. The note had been written in red ink, the block printing almost childlike. The short letter was addressed to her and signed by David. There were only two lines: *I am very sorry. I really am.*

"He was at my house to apologize?"

Mingus shrugged. "We really don't know."

"But the note…"

"The note says he's sorry and nothing more."

"So why did you take it? Why didn't you tell the police about it?"

"Because no one needs to try to guess what the kid's intent was. What was he apologizing for? Was he sorry he told? Was he sorry he ended your relationship? Or was he sorry he lied? Yesterday, you could have publicly denounced him, and he was there to justify and defend his own actions. Today, because he died on your front doorstep, people are once again looking at you sideways, wondering what you had to do with his death. That letter does nothing but fuel the negative messaging, so no one else needed to see it. I took it to protect you."

Joanna had no response. She knew Mingus was right. Now she was ready for it all to be over. She folded the note in two and passed it back to him. She watched as he held it over a metal trash can, lighting it with a match. Holding it by the edge, he let it burn until there was almost nothing left, then he dropped the remnants of ash into the trash container.

"Do you want breakfast?" she asked, the conversation done and finished. There was nothing left to discuss, she thought, trusting that Mingus knew best and would do everything in his power to protect her. He loved her and she loved him and that was enough.

He shook his head. "I have someplace I need to be."

From the time David Locklear left the district attorney's office and arrived at Joanna's front door, he had spoken to three people. Marion Talley had been the first. The surveillance video showed him meeting the teacher in the school parking lot. It also showed she hadn't been happy. The tongue-lashing she'd blessed him with looked brutal. David had been dismissive, blowing her off as he'd pulled his car from the parking lot back into traffic.

From there he'd returned to his mother's home. Loud voices had been heard coming from inside the small apartment. The disagreement had spilled out into the front yard of the family's apartment building. By then the local news station had picked up the story of Joanna's innocence and his admission that he had lied. His visit with his mother had lasted exactly twenty-three minutes. He'd left the family home with a packed duffel bag and his beloved car.

The last person David Locklear spoke with was Frank Sumpter. It had been another contentious meeting with lots of hand-waving, raised voices and bullish behavior. David had walked away from that meeting with only his duffel bag. He had taken Chicago's transit authority and had walked two blocks to Joanna's home to drop off an apology letter.

Two Vice officers stood in the lobby of the Tower Group. Neither blinked when Mingus walked past and headed to the fifth floor of the company's corporate offices. Armstrong was standing at the door when he arrived. The two slapped palms in greeting.

"How's your girl holding up?"

Mingus shrugged. "It's been a rough week." For a split second he wished he'd taken her up on that offer for breakfast.

"Just keep holding her down. It'll get better."

"I'm not used to worrying about someone else 24/7. How do you do it?"

Armstrong grinned. "She would tell you that you don't need to worry about her all the time, I'm sure. She's a strong woman, like my Danni. She's also going to do whatever she wants and all you can do is hold her down and be there when she wants you."

"I guess…"

"Look, the hard part's over, bro. She passed the sister test! They like her. Think what it would be like if they didn't!"

Mingus laughed and then he changed the subject. "When I called you, I wasn't expecting to find you here. What do you have going on? I thought the IRS audit was the only thing in play around here today."

"They're here, too! We're following up on a tip your stripper friend gave our Vice team. They've been hit with a few warrants today. Frank Sumpter has a lot of explaining to do. That is, if we can find him. He didn't show up this morning."

"Are you going to be able to make it stick?"

Armstrong grinned. He pointed toward the door and the parade of officers marching out with a boatload of boxes. "The paper trail always helps! We've got him for embezzling, a Ponzi scheme, trafficking…the list is long and not at all distinguished. Your intel helped. It was solid information."

"Glad I could be of service."

"So, what's up? Why are you here?"

"I was hoping to find Sumpter here. I need to ask him a few questions."

"About Joanna?"

"About his relationship to David Locklear."

"You think he's connected to the Locklear murder?"

"I know he is," Mingus said emphatically.

Armstrong nodded. "There's an active warrant for his arrest. Keep your ear on the scanner. I'll give you a heads-up if we find him before you do."

"I've got one more place to check. But if things go south, I may need backup."

"Just call. You know how to find me."

After slipping into a simple black dress and gold-toned flats, Joanna looked up the directions to the Locklear family home online. She hadn't been totally comfortable with the idea of just showing up to pay her respects to the young man's mother and family. She had talked herself out of it twice, but she refused to allow herself a third time to change her mind. Because she felt earnest about paying her respects, letting David's mother know how deeply she regretted his passing, how she hoped the family would eventually find peace and understanding.

She took a series of deep breaths to stall the rise of nerves then exited the vehicle. The family lived on the fourth floor of the brick apartments. As she waited for the elevator, she found herself rethinking her decision once again, but she pushed through, knocking on the door just as Mrs. Locklear was pulling it open to head to her second job at the hospital.

"What are you doing here?" Disdain for Joanna painted her expression.

"I wanted to pay my respects. I'm very sorry for your loss."

Tears suddenly misted the woman's eyes but she refused to cry. "Thank you."

Joanna pulled a condolence card from her purse. "This is just a little something to help."

"Why are you being so nice? After what my son did. My son lied about you. He lied to everybody about you and you're being so nice."

"David made a mistake. I remember making a few when I was his age, too. I appreciate that he tried to fix it."

Mrs. Locklear glanced down to her wristwatch. "I need to go. Or I'm going to be late for work." She closed her apartment door and locked it.

"You're going to work? Today?"

"My bills still got to be paid. Me sitting around crying isn't going to help that happen."

"Can I give you a ride?"

"No. You just need to leave and don't come back."

"I really do want to help," Joanna insisted.

"I don't need your help," she said as she turned toward the elevators.

Joanna hurried after the woman. "May I ask you

one question, please? And then I promise to leave you alone. Do you know why David did what he did? Why he told such a horrific lie about me?"

The boy's mother inhaled swiftly, holding the air deep in her lungs. "You really want to know?" She was leaning on the down button, pressing it as if doing so would bring the elevator faster.

"I do. I really want you to tell me. Please."

"It wasn't about you. It was all about the money."

"So someone paid him?"

"Yeah, they paid him good money to do it, and all he talked about was buying me a house. He really was a good boy!"

"Do you know who paid him?"

She shook her head. "No. He never told me. He just said they felt bad about what you had done to him and wanted to help. To make sure he testified against you, so that you couldn't hurt any more kids. They gave him that pretty car to drive and put money in his pockets."

"You do know I never had a sexual relationship with your son, right?"

"I do now. David did tell them the truth. And I'm sorry that he did that to you. That's not how I raised him."

The two women rode down in the elevator together. Neither spoke another word. Mrs. Locklear gave Joanna one last look before she exited out the conveyance doors.

Moving back to her car, Joanna couldn't begin to imagine what David's mother was feeling. She had seemed so alone and immensely sad.

After leaving the Tower Group offices, Mingus headed over to the Boys' Room. He knew that once word of the raid on their offices reached Sumpter, he would need to rally with Rourke and Talley to figure out their next steps. He was also betting that with news of David Locklear's murder headlining every media outlet, the three would be putting plans into place to flee or fight.

He'd discovered enough about the trio to know that the strip club was where they most often rendezvoused. His instincts told him they would more than likely meet there sooner than later. He'd be waiting when they arrived.

There were only a few girls in the club and none of them were dressed, or undressed, to perform. It was still early and just a few alcoholics enjoying their first sips of the day were inside. Lily slid from her seat and moved to the bar. She returned with two bottles of beer, popping the cap on his and then hers, before sitting back down.

"You really are trying to make trouble for me, aren't you?" Lily asked, her gaze skating back and forth to see if anyone was watching their exchange too closely.

"Why would you say that?" Mingus questioned.

"Because you came looking for Alicia and then she got busted. Now they say she's helping the Feds. That pimp of hers has been crazy mad since they picked her up."

"What makes you think I had anything to do with that?"

"Are you saying you didn't?"

Mingus responded with a look that ended that discussion.

Lily sighed.

"When are you going to retire from this gig, Miss Lily?" Mingus asked. He took a sip of his beverage.

"They don't have retirement plans for old strippers. When our tits start to drag around our knees, they just put us out to pasture."

Mingus laughed. "We need to get you a retirement plan, doll."

"Hey, don't knock what I do. I make an honest living."

His brow lifted as he looked at her.

"It's honest!"

"I didn't say it wasn't!"

"This job paid for my house and put my four kids through college. Now my son is headed to medical school. It has served me well."

Mingus gave her a smile as she continued.

"Better men than you have tried to put me on the straight and narrow, Mingus Black, and I don't say that to be insulting. You know my history with your daddy and I haven't met a man better than him yet! You keep walking in his footsteps, doing what you do, though, and you'll get there!"

Mingus gave her a nod and took a second sip of his brew.

"I'm glad you got Alicia out. I just hope she can stay out of this business."

"I didn't think you liked that girl."

"I don't. She's young and pretty and cuts into my money!"

Mingus chuckled.

"Seriously, though, she can do better than this dump. And that pathetic piece of trash she calls her boyfriend isn't interested in her doing better. Now, if you just put him in jail so he can't get his claws back into her, life would really be good for an old woman like me!"

Mingus wrapped an arm around the woman's shoulders and hugged her to him. At the top of each hour he slid her a hundred-dollar bill for her time. With each payment, Lily would go to the bar and bring back two beers. For four hours, the two sat and talked. They reminisced about old times, debated the political climate and Lily gave him relationship advice, excited to hear there was someone special in his life.

During their time together Lily took two bathroom breaks. This time when she left the table, disappearing into the back room, he texted Joanna, needing to check that she was doing okay. He hated that he'd left her alone, but appreciated that she understood, allowing him to do what he needed to do.

When Lily returned, her expression had changed. Her comfort was gone, her nerves suddenly on edge. She sat and gestured with her head toward the door. Kyle Rourke was coming through the entrance. Frank Sumpter was close on his heels. Neither man looked happy, both clearly frustrated. Rourke was cussing, profanity peppering their conversation. Neither was going out of his way to keep their conversation quiet, their voices raised for most to hear.

"So what the hell are we going to do now?" Rourke snapped.

"This is all your fault!" Sumpter railed. "We told you not to trust that girl." He dropped down into a chair.

"This isn't about that bitch!"

"No, it isn't. It's about your ass getting greedy, that's what it's about. Everything was perfect and you just had to have more!"

Rourke slammed his fist against the table. "Did you call him?"

"He said he was on his way."

"I can't believe he would be so stupid!"

"You're the one who told him to clean up the loose ends." Sumpter shook his head.

Rourke dragged his hands across his face. "I told him to make sure we didn't *have* any loose ends. I didn't tell him to shoot anyone! He did that shit all on his own."

"That witch he's married to probably put him up to it. She's been pulling his strings for months now."

"I definitely don't trust her!" Rourke added.

Both men suddenly shot a look around the room, cyeing the other patrons to see who was eavesdropping. Mingus was leaning into Lily's side, the two looking as if they were very comfortable and totally focused on one another. Lily giggled as she rubbed her cheek against his face, pretending to be focused on soliciting a client.

"What are you looking at?" Rourke yelled, screaming at an old man sitting at the bar.

Mingus turned to see where the man's anger was directed, visibly bristling. The old guy waved a dismissive hand and turned his attention back to his drink.

Mingus and Lily exchanged a look.

Mingus whispered. "Miss Lily, I need you to do me a big favor."

"Whatever you need."

"You know that number I gave you? I need you to call it. Tell the man who answers that I have a 9-1-1 situation and give him the address. Then I need you to come back and take Pops over there into the back room and give him one of your infamous lap dances," Mingus commanded. "Can you do that for me?"

"Boy, how many times have I told you how good I am?"

Just as Lily stood, John Talley came rushing through the door toward the table where the other two men sat.

Mingus watched as Lily disappeared behind the curtained wall. Just minutes later, she moved back into the room, directly to the bar and the old guy's side. She was giggly and flirtatious and had him laughing with her in no time. When she grabbed his wrinkled hand and pulled him from his seat, Mingus stood. By the time the two had disappeared, Mingus was standing by the table looking down at the trio. He grabbed the back of an empty chair, spun it around then lifted his leg over the seat and sat, resting his forearms against the chair's back.

"Gentlemen…" he said as he settled a look on each man.

"Who the—?" Rourke started.

"Who invited— I know you!" Sumpter barked. "You're the bastard who's been tailing me!"

John Talley looked like he was about to vomit. The color had drained from his face and he was shaking.

Mingus pulled his Glock and rested it against the table. He shook his head. "Don't think about it. Don't even flinch. We can do this the easy way. Or we can do it the hard way. Your choice."

"You're not a cop," Talley managed to mutter. "What do you want from us?"

"Smart man. I have questions and all I want is answers."

"I'm not telling you a damn thing," Rourke said through clenched teeth. "Who is this clown?" he asked, directing his question toward the other two.

"The teacher's boyfriend," Talley said.

"Do you want money?" Sumpter questioned. "We can give you money."

"You don't have any money," Mingus said matter-of-factly. "In fact, the Feds have taken most of your funds."

"I got accounts…"

Mingus laughed. He shook his head. "No, I took all the money in those accounts. You were hacked!"

The three men sat straighter in their seats.

Sumpter began to tap frantically at his cell phone.

Mingus watched as the man checked one account and then another and another. The color suddenly drained from his face, making him look like a ghost, then he became angry. Ire flushed his face a deep shade of hostile red.

"See, all gone!" Mingus said casually.

Mingus dropped his hand to his weapon and fixed his gaze on Rourke. "I would not do that," he said.

Rourke froze, his hand posed awkwardly at his side. "Here we are, having a friendly conversation, and you want to get stupid. Why don't you put your hands on the table, so I can see them? That way, we won't have any problems."

Rourke slowly lifted his arms and slid his palms to the tabletop and Mingus nodded.

"So, let me tell you what I know, and you three can fill in any blanks for me," he started. "Playground friends, right?"

"We grew up in foster care together," John Talley responded.

"Which one of you hatched the plan to bilk the Tower Group's investment money? Was that you, Frank?"

Frank Sumpter's eye was twitching, his nerves beginning to get the best of him. "We were just supposed to take a little off the top. No one would have missed it."

"I bet it was Kyle here who got greedy. You wanted more, didn't you, Rourke?"

"It was John's idea to take more," the man snarled.

"Humph!" Mingus cut his eye at the school administrator. "And I guess it was John who figured out the profit margins would almost double if the group got their hands on the Riptide property. Especially with that new hotel going up around the corner and the petition to redistrict that whole area. Those margins would probably have tripled!"

"It was an easy scam. We would have gotten rich and the investors wouldn't have been any wiser. Until this one started taking double his share!" Frank snapped as he glared at John.

"My wife and I were taking on risks you two didn't have. It only made sense. Like you didn't get your share of any extra we took!" John muttered between clenched teeth. "We all stood to make millions!"

"How did Joanna Barnes play into all of this?" Mingus directed his question at John.

The man rolled his eyes. "We needed a big scandal to help push the property sale. The school was already on the verge of closing and we figured one sex scandal would take it over the edge. Almost worked, too, until that stupid kid decided to tell the truth. The board was voting to sell this week and now they're going to wait."

"But why Joanna? Why not some other teacher?"

John shrugged. "Rumor had it she was under consideration for Teacher of the Year. Figured it would knock her down a peg or two."

Mingus shook his head slowly. "Because your wife wanted the title."

"Leave my wife out of this!"

Rourke tipped forward. "What do you want from us?"

"Which one of you killed David Locklear?" Mingus shifted his gaze between the three, his brow raised questioningly.

Rourke and Sumpter both turned to stare at John.

"I didn't kill anyone," John said, his tone snippy. "I was at a board meeting when that boy got shot. And even if I did do it, you couldn't prove anything!"

"Actually, I can prove more than you think I can," Mingus said. He stood, retrieving his firearm from the table.

Rourke suddenly jumped from his seat, pulling his own weapon. His chair fell back harshly, slamming against the floor. His two friends turned as if to run, ducking when he pointed his pistol at Mingus.

Then three gunshots fired loudly through the room. Mingus turned to see his brothers standing in the doorway. Both stood with their weapons still aimed at the man who had been deemed a threat. Both had discharged a single shot. Kyle Rourke lay dead; one shot hitting him squarely in the chest, the other blowing through his abdomen. The third shot, fired from Rourke's gun, had missed its target, hitting a bottle of Jack Daniel's on the bar behind Mingus's head.

"You good?" Parker asked. He moved to Mingus's side.

"Better now." He shot Armstrong a look. Gratitude seeped from his eyes. He was grateful that his brothers had arrived when they did. He was also thankful that Kyle Rourke had been a lousy shot. He shifted his gaze toward the body on the floor, then toward the other two men in handcuffs. He thought about David Locklear, the young man gone too soon from this world. This wasn't the ending he had hoped for, but he'd learned years ago that in his line of work you didn't always get what you wanted.

Then he thought about Joanna. He'd found the answers to finally clear her name. The Talleys and their cohorts would pay for what they put he through. She'd been vindicated, and he relished being able to hopefully put a smile back on her face. This time he'd gotten more than he wanted, determined that his win would last a lifetime. A weight had been lifted off his shoulders and he blew a soft sigh of relief. He gave his brother a nervous smile. "I see you brought the cavalry."

Armstrong gave him a smug response. "Didn't you call for one?"

"Secure the room," Parker commanded to the team of police officers who had rushed into the space behind them.

Mingus holstered his weapon and settled back against the bar. Frank Sumpter and John Talley were both in handcuffs and witness statements were being taken from the bartender and one stripper who'd been in the room.

"Did you get the evidence I sent you?" Mingus asked, referring to the surveillance tapes and digital transaction records he had on all three men.

Parker nodded. "I did. We picked up Marion Talley a half hour ago."

"She pulled the trigger on David Locklear."

"Your note said you thought it was her husband."

"I did at first and apparently so did they. But we were all wrong. He was at a school board meeting. If he wasn't the one behind the wheel of his car when the shots were fired, then it only makes sense that she was."

"I'm going to need a full statement from you."

"Whatever you need…"

"Think about coming back to the force. We could use a good guy like you."

Mingus laughed and then turned toward the door, intent on heading home.

Mingus wasn't expecting to run into his father in the club's parking lot. The police commissioner was stepping out of his city-issued vehicle when Mingus was headed to his own car. His father's presence was a surprise.

The patriarch gestured for his son's attention. "You good?"

"Yes, sir. I'm fine."

"Your brother said you almost got shot."

"He overexaggerated the situation. I had great backup from Chicago's finest."

"I doubt highly, Mingus, that someone pointing a gun at you and pulling the trigger is an overexaggeration."

"It's really no big deal, sir. I'm fine."

"You better be. We would not be able to live with your mother if something had happened to you while you were helping the police department. And if I can't live with that woman, I will bring your dead body back and kill you myself!"

Mingus laughed.

"By the way, it would seem that we've been able to recover a large portion of the money that was stolen from the Tower Group. It was transferred back into a Tower Group trust account. You wouldn't know anything about that, would you?"

Mingus gave his father a shrug, just the barest hint of a smile pulling across his face.

"Yes, Mark, good morning. It's certainly a somber morning here in Old Town. Investigators have confirmed that they have arrested Riptide High School English teacher Marion Talley for allegedly killing popular student David Locklear. Out in front of the school, students and faculty have set up a memorial here. Marion Talley faces one charge of first degree murder.

"Also arrested was school board president, John Talley. Talley faces charges for conspiracy to commit murder, embezzlement, and fraud.

"Seventeen years old, David Locklear was a star athlete and, according to his mother, had recently been accepted to the University of Chicago, where he had planned to study mathematics. David died two days ago from injuries incurred in a drive-by shooting originally thought to be random. Investigators have not said what led up to the killing. We are expecting to hear from the investigators in a news conference later this morning. We're hoping to learn more then. Marion Talley is expected to make her first court appearance later this afternoon.

"Reporting live, I'm Leanne Garner and this is ABC7 Chicago."

Joanna depressed the volume button on the remote. David's death had dominated the news since it happened and with the Talleys' arrest, she imagined it wasn't going to die down anytime soon.

She rolled to the other side of the bed, curling her body around Mingus. He was snoring loudly, but she found the rumble of air comforting. She'd been sound asleep when he'd come home and had no idea what time he had found his way to bed.

She knew there were details from the case that he needed to tie up. There had also been multiple meetings at the police department. Although Mingus hadn't shared a lot of the details, there was an active internal investigation of Parker and decisions he had made. He'd been called on the carpet for his actions, as well as the behavior of the officers who served under him. She would be grateful when things were back to normal and the Black family was no longer consumed by the issues that had taken her down.

Principal Donato had reached out about her returning to the classroom, but she wasn't sure about the idea. Returning to teaching suddenly didn't feel like it was the right thing for her to do. Thinking about being back in the classroom actually gave her anxiety and made her blood pressure rise. She had pondered the idea of taking off the rest of the school year and maybe even the next to decide what it was she really wanted to do.

She snuggled even closer to Mingus, throwing one leg over his. The heat from his body was volcanic, holding back the cold in the room. Everything about him warmed her spirit. She felt immensely blessed and wondered how she'd gotten so lucky.

Mingus opened one eye to stare down at her. "You okay?" he asked.

"I am absolutely perfect!" she said.

"What time is it?"

"Too early to get out of bed yet."

"I propose we stay in bed all day long."

"Sounds like heaven! What will we do all day in bed alone?"

Mingus laughed. "Baby, whatever we want!"

He reached for her, rolling back against the mattress until she lay sprawled above him. He hugged her close, the hard lines of his body meshing sweetly with the soft curves of hers.

"Is that a pistol in your pocket or are you just happy to see me?" she teased with a soft giggle.

Mingus pushed his hips upward. "I am very happy to see you. Extremely happy. Abundantly happy. So happy, that I about to make your entire day happy."

Joanna nuzzled her nose into that spot beneath his chin and trailed her tongue along his profile. "You could spoil a girl!"

"That's my job, baby, and I am exceptionally good at what I do."

Chapter 21

Joanna positioned the framed photo on the center of the wall. The thirty-six-by-forty-eight-inch portrait had been taken on Armstrong and Danni's wedding day. The bride and groom stood front and center, Armstrong in a traditional black tuxedo that complemented Danni's lace dress. The formfitting A-line design had fit her like a glove and she'd looked stunningly beautiful.

Jerome and Judith Black stood beside their son, beaming with joy. The brothers had flanked Armstrong's left side and bridesmaids Simone and Vaughan balanced the picture, standing next to the bride and her sister.

They were a beautiful family and the formal portrait was simply divine. It had been a month since the wedding. The memories from that day made Joanna smile. The abundance of love carried over in everything the

family did and said. She felt immensely blessed to feel
so welcomed into the fold.

Her case had been officially closed two weeks before
the wedding, the Talleys and their associates formally
charged. She'd done a round of media interviews to insure her side of the story was told and life had begun
to feel like normal again.

She and Mingus were in a very good place, the
boundaries of their relationship clearly defined. In fact,
they had no boundaries with each other, every aspect of
their lives completely entwined. She was happier than
she could have ever imagined, and she trusted that he
was as well. They had plans for their future, both wanting to travel the same path toward happiness. Both knew
that eventually there would be marriage and children
and a life of dreams come true. In the short term they
were navigating days at his home and nights at hers.
They were enjoying the hell out of each other, neither
wanting anything between them to ever change.

Mingus moved into the room and greeted her cheer-
ily. "Hey, baby, what are you…?"

He stopped short, caught off guard. He looked from
the portrait to her and back. "Wow!"

"Do you like it?"

"I love it! What a great shot of the family."

"Good. I had one framed for your parents and each
of your siblings."

He moved against her, claiming her mouth in a pas-
sionate kiss.

Joanna melted against him, her entire body like
mush. When he let her go, her knees were rubbery.
"You keep doing that to me!" she whispered.

"Doing what?"

"You know what you do!"

She giggled and took a quick step back, fanning herself with her hand. "I can't think straight, and I had something to tell you!"

Mingus folded his hands behind his back. "What's your news?"

Joanna grinned. "I got a new job. Teaching!"

"Baby, that's wonderful! Where?"

"The University of Chicago's history department."

Mingus closed the gap between them and hugged her again tightly. "I'm proud of you."

"Thank you."

He moved to his desk and the stack of unopened mail. "I appreciate you keeping me organized."

"You're very welcome. Right now, though, I need to go change my clothes. I have some errands to run and then I am going to meet your sisters for dinner. Do you need anything?"

"I don't think so. I think I'm good. Just hurry back. I'm going to miss you."

"I love you, too, Mingus Black!"

Mingus stared after her as she left the room. Everything about Joanna Barnes made him smile. Glancing back to the portrait, he couldn't help but imagine the day he would make her his bride.

Taking a seat in the leather executive's chair, he sorted through the stack of letters, separating the bills from the junk. When he was done, he slid open the side drawer and pulled out the letter he had tucked away weeks earlier. His mother's delicate handwriting, in her signature purple ink, stared back at him.

Reaching for the letter opener, he slid it beneath the

sealed flap. Inside was a letter addressed to his mother, written years earlier. Mingus read it once and then he read it a second time. He read the words over and over again until he'd committed his mother's secret to memory. Sliding the aged paper back into the envelope, he returned it to the hiding spot in his desk.

Minutes later, still pondering the ramifications of what he'd just read, he looked up to find Joanna staring at him. "You good?" she asked, concern tottering on her words.

He nodded. "I have you, baby! It doesn't get any better than that."

"Finally!" she exclaimed tossing her hands up in mock relief. "I've been telling you that for weeks now! It's about time you got it!"

Mingus chuckled softly.

Joanna moved to his side and took a seat against his lap. She wrapped her arms around his neck and brushed her lips gently against his. The kiss was sweet, the gentlest breeze between them. When they parted, both were slightly giddy with joy.

Joanna noticed the letter sitting on the desk top, her eyes drawn to the delicate penmanship on the envelope. "What's that?" she asked, her brow raised in curiosity.

Mingus fingered the correspondence between his fingers. "It's a letter to my mom. She's asked me to find the man who wrote it."

Joanna nodded her head slowly. "Is that a good thing?"

Mingus pulled the letter from inside and passed it to her to read. Her eyes suddenly widened as she looked from him to the letter and back.

"Does your father know?"

He shook his head. "She asked me to not say anything."

"What are you going to do?"

Mingus shrugged. "I'm going to do what she asked. I'm going to find him."

"Do you want some help? We do make a great team you know!"

He grinned. "I can't imagine myself being partners with anyone else!"

"Then I'm hired!" Joanna leaned in to kiss his lips a second time. "Mingus Black, did I tell you today how much I love you?" she asked sweetly.

Mingus whispered back, pressing the words gently against her lips, "Oh, baby! I love you, too!"

* * * * *

Don't miss the previous volume in
Deborah Fletcher Mello's
To Serve and Seduce miniseries:

Seduced by the Badge

Available now from
Harlequin Romantic Suspense!

ROMANTIC suspense

When Scarlett Kistler travels to Texas to meet the father she never knew, she faces a hostile but handsome ranch foreman, Travis Warren, and her father's mysterious illness. Can the burgeoning love between Travis and Scarlett survive in the face of intrigue and attempted murder?

*Read on for a sneak preview of
Karen Whiddon's latest thrilling cowboy romance,*
Texas Ranch Justice.

Scarlett's voice broke and she looked down, valiantly struggling to regain emotional control.

Travis could no more have remained in his chair than he could have stopped breathing. He took a few steps and dropped down beside her, then gathered her in his arms and held her.

Like before, his body instantly responded to her softness. And like before, he kept his desire under control. "I'm sorry," he murmured, allowing himself the pleasure of caressing her back and shoulders. "I can only imagine how much that hurts."

"And now I'm facing losing Hal before I even get to know him," she continued. "Worse, we have no idea what we're battling, so it's difficult to get together a cohesive defense."

He managed something that he hoped sounded like assent. She wiggled slightly, nestling closer to him. Desire zinged through his veins, and he had to shift his body so she wouldn't recognize his growing arousal.

How could this tiny woman make him desire her without even trying?

"Travis?" She tilted her face to look up at him, her lips parted. "Would you do me a favor?"

At that moment, he would have promised her the moon. "I'll y," he answered. "What is it?"

"Would you kiss me again?" she breathed.

Just like that, she managed to rip away every shred of the rmor he'd attempted to build around him. With a groan, he owered his mouth to her, claiming her lips with a hunger that ore through and gutted him.

Rock hard, he could barely move, never mind think. While ne wasn't entirely sure she knew what she was doing to him, ne knew if she kept it up, he'd lose the last shred of what little self-control he'd managed to hang on to.

"Scarlett," he growled.

She must have heard the warning in his voice, because her hands stilled. Though she didn't move away from him, not yet. And she had to, because right now the only movement he felt capable of making would be ripping off their clothes and pushing himself up inside of her.

"We need to stop," he made himself say.

"Do we?" Pushing slightly back, she gazed up at him, her lips swollen from his kisses and her eyes dark with desire.

Don't miss
Texas Ranch Justice *by Karen Whiddon,*
available April 2019 wherever
Harlequin® Romantic Suspense books
and ebooks are sold.

www.Harlequin.com

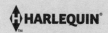
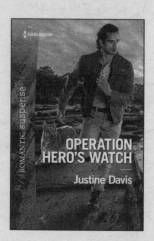